KIDS RUN
THE SHOW

Delphine de Vigan

KIDS RUN THE SHOW

*Translated from the French
by Alison Anderson*

Europa
editions

Europa Editions
8 Blackstock Mews
London N4 2BT
www.europaeditions.co.uk

Translation by Alison Anderson
Original title: *Les enfants sont rois*
Translation copyright © 2023 by Europa Editions

The translator would like to thank Michelle Bailat-Jones for her precious help
in preparing the translation.

A catalogue record for this title is available from the British Library
ISBN 978-1-78770-489-3

de Vigan, Delphine
Kids Run the Show

Art direction by Emanuele Ragnisco
instagram.com/emanueleragnisco

Cover design by Ginevra Rapisardi

Cover photo by Mircea Solomiea / Unsplash

Prepress by Grafica Punto Print – Rome

Printed and bound in Great Britain by Clays Ltd, Elcograf S.p.A.

KIDS RUN
THE SHOW

ANOTHER WORLD

"We had a chance to change the world but opted for the Home Shopping Network instead."

—STEPHEN KING
On Writing: A Memoir of the Craft

CRIME SQUAD–2019

MISSING CHILD KIMMY DIORE

Subject:
Transcript of most recent Instagram stories posted by Mélanie Claux Diore.

STORY 1

Posted November 10 at 16:35
Duration: 65 seconds

The video has been filmed in a shoe store.

Mélanie's voice: "Okay, you *sweeties*, here we are at the Run-Shop to buy Kimmy's new sneakers! Isn't that right, kitten? You need new sneakers because the other ones are getting a little tight." (The cellphone camera turns to the little girl, who takes a few seconds before agreeing, without much conviction.) "So, here are the three pairs Kimmy has picked out, size 1." (The picture shows the three pairs in a row.) "Let me show you, closer up: one pair of gold Nike Airs from the new collection, one pair of Adidas three stripes, and one unbranded pair with a red upper. We're going to have to make our minds up, and as you know, Kimmy hates having to choose. So, sweet peas, we're really counting on you!"

On screen, an Instagram mini survey appears over the image: "Which ones should Kimmy choose?"

A - The Nike Airs

B - The Adidas

C - The cheapest sneakers.

Mélanie turns the smartphone back to herself to conclude, "Sweet peas, thankfully you're here, so you get to decide!"

Eighteen years earlier

On July 5, 2001, the day of the grand finale of *Loft Story*, Mélanie Claux, her parents and her sister Sandra settled into their usual spots in front of the television. Since April 26, the day the game started, the Claux family hadn't missed a single Thursday primetime episode.

A few minutes before they were about to be set free, after seventy days locked up in an enclosed, walled-in space—a prefabricated villa, with a fake garden and a real chicken coop—the last four contestants had been brought together in the vast living room, the two boys sitting close together on the white sofa, the two girls on either side in matching armchairs. The host, whose career had just taken a turn that was as phenomenal as it was unexpected, gleefully reminded everyone that the crucial, much-awaited moment had arrived at last: "I'm gonna start at ten and when I reach zero, you're out of here!" He asked one last time if the audience was ready to accompany him, then started the countdown, "Ten, nine, eight, seven, six, five," assisted by a docile, powerful chorus. The contestants hurried toward the exit, their suitcases in hand, "four, three, two, one, zero!" The door opened as if pulled by a rush of air, and there was a burst of applause.

Now the host was shouting at the top of his lungs in order to be heard above the noise of the crowd that had amassed outside and the clamor of the impatient audience, held captive for more than an hour inside the studio. "They're out! They're on their way! After seventy days it's back to reality for Laura, Loana, Christophe, and Jean-Édouard!" Several times over, the camera showed a wide shot of the fireworks being launched from the roof of the building that had housed them all through those long weeks, while the last four contestants stepped onto the red carpet that had been rolled out for the occasion.

They were out, yes, yet it still looked strangely like indoors. An overexcited horde was pressed up against the barriers, photographers were trying to get closer, people they didn't know were begging for autographs, reporters held out microphones. Some people were waving banners or signs with the contestants' names, others were filming them with small movie cameras (back then, cell phones were rudimentary devices whose only purpose was to make phone calls).

Everything they had been promised had happened. In only a few weeks, they had become famous.

Escorted by bodyguards, they moved forward among their fans, while the host went on analyzing their progress, "They're only a few meters from the studio, take a look, they're going up the steps." The repetitive overlap of image and commentary did not reduce the dramatic tension; on the contrary, it suddenly gave it a stunning new dimension (the format would be reused in every way imaginable for decades to come). The cries grew louder, and a black curtain parted to let them through. When they came into the studio, where their families were waiting, along with the nine other contestants who had left the competition of their own free will, or been eliminated over the course of the previous weeks, the tension rose a notch. In the overheated atmosphere and growing excitement, the crowd began to chant one name: "Loana! Loana!"

Like many other viewers, the Claux family all hoped Loana would win. Mélanie thought she was simply magnificent (her sculpted silicon breasts, her flat stomach, her tanned skin); Sandra, two years older, was drawn to her solitary nature and her melancholy air (the young woman had initially been rejected by the other contestants because of the way she dressed, then, although she seemed to have integrated, she had remained the focus of whispers and rumors). As for Madame Claux, she'd been deeply affected by the elimination of Julie, a likable, joyful young contestant, far and away her favorite until she was voted out, but she couldn't help but be moved by Loana's story—her difficult childhood, her little daughter who'd been placed with a foster family—as reported in the tabloids. Richard Claux, the girls' father, only had eyes for the beautiful blonde. The pictures of Loana in her shorts, miniskirt, halterneck top, or swimsuit, along with her reticent smile, haunted him at night, and even sometimes during the day that followed. The entire family agreed they didn't like Laura, who they thought was too posh, as well as Jean-Édouard, an inconsiderate, stupid, spoiled brat.

A short while later, once the TV viewers had chosen the two winners and everyone was making their way to the secret place where the rest of the evening would unfold, a ballet of black automobiles, followed by motorcyclists equipped with movie cameras, pulled away from La Plaine Saint-Denis. A technical crew worthy of the Tour de France had taken their positions. At red lights, microphones were thrust through open windows to gather people's impressions of the winners.

"I haven't seen anything like this since Chirac's election!" said the host, whose makeup could no longer hide his exhaustion.

In the streets close to the Place de l'Étoile, it was gridlock. On the Avenue de la Grande-Armée, the crowd was converging from all the adjacent streets, and people were leaving their cars behind to be able to get closer. At the entrance to the nightclub, hundreds of eager onlookers were waiting for the *lofters*.

"Everybody loves us, it's awesome!" declared Christophe, one of the two winners, to the female host from the show who was at the scene. Loana stepped out of the car, wearing a skimpy, pale pink, crocheted top and faded jeans. Perched on her platform heels, she unfolded her spectacular body and looked all around her. Some people thought they could detect a sort of absence in her eyes. Or bewilderment. Or else the tragic intimation of a destiny.

Mélanie Claux was seventeen years old at the time, and had just finished her second year in the literary section at the lycée Saint-François d'Assise in La Roche-sur-Yon. Something of an introvert, she didn't have many friends. Although she had never really imagined that her future could, in any way, be tenuously linked to the uncertain pursuit of her studies, she was hard-working and got good grades. Television was what she liked more than anything. The empty feeling she had—something she couldn't describe, perhaps a sort of anxiety, or the fear that her life might slip away from her, a feeling that sometimes hollowed its way into her gut like a narrow, bottomless well—that only ever left her in peace when she settled down in front of the small screen.

A few hundred kilometers away, in Bagneux, in the Paris region, Clara Roussel was watching the finale of *Loft* on her own and in secret. She was in the first year of lycée. Her obvious skills and the very average level of her lycée meant she could get satisfactory grades even though she didn't do a bit of work at home. She was interested in boys more than anything, with a preference for short-haired blonds; the competition seemed less stiff in this category, because the trend was undeniably in favor of dark, brooding types. The way she expressed herself— she was often teased about her choice of vocabulary and her penchant for convoluted sentences—was not common for her age, but it turned out to be an asset when it came to flirting. Her parents, both teachers who were very involved in the local community and public activism, were founding members of a collective that went by the name of Smile, You're On Camera. It consisted of people who didn't want to end up in a society of repressive technology, and who were very active in the struggle against any form of video surveillance. The collective had called on television viewers to boycott *Loft Story* and, a few weeks earlier, to empty their garbage cans outside the head offices of M6, the television channel airing the show. That day they threw eggs, yogurt, tomatoes, and a great deal of garbage. Naturally, Clara's parents had taken part in the protest and subsequently joined another major operation piloted by Zaléa TV (an alternative channel which, in the early 00s, had conducted an unprecedented experiment in free television). No fewer than two hundred and fifty activists had managed to get near the Loft, in order to free the participants. They had even managed to climb over a first protective wall. Philippe, Clara's father, actually appeared in a short segment that was broadcast on the France 2 newscast.

"The Red Cross is allowed to enter prison camps, we demand the same right! The participants are underfed, exhausted, exposed to the glare of projectors, they are constantly in tears—free the hostages!" he declared, to a journalist's microphone.

"Let them out!" they all chanted in chorus, when a riot squad prevented them from going any further.

Suffice to say that Clara's parents, who were busy the night of the finale at a meeting held by the collective on the question "What sort of society do we want to live in?" would not have appreciated the fact that their daughter, who was barely fifteen years old, was taking advantage of their absence to sprawl in front of that diabolical program, the manifest symptom of a world where everything had become merchandise and was governed by ego worship.

Eleven million viewers were tuned into the finale of *Loft Story* that night. Never had a television program aroused so much passion. The print media had initially focused on the arrival of the format in France, then, from one revelation or plot twist to the next, they were hooked, devoting columns and op-eds and front pages to the program. For several weeks, sociologists, anthropologists, psychologists, psychiatrists, psychoanalysts, journalists, editorialists, writers, and essayists dissected the program and its success.

More than once they wrote, "There will be a before and an after."

They wanted to be on television to become famous. Now they were famous for having been on television. They would be the first, forever. The pioneers.

Twenty years later, the iconic moments of the first season—the famous "swimming pool scene" between Loana and Jean-Édouard, the arrival of the contestants at the Villa, and the finale in its entirety—would be available on YouTube. Under one of these videos, the very first comment written by an Internet user resonated like an oracle: "The era when they opened the doors of hell."

Maybe it really was during those few weeks that everything began. The permeability of the screen. The new possibility of transitioning from watcher to watched. The determination to be seen, recognized, admired. The idea that it was within anyone and everyone's reach. No need to make things up, create, or invent, to be entitled to your "fifteen minutes of fame." All you had to do was show your face and stay in the frame, or facing the camera lens.

Before long the arrival of new platforms would exacerbate

the phenomenon. From now on, everyone would exist through the exponential multiplication of their own traces, in the form of images or comment. Traces, they would learn soon enough, that could not be erased. Accessible to all, the Internet and social media would quickly take over from television and multiply the range of possibilities. Put yourself on display—indoors, outdoors, from every angle. Live to be seen, or live vicariously. Reality TV, and all the various ways it could provide personal testimonies of life, would gradually expand to many domains and continue, for a long time, to dictate their codes, their vocabulary, and their narrative models.

Yes, that was when it all began.

When Mélanie's mother spoke to her, she generally began her sentences with "you," immediately followed by a negative, so she wouldn't have to come straight out with her own feelings. *You never do a thing, you won't change, you didn't tell me, you didn't empty the dishwasher, you aren't going out looking like that, are you?* "You" and "n't" were practically inseparable. When Mélanie decided to enroll at the faculty of English, once she'd obtained her baccalaureate (without any honors but on her first try), her mother said: "Don't you go thinking we're going to pay for ten years of university!" Studying, having a career, was something boys did (Madame Claux, to her great regret, had not had any sons), whereas the main priority for girls was to see to finding a good husband. As for Madame Claux, she had devoted herself to bringing up her children and had never understood why Mélanie wanted to leave the region, suspecting that a certain snobbery lay behind her decision. "It's not nice to go around with your nose in the air," she would add, exceptionally departing from the "you and n't" rule. Despite this warning, the summer she turned eighteen Mélanie packed a suitcase and moved to Paris. Initially she lived in the seventh arrondissement, in a maid's room with a shared sink and toilet outside in the corridor, in exchange for four nights a week babysitting, then she rented a tiny studio in the fifteenth (she had found a job at a travel agency and her father sent her two hundred euros a month).

How she had come to leave university in order to work full time at the agency was not something she could have easily explained, other than to say that sometimes everything seemed preordained, both success and failure, and she'd received no signs encouraging her to go on with her studies: she had decent results, but other students already spoke without an accent and wrote perfect English. Above all, when she tried to project herself into the future from the *present continuous* she couldn't see a thing. Nothing at all. When the position for an assistant became available at the agency, the manager offered it to her: it would combine both human and administrative aspects, so Mélanie said yes. The days went by quickly and she felt she was where she belonged. In the evening she went back to her little studio on the rue Violet, which she could now pay for on her own, fixed herself a TV dinner, and never missed a single reality show. *Temptation Island*, though a little too immoral to her taste, and *The Bachelor*, more romantic, were easily her favorites. On the weekend she went out with her friend Jess (they'd met in secondary school, and Jess had also moved to Paris) to drink beer at a bar or vodka orange at a nightclub.

A few years later, due to increased competition from online tour operators, the travel agency that had given Mélanie her start in the world of work entered a difficult period, and ended up on the verge of going out of business.

One evening when she was visiting a website specialized in recruiting reality TV contestants (in fact, over time she had replied to several ads, without ever being contacted), she came upon a new offer. The only requirements were to be between twenty and thirty years of age, to be single, and to send two photographs: a portrait, and a full-length picture, preferably in a leotard or bathing suit. After all, she thought, a few days of hope, a few days nurturing her dream, that would already be something. A week later they contacted her. A young voice—it took her several minutes to determine the gender—asked her twenty or more questions about her tastes, her figure, her motivation. She lied about two or three details and acted more brazen than she actually was. She would have to show more originality if she wanted to be chosen. They gave her an appointment for the following week.

On the day, it took her over an hour to choose her outfit. She knew she had to express a certain style, both readable and striking, a style that would immediately reflect an important aspect of her personality. The problem was that she wore the same thing every day: shirt, sweater, jeans—and the more she thought about it, the less sure she was that she had any particular personality to reveal.

Mélanie Claux dreamt of being flamboyant and irresistible; but for now she was still the reserved young woman, discreet in appearance, that she hated.

In the end, she chose her tightest trousers (she had to lie on the floor to close the zipper, even though there was Lycra in the material), and a promotional T-shirt from Nestlé—where her father had just been promoted to senior executive—which she cut above her chest to make the brand's logo disappear. She put on her sneakers and looked in the mirror. She'd gone a little too far with the scissors: a sizable part of her bra was visible, but it gave her a look, no doubt about it. Her appointment was for 6 P.M. To make sure she wouldn't be late, she'd asked for the afternoon off.

She arrived at the production offices five minutes early. Her nails were painted pale pink, and her makeup—faint blush, a light touch of mascara—made her look very young. They ushered her into a huge square room where a stool and a movie camera on a stand had been set up. The young man who had led her silently along a labyrinth of corridors left her on her own. Mélanie waited. Several minutes went by, then a quarter of an hour, then half an hour. Certain that the camera was filming her without her knowledge, she refused to show any signs of irritation or vexation. Patience was, without a doubt, one of the prerequisites for a good reality TV contestant, and so she decided to go on waiting without speaking up, convinced that this was some sort of test.

After an hour, a furious woman burst into the room.

"Honestly, couldn't you have let me know you were here? If no one tells me, how am I supposed to know?"

"I—I'm sorry. I thought you . . . you knew."

When she was upset, Mélanie instantly became short of breath, which reduced her voice to a near-whisper.

The woman calmed down.

"You have to make more noise if you want people to hear you. How old are you?"

"Twenty-six," she replied, scarcely any more loudly.

The woman asked her to stand facing the camera. Then in profile, from the back, and again in profile. She asked her to walk. To laugh and arrange her hair. She asked her a slew of questions: how much she weighed, what her qualities were, what she liked best about her appearance, what, on the other hand, she despised, what people most often reproached her with, whether she had any complexes, how she would describe her ideal man, whether she could change her look, her atti-tude, or her physique for love. Mélanie tried to answer all the questions as best she could. She thought she was a little on the plump side, but not bad-looking, she was frank and had a joyful temperament, she dreamt of falling deeply in love with a tender, attentive man, she wanted children (at least two), yes, she was prepared to do a lot of things for love, but not just anything.

The woman showed she was annoyed, but didn't actually stop the interview (she'd been trained by Alexia Laroche-Joubert, an emblematic producer of reality TV in France, whose motto was,

"A good contestant either charms you or annoys you; if they bore you, forget it"). Mélanie exasperated her. Maybe it was the squeaky voice, which became high-pitched when she was upset, or maybe it was those big eyes that reminded her of a cartoon cow. Gone were the days when producers of so-called confinement reality TV were content with merely filming the abysmal boredom of a handful of young guinea pigs around the clock. Other ingredients had to be added to the founding principle of exhibition: fabrication, disinhibition, exacerbated sexuality. Physiques and figures had changed as rapidly as names, real or borrowed. Dylan, Carmelo, Kellya, Kris, Beverly, and Shana had replaced Christophe, Philippe, Laura, and Julie.

More than once, the casting director thought she ought to cut the interview short. She wasn't looking for a well-mannered young woman. She needed caricatures, lies, manipulation, and people who were trash. She needed antagonism and rivalry, future little soundbites of the kind people would pick up on while flicking through the channels. But she didn't stop the interview. It briefly occurred to her that the contestant sitting before her was far more formidable than she first appeared. What if, beneath that deceptive banality, there hid the most brutal, wildest, blindest ambition she'd ever encountered? All the more dangerous in that it was so well camouflaged. Then the thought faded and once again she saw Mélanie Claux there before her, a rather lackluster young woman who was swaying from one foot to the other and didn't know what to do with her hands.

Good reality TV casting always used the same ingredients, which the professionals summed up as follows: one vixen + one bimbo + one funny man + one dishy guy + one big-headed jerk. Experience had shown, however, that a less assertive personality was not altogether useless. A scapegoat, a mediator, an airhead, a village idiot, could always come in handy. But even for this kind of role, Mélanie wouldn't be the first choice.

On the pad in front of her, she scribbled in red:

Little Miss Average. Reply: No thanks.

"We'll call you," she announced firmly, heading for the door.

Mélanie picked up her bag from the chair and followed her out. When she raised her arms to put on her jacket, her breasts, which the casting director had noticed straightaway, given their fullness, seemed to spill out of her T-shirt. Mélanie really did have very big breasts, real ones, supple and apparently soft, and the lace on the pink bra seemed unable to contain them. Whether it was a sudden doubt or her intuition, as the young woman was meekly preparing to leave the room, the casting director stopped her with a faint wave of her hand.

"Tell me, Mélanie, how many boyfriends have you had?"

"What do you mean by *boyfriend*?" asked Mélanie, aware that she was playing her last card.

"Let me put it more bluntly," sighed the woman. "How many guys have you slept with?"

A few seconds of silence followed, then Mélanie looked her straight in the eye.

"None."

After Mélanie had gone, the director wrote in red under her photo:

26 years old. Virgin.

And underlined it three times.

CRIME SQUAD – 2019

MISSING CHILD KIMMY DIORE

Subject:
Transcript of most recent Instagram stories posted by Mélanie Claux Diore.

STORY 2

Broadcast November 10, 16:55
Duration: 38 seconds

Mélanie Claux is in her car. She is holding her cell phone in her hand and speaking, facing the camera. The name of the filter she is using ("doe eyes"), is written on the screen, top left.

She turns the device toward her children, both sitting in the back of the car. Sammy smiles to the camera, Kimmy is sucking her thumb and rubbing her nose with a stuffed camel toy in her hand. The little girl ignores the cell phone trained on her and doesn't smile.

Mélanie: "Hi there, kids, thank you so much! So many of you voted to help us, and you chose the gold Nike Air sneakers for Kimmy! Of course, as always, we took your advice and those are the ones we bought! They are a-ma-zing! Thank you for your help and participation. I'll share them with you later on, so you can see them on her feet. They suit her to perfection!!!

"Now we're on our way home! But we're not leaving you behind! We'll see you very soon, you angels!"

Clara Roussel was finishing her law degree at the Sorbonne when she decided to take the entrance exam to the national police academy. She was twenty-four. She was at a loss to explain how the idea had come to her one morning, when only a few days earlier there had been nothing to suggest such a sudden change of direction. The best explanation she could come up with was a desire for justice, an urge to feel useful, her idealism when it came to protecting and defending her fellow citizens—so many banal arguments which in reality were mere pretexts. Because she couldn't come out and say, as she would later, without the slightest embarrassment or scruples: I want to see blood, horror, and Evil closer up. And yet she hadn't read that many crime novels (with the exception of a few Agatha Christies during a rainy summer in Brittany) and she didn't watch any series. She was a teenager by the time her parents agreed to buy their first television set, to be used solely for watching panel discussions and documentaries. But there were two films she'd seen at the cinema that had really captured her imagination: Sydney Lumet's *Serpico* (one of her father's favorite cult films) and *Police* by Maurice Pialat (her boyfriend at the time had just started at La Fémis film school and had made it his business to introduce her to French cinema).

Clara left the family home after her second year of university for a shared apartment in the thirteenth arrondissement, a stone's throw from Porte de Gentilly. The rent was low and the apartment was furnished. She had two roommates. They were officially a couple, but she found that hard to believe: not only did they have nothing in common, but there did not seem to be any sexual chemistry between them at all. And for good reason. It didn't take Clara long to get to the bottom of things: it turned out that each partner had a true love relationship on the side with a person of the same sex, and their association was merely a screen for the benefit of their narrow-minded parents. As for Clara's parents, they wouldn't have batted an eyelash, if they'd found out that their daughter was a lesbian (which didn't seem to be the case), but they did think she was telling them a tasteless joke when she informed them she had applied to take the competitive entrance exam for the national police academy.

"The first test is an essay on general culture," Clara told them, after explaining that the external competition for officers was reserved for people who had at least a university degree or equivalent diploma. If she passed, she would start at the academy soon after the competition.

On hearing these details, and the tone his daughter adopted, which ruled out the initial hypothesis of a post-adolescent practical joke, her father had to sit down. For a few minutes he had trouble breathing and Clara thought about the expression, "to have your breath taken away," which he often used. Her mother, hands trembling, wouldn't look her in the eye.

"Should there be complete freedom of speech on the Internet?" was the general culture topic assigned to candidates that year. Clara then took a test where she had to solve a practical case on the basis of administrative documentary records, then came a questionnaire requiring short answers about general administrative law and public liberties, another questionnaire about general knowledge, and a final admissions test regarding criminal procedure. After that she was summoned for physical tests: a cardio-respiratory endurance test and a motor skills obstacle course. She passed the first test with flying colors, but the second one left her with mixed feelings. Clara was a small person. "What a feisty little lady," her uncle Dédé liked to say, an expression that drove her crazy. As a child, she'd had all sorts of medical tests to determine why she was so small. For a few months there had even been talk of a growth hormone treatment, then Réjane and Philippe, with their daughter's consent, had decided to let nature take its course. By the time she was an adult, Clara stood just over five foot tall. She was small but perfectly proportioned. Agile and sporty, she had plenty of stamina and was not particularly anxious about the test. That day, after a promising beginning under the watchful eye of Commandant M., a blond man in his forties whose bearing and charisma did not go unnoticed, she lost her balance on the beam, fell, got back up, then set off again in the wrong direction.

In the gym there were peals of laughter, and a loud voice saying, ironically, "The exit's over here." Clara stopped and took a few seconds to catch her breath. She looked the commandant in the eye, searching his face for permission to continue. The man's expression was inscrutable. Proudly, not saying a word, she continued on the course.

When she got home, Clara thought that despite her clearly iffy motor skills, she'd managed to display an undeniable tolerance to ridicule—which, in the police force, was bound to come in handy.

M élanie got the call one morning at nine. She'd been chosen for the very first season of *Meet You in the Dark!* Chosen, selected, elected. She jumped for joy, saying over and over, "I can't believe it! I can't believe it!," then she was overcome by a wave of nausea so strong that she had to lie down on her stomach. Later, she called her mother, who initially thought she was making things up, but eventually concluded, "Don't you go getting ideas in your head!" A little later, Mélanie had to fill out a request for unpaid leave, as the shoot would take place in the middle of the week. The timing wasn't ideal, but her boss agreed to let her go.

On the appointed day, a contestants' assistant drove Mélanie to the town of Chambourcy, where the production company had rented a house.

A description of the program is still available on Wikipedia:

"*Meet You in the Dark* was a French television program aired on TF1 from April 16, 2010 to April 11, 2014 (three seasons)."

The page includes a succinct explanation of the show's formula:

"Would they find love? Three women and three men, all single, convened in a big villa, the men on one side, the women on the other. The only common room was a dark room, equipped with infrared cameras, where the participants were brought to get acquainted in complete darkness. They went on to choose a partner they'd be alone together with in the dark room. At the end of the show, their chosen partner was revealed to them in the light and at that point they had to decide if they wanted to take things further.

"After disappointing audience ratings, the program was replaced by *Who Wants to Marry My Son?*"

Of the three girls, Mélanie was the first to arrive. In the wardrobe, a label with her name on it marked out her territory, and she arranged her belongings in the designated area. She had brought her showiest clothes, although she'd been warned that the production company could suggest other outfits adapted to her style and personality if they thought it was necessary. Another contestants' assistant poked his head around the door to inquire whether she needed anything, to which Mélanie replied in the negative, although she was famished, terrified, and frozen (the assistant director had forgotten to plug in the space heater in the room). The assistant asked her to go to the living room where the other two female contestants would soon join her. Now it was time to meet her rivals. Naturally their reactions would be filmed as they were introduced to each other. Sitting on the huge sofa upholstered in pink fabric, Mélanie had a thought for Loana. But this time she, Mélanie Claux, was the one facing the camera, on the side of the screen where she should be. She was the one in the middle of the frame, who would soon be watched by millions of TV viewers, who'd be recognized in the street, pursued, worshipped. A wave of emotion came over her, and for a few seconds she saw herself climbing out of a luxury car, submerged by a tide of fans waving notebooks or photographs in hopes of an autograph. She could feel, physically, that onslaught of love and admiration, and the joy it would bring her—a state of grace, an ancient void filled at last. But very quickly, aware that her reverie was going too far and beginning to release a powerful, addictive molecule into her brain, Mélanie swept the vision aside.

From the picture window she saw a young blonde woman heading toward the front door, dragging a big suitcase behind her. For a few seconds, Mélanie couldn't take her eyes off the woman's legs, endless legs, slim and smooth, made longer still by stiletto heels that were at least four inches high. She felt the blood draining from her face, pooling in her feet. It looked like the competition would be tough. Savane came into the room and delivered a *Hello* in a tone that revealed both arrogance and the awareness of incarnating a male fantasy: a sensual, erotic superiority, that few women could equal. She was wearing a leopard-skin bustier and a black leather miniskirt, that Mélanie thought looked more like a belt. She struggled to hide her anxiety and clenched her fists. She'd stopped biting her nails a few years earlier, but there were times when the urge came back, with all the authority of compulsion. The two women gave each other air kisses and made small talk for the avid eye of the cameras. Reality TV had long given up on the principle of live broadcasts, which were cruelly lacking in dramatic tension. Still, both women knew that every word or gesture could be chosen during the editing process. Then the third contestant arrived, as dark as Savane was blonde, "and every bit as vulgar," thought Mélanie, fascinated all the same by her hair (long, straight and shiny, the color of ebony), and her denim shorts, the frayed edge not quite hiding the bottom of her buttocks. She too was beautiful, with that highly alluring, sexual beauty that Mélanie would never have. More than anything she envied their power to subjugate.

Once the introductions were over, they were each asked to put on their sexiest outfit and proceed to makeup. They would meet again in the living room. On her bed, Mélanie found a short skirt and a halterneck top, which she put on without a second thought. The makeup artist then set about making her look good. Mélanie worried about the amount of foundation she was using, but the assistant gently reassured her: they knew how to do their job. A hair stylist smoothed her hair with a straightener and waxed rhapsodic over the color: he'd rarely seen such intense chestnut brown. Night had just fallen when Mélanie looked at herself in the mirror. She got the impression she was seeing another version of herself. A magnified, transformed, idealized version, one that could not survive. "Because the carriage always turns back into a pumpkin," she thought, "and the ball gown goes back to rags."

They were served a first cocktail in the living room. The blue liqueur—unfamiliar to Mélanie, mixed with soda and garnished with a slice of lemon—gradually relaxed her neck, shoulders, and limbs. The men had arrived and were on the other side of the villa, in a part of the building that was closed off from the women. After a few drinks, the girls began to laugh, and they lapsed into an easy closeness. A voice from production came over the loudspeaker above the sofa, which was essentially there to direct their conversation, after a fashion. The Voice asked them to describe their ideal man, or to explain why they were single. Vanessa and Savane liked sturdy, muscular men, Mélanie had a weakness for the rounder type with extra padding. "A bit like a Teddy bear," she added, and all three burst out laughing. Savane had a child she was raising on her own, Vanessa had just left a jealous partner (a fleeting expression of pain clouded her face), and Mélanie explained that she was a romantic and was waiting for her *other half*, the man with whom she could start a family.

Three or four cocktails later, they gave a start when the Voice interrupted them again:

"Savane, Vanessa, and Mélanie, they are waiting for you in the dark room . . ."

Mélanie had not imagined the darkness would be so opaque. She groped her way forward, her hands held out in front of her. Finally, she bumped into something, realized it was an arm-chair, and sat down. The only thing she could see, in each corner of the room, was the indicator light of an infrared camera. Savane and Vanessa came in after her, and she helped them find the armchairs on either side of her own. When the women were seated, the men were ushered in. A strong, musky perfume immediately spread through the room.

Never had darkness seemed so dark to her. They all said their names, first the women, then the men. Once the formal introductions were over, the Voice invited them to stand up and become acquainted in a more tactile way.

"You can touch, feel each other, get to know each other! You can't see, so you have to use all your other senses to get acquainted."

One of the men came over to Mélanie and put his arm around her waist. The young woman stiffened. Yoann was able nevertheless to gauge the size of her breasts; just to make sure, he held her a little closer. When he lowered his nose to her neck to breathe in her scent, she could not help but pull away.

"Whoa . . . we've got a shy one on our hands!" he exclaimed, a bit too loudly.

The Voice intervened.

"Mélanie, don't hesitate to get to know your admirers."

Just next to her she could hear sighs and giggles. Savane and Carmelo had gotten significantly closer.

Yoann, put off, walked around her to look for Vanessa.

Throughout the rest of the session, women and men touched, sniffed, caressed each other. The three men had clustered around the other two girls, hands roaming, slow and sensual. It was all about seduction, domestication; their fate depended on it. Around her, Mélanie caught a whiff of sweat mingling with other perfumes; the powerful, acrid smell of desire had gradually pervaded the room. A few minutes had sufficed to eliminate her from the game. Several times over the Voice asked the men to go up to her, and they did, but they never touched her again.

After what seemed to Mélanie an endless amount of time (after editing, the sequence would only last ten minutes or so), the Voice ordered them to leave the dark room and return to their respective areas.

Later, in the confession box, each of the men had to announce to the camera which young woman he wanted to see again in private. Not one of them chose Mélanie.

She left the game the following day, escorted by a contestants' assistant. The production company had allowed her to keep the skirt and halter neck, and gave her, pointedly, a makeup palette compliments of the cosmetics brand that sponsored the show.

In the car, she began to cry. Realizing it would be the least embarrassing solution for both of them, the contestants' assistant turned up the volume on the car radio.

Mélanie watched the trees and fields and villages go by, and as they came closer to Paris, the first warehouses and high-rise apartment buildings appeared. When the car merged into the traffic on the beltway, her gaze landed on a giant billboard hanging from the top of a brand new building, advertising the lipstick *Color Riche* by L'Oréal. For a moment she stared at the mat color and apparent thickness of the substance. The lipstick seemed as erect as a monument, or a penis, or a flagpole. Behind it, Laetitia Casta's face reflected a light that seemed to have come out of nowhere, as if it were for her alone. And then everything became clear. She would become one of those women. She wanted that warm light, shadows sculpting her face, a luscious mouth. In a few months the agency would be closing and she'd be unemployed, but she wouldn't go back to La Roche-sur-Yon. No. She'd stay here, in Paris, because it was here that *everything* happened.

She would stay here and one day she'd be famous.

MISSING CHILD KIMMY DIORE

Subject:

Transcript of most recent Instagram stories posted by Mélanie Claux Diore.

STORY 3

Posted November 10 at 17:18
Duration: 42 seconds

Mélanie Claux is facing the camera. Only her face and upper body are visible. All through the video, gifs or animated emoticons are superimposed on her: hearts of various colors, characters from *The Little Mermaid*, *Frozen* and other Disney films (a bear?) waving a sign with a beating heart.

Mélanie: "Hello you *sweeties*, we just got home from the mall and would you believe it, Kim and Sam have already gone out again! That tired spell in the car didn't last long. Some of their friends were playing in the courtyard and they went down to join them. I think they're playing hide-and-seek, and I'm going to use the time to put away the shopping and make some crepe batter for this evening. You heard right! Like I told you this morning, it's

Wednesday night and as you know, one Wednesday a month, it's . . . crepe party! And of course, we'll have Nutella! (*An animated Nutella jar appears, superimposed.*)

You know Sammy! No crepes without Nutella! I'll give you the recipe, those of you who haven't written it down yet.

There you are my angels, we haven't forgotten you! See you later!"

A shower of multicolored hearts pours over the image.

Every family cultivates its own myth. Or at least an epic version of its history, enriched over time, to which exploits, coincidences, and remarkable details are gradually added, and even some pure fabrication. Clara's family—her parents, grandparents, aunts and uncles and, later, her cousins—liked telling the stories about the strikes, the demonstrations, the rallies, in short, the whole range of mostly pacifist battles, won or lost, that anchored their family history in a time-honored tradition of social struggle. The dates had their own significance: Réjane and Philippe had met in June 1985, during the huge celebration organized on the Place de la Concorde by SOS Racisme. Clara had been conceived the night of the protest against the Devaquet bill on university reform, and her parents got married when Clara was already nine years old, the day after the Juppé plan to reform the funding of Social Security and special retirement regimes was scrapped.

Over time, the various versions of the story had been enriched with romantic subtleties, to the occasional detriment of chronological coherence. Because on closer inspection, the dates didn't always match up. For example, how could Clara, who was born in 1986, have been conceived in November of the same year?

Clara, however, had a clear memory of the famous strike and unrest in 1995. Her father, busy trying to keep things from getting out of hand toward the rear of the procession, inadvertently let go of her hand. Instead of allowing herself to be carried further along on the tide and continuing the march, she'd been pulled off to the side (or had she left the march of her own accord?), and then she'd stood on the sidewalk waiting for her father. It had taken her several minutes to realize that she couldn't see him anywhere and that she was lost. She couldn't call for help; the people shouting slogans through their megaphones were making too much noise. She decided to sit down on the ground, saying over and over to herself a sentence the demonstrators had been chanting, one she liked better than the others: "Sow poverty and you'll reap anger! Sow poverty and you'll reap anger!" Gradually the last marchers filed past the little girl, brandishing their banners and banging on casseroles. She wasn't afraid. Two or three kindly people had stopped to ask her what she was doing there, and she always gave the same poised, well-behaved reply: she was waiting for her mommy who had gone to use the restroom. In fact, Réjane had insisted on marching in the middle of the procession with her colleagues from the Collège Romain-Rolland, and she'd left Philippe in charge of their little girl. Clara knew that she was not, under any circumstances, to go off with a stranger.

She didn't know Paris very well, so for a while she sat looking around her at the façades of the Haussmann-era buildings. She was beginning to get cold when she saw two policemen in uniform coming toward her. She'd always heard you shouldn't trust cops, so she leapt to her feet and tried to run away, but the younger of the two quickly caught up with her. How long it had been since her father disappeared, she couldn't say. In the early versions of the anecdote, it was twenty minutes, then half an hour, then everyone settled more or less definitively on the story that she'd been waiting two hours—less probable but more sensational.

What was certain was that Clara ended up at the police station in the twelfth arrondissement, while several policemen tried to reach her parents. She played chess with a young intern, and a gentleman with a big mustache, who seemed to be the boss, gave her a lollipop.

Those are the images that came back to her that day in June when she had to inform her parents that she had indeed passed the admissions exam to enter the National School of Police Officers. For several weeks, Réjane and Philippe had been surprised to find themselves hoping she would fail, while Clara told them about the successive tests: once she was pre-admitted, she had to take written psycho-technical tests, then an individual simulation exercise, then there would be an interview with the jury and, to conclude, an oral English test. While she enumerated the various stages, her father had to refrain from asking her why cops turned out so damn stupid after such a difficult selection process.

The day Clara received the letter telling her she'd been accepted, she decided she'd go and see them to give them the good news. Part of her was dreading it, another part told her to have faith. Her parents had always shown her that they cared about her self-fulfillment, and respected her personality. Hadn't they let her go to London after her baccalaureate exam, instead of starting her studies right away? Hadn't they reacted with humor and indulgence, two years later, when they found out that she wasn't exactly an au pair girl for a family in a residential suburb anymore, but more of a hostess in a nightclub?

Clara walked through the archway of the first building and across the garden of the residence. She reminisced about the games she used to play as a child, and all the firecrackers she'd loved setting off in the bushes, or even, when the opportunity arose, in dog turds. She went into the second building and sped up the stairs. Her throat felt tight and apprehension spread through her entire body. When she reached the third floor, she could hear music. At this time of day, it wasn't at all in keeping with her parents' routine. She rang a first time, but no one came to open. She assumed her mother must be at the back of the apartment. She rang a second time, then took out her key. When she walked in she found her parents, her uncle Pascal, and his wife Patricia, all dressed up as police officers. They were standing in a line, a sort of merry, unruly guard of honor. Where had they unearthed those kepis and whistles? They looked authentic! She never found out.

"Show us your ID!" demanded Pascal.

They collapsed in laughter and let her go by. Her roommate must have let the cat out of the bag and told them she was coming. On the table there were bottles of wine and champagne, as well as all sorts of quiches, pies, and spreads, which her parents, who regularly attended parties, rallies, and other community picnics, had a real knack for making. A way to show her, despite their failure to comprehend—not to mention their sense of betrayal, which they tried to keep hidden—that they were prepared to celebrate her success with her. They raised their glasses. Her cousins Mario and Elvira, their wrists bound in handcuffs, improvised a dance.

At the end of the evening her uncle Dédé, who had joined them for dinner, picked up Réjane's guitar and began singing Renaud's *Hexagone*:

France is a land of cops
With hundreds on every corner
They kill and go unpunished
In the name of law and order.[1]

Just as she was about to protest, Philippe led his daughter into the kitchen. He pointed to a chair, and took the time to

[1] Hexagone, lyrics and music by Renaud Séchan, © Warner Chappell Music France – Catalogue Mino Music. Translation Alison Anderson.

open the window before he sat down across from her, cleared his throat, and lit a cigarette. He opened his mouth to say something, something serious he had no doubt prepared—a sentence, a piece of advice, some encouragement, something powerful and definitive. But nothing came out. Tears rose to his eyes. He sighed and merely gave her a smile, his palms spread in surrender.

Long afterwards, that smile was still there in Clara's memory, clear and precise, eclipsing all the others. Her father was the king of maxims and aphorisms, professions of faith and wooly theories, elaborated on the basis of mathematical formulas he enjoyed applying to the vagaries of everyday life. That evening, however, the words he wanted to say were so simple that they failed him. He wanted to say: *Look after yourself.*

A few months later he was dead.

When the two women met for the first time, ten years had passed since Mélanie Claux had moved to the Paris region and Clara Roussel had entered the National School of Police Officers. Ten years, like a gust of wind or the whack of a police baton, the kind of years you look back on, stunned and groggy, and wonder where on earth they went. Ten years of youth, quick and decisive, that both women would have found hard to describe if anyone had asked them to. Or maybe they would have said: those years were both happy and sad. Years that would vanish into a sort of mist, growing ever thicker, but from which a few dates would emerge—administrative, emotional, or symbolic.

In 2011 Mélanie Claux married Bruno Diore, whom she'd *matched* with a few months earlier on the Attractive World website. For a while she'd thought about taking her husband's name, and even of initiating a procedure to have the final silent *e* removed (Dior seemed more chic, and would undeniably have placed her in a different sphere) but given how complex the formalities would be, and the fact that she would have to provide a legitimate motive, she had decided against it. In the end she kept her maiden name. That same year she gave birth to a little boy, Sammy. Her husband, who was slightly older than her, was working for a computer engineering company at the time, and had just been given a significant raise. So she decided not to go back to the job as administrative assistant she'd had for some time in the same company, in order to devote herself full time to her son. After the wedding they had moved to Châtenay-Malabry—where Bruno's parents lived, and where he'd spent part of his adolescence—into a huge apartment in a recently-built residential complex a stone's throw from the park in Sceaux. A little girl they called Kimmy was born two years later, when the couple was going through a difficult period. Mélanie had decided she'd go on being a stay-at-home mom, a situation she fully enjoyed, while waiting for some hypothetical destiny.

After a few years working for the community policing and citizens' complaint bureau in the fourteenth arrondissement, where her superiors had appreciated her anticipation and deduction skills, and her unusually strong writing skills, Clara Roussel joined the Paris Crime Squad. The preliminary trial period she'd completed there, which was part of the recruitment process, had confirmed her determination to work for the criminal investigation department. While at the beginning she'd considered working for the Child Protection Squad, the little she had seen of child abuse cases had dissuaded her: her nerves were not strong enough. During her first two years with the Crime Squad Clara became fully acquainted with the famous premises of 36, Quai des Orfèvres. The regional headquarters were then transferred to the rue du Bastion, in the seventeenth arrondissement. Not everyone appreciated the move, and it triggered a number of departures and transfers. Several legendary figures from the squad chose that particular moment in time to leave. In the course of the reshuffle, and sooner than expected, Clara obtained a position as an evidence custodian. At the same time she joined the Berger Team, one of six teams that focused on criminal investigations.

The job title of evidence custodian was not exactly the stuff of dreams, but it was Clara's dream. The name evoked a nitpicking, fastidious occupation, something even a bit tedious, but she thought it was fun. It was a far cry from the imaginary depictions in TV series—high-risk manhunts, forceful arrests, networks of informers, and nights spent infiltrating unsavory milieus. And yet, no manhunt could take place without her. From the very first moments until the end of the investigation, Clara recorded every stage, in images or in writing. She loved to describe the nature of her job, something that only existed as such in the Crime Squad. The evidence custodian was the guarantor of the file that landed on the desk of the judge or prosecutor, and was responsible for its coherence, for making solid arguments, and for ensuring the absence of flaws or gaps. She began by overseeing all the findings from the crime scene, gathering all the traces and clues, and was in charge of the sealed evidence. Then, very often, she was called on to attend the autopsy in order to give the coroner the information they needed. Subsequently, she was responsible for all the research entrusted to third parties, and all the elements submitted to the court. She made sure they were pertinent and compliant. In addition to her own writing, Clara reread her colleagues' reports. She pointed out the weak areas and murky spots, asked for greater precision, and questioned certain turns of phrase. Occasionally she voiced her surprise when a lead had been too hastily abandoned.

The legal account would have to stand up in court . . . and if possible, in a binder as well: that was her role. It had to be legible, comprehensible, irreproachable. Rock solid. So that no lawyer could turn up an irregularity, nothing could be left to chance, every door still open had to be closed. A profession for an obsessive, persnickety pencil pusher, she would sometimes tell people with a smile.

Her reputation was firmly established. Nothing escaped her watchful eye, whether it came to content or form. She was capable of rejecting a report simply because there were problems with the syntax; she could detect a flaw in an alibi from a mere turn of grammar.

On a more personal level—a subject she never spoke of—Clara had been in love twice. And both times she had backed out. A feeling, a disposition, a weakness typical of the love-sick condition, a physical or physiological state brought on by waiting and dependency, or simply a change in her cycle—something that seemed to diminish rather than enhance her faculties—always ended up getting the better of her passion. And then fear would set in, a brutal, irrational fear that forced her to distance herself. All that remained of her most recent affair—the strongest and most obsessive—was their email correspondence. Clara had written letters to the man she once loved, and after several months of silence, he finally gave in and replied.

Ever since she'd started at the Squad, Clara had been living in Saint-Mandé, in a building that belonged to the police and where most of the tenants were cops. In her entourage, families were forming, bellies getting round. Having a child was not on her agenda. Not only was she not sure that she herself was fully adult, but the times seemed resolutely hostile as well. She got the impression that a deep, silent, insidious mutation of unprecedented violence was occurring—a step too far, a disastrous threshold being crossed in the great march of time—and no one could stop it. And to thrust a child into the thick of this gigantic web devoid of dreams or utopia seemed like sheer folly.

When she was three or four years old, her parents had taken her to stay with Philippe's mother near the Belgian border. Clara loved her granny very much, but the old woman lived in a dark apartment full of objects, knick-knacks, and oil paintings that frightened her. Her granny was delighted to have her granddaughter for a few days (Réjane and Philippe had plans to take some vacation on their own), and to welcome her family she'd prepared an afternoon tea. In spite of her fear that her parents would soon be leaving, Clara sat docilely on a stool with her hot chocolate. Then, just after she'd finished her snack, she said as tactfully as she knew how: "Granny, your place is very pretty, but you know . . . I won't be able to stay."

On evenings when Clara'd had a few drinks, in addition to the usual arguments she trotted out to justify her solitude or her celibacy, she would think of the times they lived in and the state of the world. This sense of being out of step, and the awareness, both futile and necessary, of being on the right side, in spite of everything. Sometimes, to conclude the conversation, as if it were a private joke she was sharing with herself, whose impact she herself refused to gauge, she would murmur: ". . . besides, I'm not sure I'll be able to stay."

On November 10, 2019, at around six o'clock in the evening, Mélanie Claux's six-year-old daughter disappeared while playing hide-and-seek with the other children from her apartment building.

When her son raised the alarm, Mélanie walked around the garden several times, and before long a few neighbors joined her. Everywhere they went they shouted the little girl's name, then, methodically, building by building, they knocked on every door. They made the rounds of basements and corridors, split into two groups, and asked the caretaker to open the common room. After more than an hour of fruitless searching, he suggested they call the police. Mélanie burst into tears. A tenant on the ground floor took charge of calling the police station and explaining the situation.

Half an hour later, ten or more policemen were deployed at the location to search for the child. Kimmy's "Dirty Camel" (a little threadbare cloth cuddly toy) was found on the ground near the play area.

After an hour of searching, where still more neighbors joined to go over every stairway, pathway, and nook and cranny of the garden with a fine-tooth comb, they had to conclude the child was truly missing.

At around 9 P.M., Mélanie and Sammy were taken to the police station in Châtenay-Malabry. Bruno, Mélanie's husband, was away from Paris on a business trip. As soon as he was informed, he jumped in his car, but according to his GPS he wouldn't be able to make it back before midnight.

A policewoman questioned Sammy in greater detail about the circumstances of the disappearance. The boy, who was eight, seemed in too great a state of shock to make a proper statement. Not without difficulty, the young woman encouraged him to tell her how the game of hide-and-seek had gone. According to what she managed to find out, the last time he'd seen her, Kimmy had been running toward the waste room where the trash cans were kept. He was very worried about his sister, and he seemed exhausted. After a short while the child rubbed his eyes, and fell asleep all of a sudden, sitting up. The young woman went to get his mother. Mélanie Claux gently lowered him onto the adjacent chair, stretched out his legs, and covered him with her down jacket.

A short while later, in the office of Commissaire S., Mélanie Claux was given a hot drink and questioned for the first time. The Commissaire typed rapidly on his computer keyboard while she went over the chain of events in detail: the three of them were on their way home from the Vélizy 2 shopping center when Sammy and Kimmy spotted the other children playing hide-and-seek. One of them, little Léo, immediately asked them to join in. Sammy and Kimmy turned to their mother, waiting for permission. At first she hesitated, then agreed.

As the hot drink didn't seem to have warmed her up in the slightest, Commissaire S. asked for a blanket to be brought. A minute later, she was wrapped in a woolen shawl that had been forgotten on the coat rack, and her hands were cupped around her mug. Commissaire S. let the silence take over the room. Not a suspicious silence, even though parents are always the first suspects in cases where children have gone missing; rather, something neutral and vacant asking to be filled. The husband was on his way, and as soon as he arrived the commissaire would set about questioning him himself.

Mélanie eventually looked up at him.

"We're famous, you know. The children and me. Very famous. I'm sure that has something to do with it."

A quick glance at his assistant confirmed that Brigadier F. had never heard of this woman or her children either. When it came to psychiatric disorders, Commissaire S. had seen others—much worse even—people who thought they were God, Céline Dion, or Zinedine Zidane. But experience had shown him that the best strategy was to let them talk. Mélanie's voice now seemed more high-pitched, somehow out of tune— fairly unpleasant, he would have concluded, under different circumstances.

"Most people love us. And they tell us, they write to us, they come hundreds of miles to see us. It's crazy how much love we get. You can't imagine. But recently, there've been rumors, some bad gossip, and now there are people who are full of resentment. They want bad things to happen to us. Because they're jealous."

"What are they jealous of, Madame Claux?" he asked, as gently as possible.

"Our happiness."

Aware that she had hit a wall of incredulity, Mélanie took out her smartphone to show the commissaire and his assistant her channel on YouTube, with its five million subscribers. Every one of the videos she published on Happy Recess had several million views. Then she connected to her personal Instagram account. She explained the figures: in addition to the number of subscribers and views, what mattered was the total number of likes and comments. It all represented a great deal, she insisted, it all meant that they were . . . she hesitated for a moment, searching for the right word, but she couldn't find anything else: yes, it all meant that they were stars.

When asked about the income generated by this activity, she refused to answer. She had a contract with the platform, she didn't have the right to divulge that information. Curtly, the commissaire reminded her that her daughter was missing. "We're afraid she might have been taken for unscrupulous reasons," he explained, a theory which gained traction in his mind when she eventually admitted to an annual income "of over one million euros." The commissaire could not help but let out a whistle. As he was obliged to do in these circumstances, he called the prosecutor on duty.

At 21:30, Mélanie Claux received a short private message on her Instagram account. The sender, whose name was unknown to her, had no followers of their own. Everything indicated that the account had been created with the sole purpose of sending her the following message: "Kid missing, deal coming," which confirmed the theory of a kidnapping for ransom.

At 21:35, in light of the initial developments, and given the family's notoriety (the mother's assertions had been verified), the prosecutor's office in Nanterre decided to refer the case to the Crime Squad.

At 21:55, the members of the Berger team, on call since that morning, entered the Poisson Bleu residence. Clara Roussel and her team leader were among the first to arrive, quickly joined by the section leader and the head of the Squad. For this sort of case, the entire team had to be ready to go at the drop of a hat.

Half an hour later, twenty or more investigators were deployed. While they began making inquiries in the neighborhood, Clara Roussel marked off the areas for forensic sampling and gave her instructions to the crime scene investigators.

She established a wide perimeter around the area where the child's cuddly toy had been dropped, and cordoned it off with police tape. Access to the parking lot and waste room was also taped off.

The cuddly toy, a few used tissues, twenty or more cigarette butts, a paper bag from a bakery, a long-haired Barbie doll head, and a broken compass were placed in sealed evidence bags. Photographs were taken of the footprints found on patches of earth, even though there were a lot of them and they were hard to follow.

Once the samples had been collected, the section head decided to send for search dogs. After being shown an item of the little girl's clothing, both dogs retraced exactly the same itinerary: they followed a trail that led through the waste room and came to an end in the parking lot.

While her colleagues continued questioning neighbors, hoping to find key evidence, Clara stayed in the common area.

During the night she would freeze-frame the crime scene. Describe the place as painstakingly as possible. Write everything down, record every single detail. Search for blood, sperm, hair, any trace left behind. Or else point out the absence of traces. As if the child had flown away.

She drew up a map of the apartment complex, indicating the entrances, the location of each of the three buildings, the playground, the waste room, and the underground parking lot. Then she inventoried the sealed bags containing evidence that had been found outside, as well as the elements collected in the apartment, with a view to collecting the DNA of the four family members. Investigators had gone through both children's rooms, searching for any possible clues to indicate whether the little girl had planned to meet someone, but they didn't come away with anything.

At this point, while the police were leaning toward the theory of a kidnapping for ransom, they could not rule out revenge, a pedophile network, or an unfortunate chance encounter. Given the child's age, she was unlikely to have run away.

Whatever the case may be, the clock was ticking. The statistics were categorical: when the abduction of a minor also led to a homicide, in nine cases out of ten the homicide occurred during the first twenty-four hours.

Shortly before two o'clock in the morning, as the police were about to take the parents home—escorted by a negotiator in the event the kidnappers got in touch with the family—Clara went up to them and introduced herself.

The first time Mélanie Claux and Clara Roussel met, despite the extreme tension both were under, Mélanie was astonished by the authority that emanated from such a tiny woman, and Clara noticed Mélanie's fingernails, with their sequined pink polish that shone in the dark. "She's like a little girl," thought Mélanie; "She's like a doll," thought Clara.

Even during the most dreadful, dramatic moments in life, appearances have their role to play.

Ever since the death of her parents Clara Roussel had been acutely aware of human fragility. At the age of twenty-five she had understood something that would stay with her for the rest of her life: you could leave the house one morning serene and confident, and never go home again. That was what had happened to her father, run over by a van one Saturday morning at half past eight, on his way to buy some croissants. More precisely, the vehicle only grazed him, but the side-view mirror hit his head so violently that it was partially torn from his body. A few months later her mother died of a ruptured aneurism while walking down the street. Since that day, whenever she was called to a crime scene, whenever she happened to go by one of those clusters that form in only seconds around a malaise or an accident, whenever she saw an ambulance or a fire truck stopped somewhere along the street, she was starkly reminded that every day, every minute, every second could witness the sudden reversal of a life. This was not a given, a fact she merely acknowledged intellectually the way most people did. It was a physical, oppressive sensation of terror that would stay with her for hours. Sometimes longer. That was why, when she was called on a case, the first conversation with the victim's family was extremely difficult for her. She couldn't help but feel the surge of adrenaline that was circulating in their blood as a physical echo in her own body. For a few seconds she was that woman who'd been told her child was dead, or that husband whose partner had been stabbed, or that old lady whose son had just been arrested.

For all the police officers at the Quai d'Orfèvres who'd seen their colleagues come back from the terrorist massacre at the Bataclan, the month of November was a dark time. Clammy. On the evening of November 10, 2019, Clara had just gone to meet her friend Chloé at a bar in the thirteenth arrondissement when she got the message from her boss, Cédric, on the team's WhatsApp. That very day she'd wound up a triple first degree murder case they'd spent weeks on. She would have liked to have time to toast the successful outcome of the procedure, one of the most complex she'd ever had to deal with, but her team had just gone on duty and calls rarely came at the right time. "Back to work," she thought, cracking her knuckles, a bad adolescent habit she'd never managed to break.

Calls in the middle of the night or at dawn, interrupted meals, holidays frittered away in the cold or the neon lights of her office, vacation time postponed . . . she'd prepared herself for all that vaguely heroic mythology that went with her profession, and was used to it. What she had not foreseen, however—something that took on more of a concrete reality with each passing day—was the degree of tension her body would be subjected to over the years. Even in her sleep her joints and muscles were primed and ready. As a result, at any time of the day or night she could jump to her feet, get dressed, and get going at the drop of a hat.

Once the first impression had worn off, during the few minutes they stood opposite each other in the yellow light of the residence's streetlamps, Clara saw the extent of Mélanie's distress. A brutal, absolute distress. While the young mother was looking around one last time, as if her daughter might suddenly emerge from a grove of trees, as if all this—the police scouring every corner of the garden, the plastic tape strung between the trees—could not possibly be happening, Clara felt as if she were absorbing Mélanie's deep distress. In the time it had taken to exchange a few words, she felt she could see with her naked eye the terror colonizing every cell in her body. Clinging to her husband's arm, Mélanie was reliving for the tenth time those minutes that were now inaccessible, minutes she would have liked, with every ounce of her being, to subtract from reality, minutes that were impossible to erase, and against which the greatest sorrow, the darkest regret were powerless: the moment when her son came back up from the garden to tell her that he couldn't find his sister.

At around two thirty in the morning, once she'd collected the first reports and all the sealed evidence, Clara finally went home. She knew she had to try and get at least two hours' sleep before heading back to the rue du Bastion.

But instead of going to bed, she turned on her computer, and searched for Happy Recess on the Internet. On the YouTube homepage, thirty or more thumbnails appeared, corresponding to the latest videos the family had posted. Under each one, the number of views was listed: between five and twenty-five million. Clara scrolled through the thumbnails; the list seemed endless. She was too tired to count them. There must have been at least several hundred videos of Kimmy Diore and her older brother. She stared for a while at the child's face, her blonde curls, her big dark eyes, "an adorable little girl," she thought, banishing all the visions that were beginning to besiege her, then she watched two or three videos at random.

In the short night that followed the child's disappearance, Clara awoke with a perfectly formed sentence in her mind. This happened to her from time to time: clear, ordered words, as if they were coming from her own lips, would rouse her brutally from her sleep. Each time, these sentences emerging from a dream, her unconscious, or some inaccessible place in the night, later took on meaning and sometimes even the form of an omen.

At 5:20, she sat up in bed, and in the silence of her room she heard herself say, out loud: "It's a world whose existence is beyond us."

This little six-year-old girl had disappeared in the world, the real world, and Clara knew its dangers only too well. But Kimmy Diore had grown up in a parallel universe, a world of make-believe, from start to finish, a virtual world Clara did not know. A world that obeyed rules she knew nothing about.

The terror penetrated Mélanie's body in a fraction of a second—acid, burning—before spreading through all her limbs. The terror was in her blood, powerful, much more powerful than anything she could have imagined. And yet she'd seen a fair number of those stories about missing children and mothers sick with worry on television and on Netflix. A box of tissues within reach, she'd identified with the protagonists. She'd suffered along with them and for a second, just a second, she'd considered the possibility that something like that could happen to her. Just long enough to conclude, "I wouldn't be able to bear it."

But this time she wasn't looking at one of those characters she'd so admired for their composure or their courage. Tonight she was the one standing there in her living room, stiff, tense, unable to sit down, unable to bear the slightest physical contact, not even her husband's hand on her shoulder.

Etched forever in her memory was Sammy's strangled voice, his pale face, his breathlessness.

Then there was all that agitation around her, questions asked twenty times over, hot drinks in plastic cups, her son's little hand in hers, the cold air, the shawl they draped over her shoulders, the scent of a woman's perfume, something like the one her mother wore and which made her feel sick. Shortly before midnight, Bruno arrived at last. He too had to answer a load of questions; it was as though they suspected him of having taken Kimmy somewhere. You only had to look at Bruno to see he wouldn't hurt a fly—Mélanie had understood this from the first glance, the first day, the moment she set eyes on him. Her husband answered their questions calmly and patiently, not showing the faintest sign of irritation. He waited until they got home and had carried Sammy, fast asleep, to his bed before allowing himself to cry. The whole thing only lasted a few seconds. He sat down on the sofa and let out a stifled sob, a choking sound that made Mélanie's blood run cold.

After all the coming and going in the apartment complex, the dogs, the searches, the samples and fingerprints—everyone left except the guy they were told would stay there, in their house, until Kimmy came home. A guy who was with an intervention squad, or something like that, whose role was to escort them and advise them in the event that the kidnappers should contact them. The guy went into the room at the back they'd planned to make into a study and which was used as a junk room for now, and where, fortunately, they'd stored a sofa bed he could open out. If any unknown number called either of their cell phones they must tell him immediately, before they even answered. Once he'd given his instructions, he slipped away and Bruno and Mélanie managed to have a moment together the two of them, alone in the kitchen; neither one could think of going to bed. In the silence, the humming of the refrigerator had started up again, as if it were all only a bad joke, a hoax, and for a moment she thought she would pass out. She stood there holding the table, closed her eyes, imagined her breath following the straight line of a rail, and the dizziness faded. Bruno sat on a chair, his head in his hands. She could hear his breath again, irregular, halting, a restrained moan.

That morning, they'd gotten up like every morning, with no idea they had only a few hours of happiness and serenity left, or how that very same evening their life would be shattered by a catastrophe that had no name. Who could imagine such a thing? She would give anything to be able to go back in time. A few hours. Just a few hours. To say no. That was all. *No, you can't go play outside.* It would have taken so little, next to nothing. Someone, somewhere, could surely grant her that favor: let her go back in time, let her say other words. Words she'd hesitated to say, words that had been on the tip of her tongue and which, in a moment of weakness, had yielded. She'd wanted to say no. No, we don't have time, you have to finish your homework and record a video for Instagram. But Kimmy and Sammy both seemed so happy at the thought of being with their friends. And so she thought, "just this once," and she said yes.

Once, just once, and their life was destroyed?

Mélanie had to grasp the impact of the event. For the moment she was like those foreigners who understand only half of what the person they are talking to has said, and have to make a huge effort to adapt their thoughts in order to construct some sort of meaning. She could tell very clearly, without being able to express it, that part of what was being said was inaccessible to her. The truth was beyond her. The resilience she'd shown over the last hours had enabled her to put on a brave face and answer questions. That was already a lot.

Now she was standing there in the kitchen, playing that scene in her mind over and over, pleading out loud with a higher authority not to let it happen.

In the end, though, she would have to sit down. Maybe even sleep. And accept the fact that her daughter had disappeared.

MISSING CHILD KIMMY DIORE

Subject:
Statement from first interview with Mélanie Claux Diore.
Recorded November 10 at 20:30 by Commissaire S. on duty
at the central commissariat in Châtenay-Malabry.

(Excerpts.)
Question: You said you left the window open to be able to
hear the children, were you worried about them being outside?

Answer: No, no, not really . . . I didn't want them getting yelled
at. Some neighbors won't let their children play in the garden because they make too much noise. Every time we have a meeting
with the other co-owners, there's conflict over this issue, com-
plaints about trash cans overturned and trampled flowers. And
anyway as a rule I'd rather they stayed inside. There's this guy,
Monsieur Zour, who hangs around with his yellow dog, and he
scares the kids. But he's not here at the moment. Apparently
he's in the hospital, so that's also why I let them go . . .

Question: Other than your neighbors, is there anyone else
who might have known the children were playing outside?

Answer: Well, no . . . wait, yes. Because I posted a story.

Question: A what?

Answer: A story. It's a little video you can post on Instagram.

It's not permanent. It only stays online for 24 hours. But posts with photographs or videos are there for good.

Question: Is the story an actual story?

Answer: No, not really . . . it's just moments from your everyday life that you share with your community, you know what I mean? I mean the people who follow us, the subscribers. I posted one when the kids went downstairs and I just said it would give me some time to catch my breath and make dinner. I also posted one at Vélizy 2, when we were buying Kimmy's sneakers, because we have a partnership with Nike, so I have to show their products, you know? It's kind of hard to explain . . .

Question: Can we see these videos?

Answer: Yes, they're still on my Instagram account. Until they go into my "archive" folder, and I'm the only one who has access.

Question: At what time exactly did you post the story where you said the children were playing outside?

Answer: I don't remember . . . I guess around 17:15 or 17:30.

Question: Do the people who follow you know your address?

Answer: No, no. Not at all. Well maybe some of them do, because people at the school know, and here in our apartment complex, people know who we are. We're well known, so maybe they talk about us to other people, brag about living in the same building as Kim and Sam. I don't often let them play outside because some of the children make fun of them. Children are cruel to each other, you know. Or else the parents will go and say any old thing and then their children repeat it. One day, some kids from the residence turned on Sammy, they said mean things to him, really horrible even. I told him he wasn't allowed to see them or speak to them anymore. But today it wasn't the same gang playing outside, Kevin Tremplin and his friends, it was the younger children that Kim and Sam really like: little Léo, little Maëva, the Filloux family's son, I can't remember his name, he's a really nice boy . . . that's why I said yes . . . (*Interruption sobbing / several minutes.*) I take the car and go to pick my kids up from school every day, I'm a mother hen, you know. I didn't think anything could happen here, this is a luxury residence. Maybe Kimmy's hurt, maybe she fell somewhere, maybe we should search some more.

Question: You posted the story between 17:15 and 17:30 and at 18:15 your son came to tell you he couldn't find his sister, is that correct?

Answer: Yes, I think so. When he came back up, I had just checked the time and I was about to call to them from the window. We're on the third floor and I heard them down below just a few minutes earlier. Sammy had homework, and even during vacation, I'd rather he didn't fall behind, and normally on Fridays it's the day where we post our video on YouTube, so we have to make a story for Instagram to let people know we've uploaded the video.

Question: How did you react when your son told you?

Answer: I went downstairs right away. I shouted my daughter's name in the garden and everywhere in the complex she might've hidden. I checked with a few neighbors who have children, where she might've gone. I . . . I was in a complete panic.

Question: You say you "have to" make these stories or these things, does someone ask you for them?

Answer: No, no, no one. I do it, because I'm the one who's in charge of everything, what you have to do on YouTube and Instagram is really be there. It's a lot of work and I'm the one who takes care of it all.

Question: So you had to film a story to say a video was coming, is that it?

Answer: Yes. As a rule, on our Happy Recess channel, we publish two or three videos a week. These videos are very elaborate, particularly the recent ones. They're carefully edited. It's my husband who takes care of that. But those are the family videos that go on our YouTube channel, the one I showed you, which has five million subscribers. The stories are something else. They're on Instagram and I post them all day long, to show people how we live. I describe what we're doing, where we are, where we're going. The fans love it. That way we can also tell them when new videos are on the way. I don't know if this makes sense, I'm tired, I'm sorry . . . When my husband gets here, he can explain better than me.

Question: Does Kimmy enjoy filming these videos?

Answer: Oh yes, she loves it. Sometimes she fusses a little, when she's tired, but she's actually really happy to have so many fans, as you can imagine, at her age . . .

Question: Do you see any reason—a conflict, an argument—that would explain why Kimmy might have hidden somewhere, rather than go home?

Answer: No, no, not at all. Nothing. Everything was fine.

* * *

Description of the child at the time of her disappearance:
Six years old.
Blond hair, shoulder length, curly.
Height: 3'11", Weight: 44 pounds (slim build).
Pink down jacket with fake fur collar.
Pale pink sweater.
Slightly faded jeans.
Navy blue socks.
White sneakers.

The day after Kimmy Diore went missing, before it was even six in the morning, Clara prepared the evidence bags from the night before to send to the various labs, then turned her attention to Mélanie Claux's first police interview, written up at the police station in Châtenay-Malabry.

On rereading the document, a strange feeling came over her. Something was missing. Something that should have been said, and that had been passed over in silence. She thought for a moment, and summoned her memories of Mélanie Claux. The woman was terrified, that much was certain. But in her terror, there was hope. Faint, insane, and unspeakable, but hope all the same. Briefly, Clara's mind began to wander, then she pulled herself back to the task at hand.

The process of becoming—then continuing to work as—a cop had brought about a progressive change in the way her mind worked. Suspicion and mistrust had found their way into her thoughts, colonized her emotions, and spread like a slow and ineluctable disease. It was her job to doubt, to constantly call things into question. To look for the flaw, the incoherence, the lie, rather than taking what seemed like proof or evidence for granted; cross-examine every hunch, every impression. Track down the gray zones, the hidden recesses. She often said to herself, "This is bringing about a profound change in my way of seeing things." She sometimes comforted herself with the notion that this seepage from her profession into her life was something no cop could avoid.

*

When children went missing, the first lead was always the family. Conflict, jealousy, adultery, plans to separate or break free: there were so many motives for abduction that would have to be eliminated. Over recent years the Diore family had been making money. A lot of money. Probably much more than Mélanie and her husband had been willing to own up to. That could have given people ideas. In accordance with the prosecutor's investigation department, the child rescue alert plan had not been set in motion. In addition to fears it would fuel a media circus, the mass distribution of Kimmy's photograph could easily alert the abductors and prompt them to get rid of her. After a thorough discussion, it had become clear that discretion was the best policy.

During the night, a crisis room had been set up. "Battle ready" was how they put it, like prepping a battalion, a squadron, an armed vessel. Under the orders of the deputy director of the Crime Squad, they'd been organized into various working groups: one team of investigators in charge of the neighborhood door-to-door, another to deal with witnesses, a third to take care of telephone research, yet another devoted to CCTVs. All these teams worked in conjunction and as quickly as possible: hunting for witnesses, observing the schedules and movements of everyone close to the family, identifying any suspicious cell phone numbers that might have signaled a position in the vicinity, studying the CCTV images recorded by local authorities and neighborhood shopkeepers. Information was shared in real time on the server. A final working group was being put together that would be in charge of tracking any possible leaks on social media, and of thorough examinations of all the comments addressed to Mélanie Claux over recent months.

The case had been referred to the Crime Squad because of its strike force. In addition to its ability to mobilize several dozen investigators in one night, it was able to muster experts in every domain. At eight o'clock in the morning, department heads, the team leader, his deputy and his evidence custodian were summoned to the crisis room, next to the boss's office. Everyone took a seat at the long table. At the back of the room, a dozen screens were beaming images in real time from around the city.

Lionel Théry, the head of the squad, hurriedly greeted the gathering. No one was in the mood for digression. The firmness of his tone and gestures, along with the crease in the middle of his brow, indicated the degree of stress he was under. Every minute was precious and they could not afford to get anything wrong. The slightest error of assessment could be disastrous. The disappearance of a child, beyond the emotional charge it involved, could have major repercussions in the media, including the potential to harm the image of the criminal investigation department, as had so often been observed. The life of a little six-year-old girl was at stake. They had managed, after a hard-fought struggle, to negotiate silence on the part of all the media, until further notice. How long this truce would last, he had no idea, but for the time being they were lucky to be able to work without a horde of journalists clustered beneath their windows. One colleague from the Research and Intervention Squad had spent the night at the parents' place, and would stay on in order to oversee any eventual contact from the kidnappers. During the morning a psychologist would be joining him, to be of assistance to Mélanie Claux and her husband as well.

To conclude, the boss recalled the principles of crisis management: gather as much information as possible, analyze it, and share it. He insisted on this last point, stressing the word "share": petty squabbles between working groups or individual cops drove him up the wall. A quick briefing every two hours would allow them to adjust their priorities.

The main lines of the investigation had been set out. Cédric Berger looked at Clara: an imperceptible exchange told him it would be fine by her, so he took over to sum up their initial findings from the night before.

"There are two ways into the residence: one for pedestrians, and the other for vehicles. In theory, all foot traffic is being monitored via CCTV. We've made a request to see the tapes and should be able to view them sometime during the day. The vehicle entrance, however, is not from the same street and there's no video surveillance. The first camera is three hundred meters from there and faces the other way. A remote is required to open the entrance to the parking lot, which is located under building A and leads to the basement storage area and the waste room. There are only forty spaces, for eighty-five apartments in the residence. Unfortunately, the system doesn't keep a record of either incoming or outgoing vehicles. Later today we'll get a list from the superintendent of the residents who currently have a remote. Let me remind you that a certain number of items found on the premises were sealed as evidence last night, principal among them the little girl's stuffed toy, which was found outside, near the playground. Clara has drawn up maps of the residence, the grounds, the basement, the parking lot and the surrounding streets, and they're available on the server. Regarding the first witness statements, one of the neighbors said she heard a child calling for help at the end of the day. We took these statements last night, and the woman has been summoned for questioning this morning. Mélanie Claux was at home, her window was open, and she says she didn't hear anything. The father was at a training session in Lyon and came home at 23:55; we are currently checking how he spent his time."

He paused briefly, noting his listeners' exceptional attentiveness, then continued.

"A team will be going back there this morning to finish the neighborhood investigation. A number of summonses were already handed out yesterday and several neighbors are scheduled for questioning here during the day. For the time being we're leaning toward the hypothesis that the little girl was taken from the parking lot, by car. That's where we lost all trace of her, after she passed through the waste room, as has been confirmed. Since no one saw her leave the premises, there is still a possibility that she could be sequestered somewhere in the residence. The caretaker and his wife have been summoned for questioning this morning. We want to know everything. Who is friends with who, who has fallen out with who, local quarrels, old scores not settled, episodes of jealousy or petty squabbles. Little Sammy and all the other kids who were playing the game of hide-and-seek will be interviewed up on the fourth floor today by our colleague from the Child Protection Squad. We had no difficulty finding the IP address of the author of the message about an imminent deal that was sent to Mélanie Claux under a pseudonym at 21:30 from an apparently recent Instagram account. It belongs to a fifteen-year-old boy who lives in the residence. A team left fifteen minutes ago to take him in for questioning and to search his house. I confess that given the context, this seems a bit too easy."

"Maybe he has co-conspirators somewhere else," suggested one of the team leaders.

"It seems unlikely. If that's the case, we're not dealing with real professionals. Clara has submitted a request to the prosecutor's office to tap the cell phones of both of Kimmy's parents."

Cédric turned to Clara to see if she had anything to add, but before she could reply, Lionel Théry began speaking again, to end the session.

"Right. We'll meet here again in two hours for the next briefing."

Murmurs of consent could be heard, and a draft of air from the corridor was already coming through the door when Clara spoke up.

"Who's going to watch the videos?"

Cédric Berger looked at his evidence custodian, puzzled.

"You mean the comments? We just said there was a team—"

"No," she interrupted. "I mean the actual videos. What they do on YouTube that has made them so rich and famous. And why it works . . ."

Cédric Berger was not the type to be caught off guard.

"Well, you can do it. Send off your evidence bags, then get started. And don't forget to tell us if they speak French correctly!"

At any other time, they would all have laughed, Clara among them.

In that in-between state where she'd spent the rest of the night, not even drowsy, at best in a state of dullness, images of her daughter had arisen one after the other. And whenever Mélanie felt herself lapsing into a state close to dropping off, she would start awake in terror—a brief rush of adrenaline repeated ten times over—and she was called back to reality. Kimmy was missing. Still, at around five or six o'clock, thanks to an expired sleeping pill she'd found in the medicine cabinet, she managed to fall asleep for an hour, maybe a bit longer.

In that in-between state, one of the moments that came back to her with terrifying clarity, as if fear were offering her unprecedented access to memory, was that day when Kimmy had learned to look at the camera. At the time, Mélanie was still filming in her living room. She had explained to Kimmy that if she wanted to be like the ladies who gave the weather forecast, she had to look at the camera. It wasn't easy for such a little girl to understand that she had to stare at the lens rather than at her mother, even when she was answering her questions, and that this way she would give the viewers the impression she was speaking to them. Because every child, every teenager bent over a tablet or a computer, had to be able to imagine that Kimmy and Sammy had a special relationship with them. Eager to do things correctly, Kimmy started over several times before she was able to train her gaze in the right direction. When her eyes wandered, Mélanie waved her hand to draw her attention, then pointed to the camera lens. Before long, after a few hesitant starts, Kimmy had learned how to follow her mother's directions. In a few days it became second nature, and she no longer thought about it. She learned so quickly. In the beginning, Mélanie didn't appear in the videos. She guided her children, asked questions, interacted with them, but didn't show her own face. Kimmy was so serious, so focused. She learned her text diligently, and would start over more than once if need be. She wanted to please her mother. She wanted her to tell her how good she was.

One evening a few weeks later, Kimmy said, "Why don't you come in front with us?"

Mélanie smiled, then went closer to her.

"Because you're the prettiest one, sweetie."

Preoccupied, Kimmy didn't let up.

"Are you afraid?"

"No, not at all, what would I be afraid of?"

"Of being locked inside."

"Locked inside what?"

Kimmy pointed to the computer screen. What she meant by that exactly—Mélanie didn't know. Her daughter had always had a great deal of imagination, and she occasionally had nightmares.

"Of course not, sweetie, no one gets locked inside."

Another day, when she was getting ready to film a video where Kimmy would look straight at the camera and present the newest Dolly Queen dolls, Sammy began crying because he wasn't included in the filming. He was inconsolable. Kimmy, upset at seeing how sad her brother was, suggested he open the boxes for her, and even choose, in front of the camera, which doll was the most beautiful. Sammy calmed down, happy to have a role to play, but Mélanie had to say no: the doll manufacturer had clearly insisted that the dolls should be unwrapped and displayed by a little girl. So Kimmy went over to her big brother and put her arms around him, the way a mother would.

Why was it only these melancholy moments that came back to her, when there were so many others full of laughter? Because in reality, for four years they'd been having so much fun. Happy Recess was the gift she'd given her family. A gift that had lit up their lives.

At around seven o'clock, as day was breaking, Mélanie got up and headed quietly toward her son's bedroom. She found Sammy lying on his back, his eyes wide open and the sheet pulled right up to his chin. She went over to the bed, knelt down on the carpet, and stroked his forehead. The boy's face seemed to relax beneath her palm.

Mélanie didn't dare say anything, worried her voice might betray her fear.

"Do you think Kimmy is going to come back?" he asked, after a few seconds.

"Of course she is, darling."

He let another moment go by before adding, "Is it my fault?"

"No, sweetheart, not at all. It absolutely is not your fault. You're a very caring older brother."

She couldn't go on speaking. Her voice was beginning to tremble. She caressed his cheek one last time, then stood up, without another word.

In the kitchen, she came upon Bruno and the police negotiator seated at the table drinking coffee. Bruno hadn't gone to bed; he'd spent the night in an armchair in the living room, where he'd probably eventually dropped off. When she came into the room, they stopped talking, and the man, whose name she'd forgotten, stood up to give her his seat.

We'll have to put up with this guy all day long, she thought as she flopped into the chair.

She wasn't sure she had the strength.

To eat, and drink some water.

To answer questions, over and over.

To see the psychologist.

To drive Sammy to the Crime Squad so they could take his statement.

To survive the day.

MISSING CHILD KIMMY DIORE

Subject:
Transcript of Sammy Diore's interview.
Recorded November 11 by Aude G., police officer from the Child Protection Squad, assisted by Nicole B., psychologist.

(Excerpts.)

Question: Can you tell me about the game of hide-and-seek you were playing when your little sister disappeared?

Answer: Well . . . it was the third game and it was my turn to seek. I started counting, then when I got close to thirty, I turned around a little. I wasn't cheating, but I saw Kimmy running to the room with the garbage cans. I thought she was going to hide there, instead of staying in the garden like we'd said, I didn't like it because that garbage can room stinks and I don't like going in there. Then I went on counting up to three hundred like we decided. Before, we only counted to a hundred, but that wasn't long enough. After that I shouted "three hundred," and I started looking. I found Maëva in the garden right away, behind the playground, and then I saw Ben. He came out of his hiding place because he was afraid of being all alone, and then Léo. We all started looking for Simon together because it was already kind of late. It was Maëva who spotted him lying on the ground behind the bicycles. After that there was only Kimmy left so we all went down to the garbage can room, but she wasn't there.

Question: What did you think then?

Answer: I thought she'd found a really good hiding place.

Question: So where did you think she was?

Answer: Under a car in the parking lot, because you can get there straight from the garbage can room. I figured that Mommy would give her a hard time if she'd been lying on the ground or something, because sometimes she does it on purpose to get dirty and that really annoys my mom . . .

Question: So did you go into the parking lot?

Answer: Yes, with Maëva and Simon. Ben stayed outside with Léo because he was too scared. We went around once, we looked under the cars but we didn't see her. I didn't want to stay there too long, because our parents don't like us hanging out in the parking lot, it's really dangerous.

Question: And after that you went to tell your mom?

Answer: Yes.

Question: Were you afraid for your little sister?

Answer: Yes. I started to get scared because usually she's not very good at hiding.

(Pause.)

Question: You told me that Kimmy sometimes got herself dirty on purpose, do you know why?

Answer: Uh-huh, like, when we're making the videos, on Wednesday, or Friday after school, or on Sunday, Mom always tells us what we're supposed to wear for the shoot. She does our hair, she gets us ready and everything. But Kimmy, she, like, makes a huge spot on her T-shirt or her dress just before we start. Either it's all wet, or splattered, or she spills something on purpose, like her grenadine syrup. Mom gets really mad. It's the same thing when Kimmy pretends she didn't hear Mom calling her to tell her it's time to make the videos.

Question: Why do you think Kimmy does that?

Answer: Well, I don't know . . . she's stubborn. Like, she won't play games she doesn't like anymore, she doesn't want to start over when we're filming and she gets the words wrong, she doesn't want to dress up like a princess anymore, she doesn't like Elsa even though Mom loves her. Sometimes she says she's tired, she doesn't want to do anything, or she's fed up . . . so Mom gets mad.

Question: And what does she say, your mom, when she gets mad?

Answer: She says it's really not nice to do that. That we're really lucky to do what we do, with millions of subscribers and all that, and all the kids who love us, who want to take selfies with us and get autographs when we have meet-ups, they stand in line for a really long time to see us, sometimes as long as two hours, and they can only dream of being like us, and on top of it we're number one now, the YouTube favorite of all the kids in France, even more favorite than Mélys and Fantasia, even more than the little kids in the Toy Club, more than Liam and Tiago from the Cuddly Toy Gang, now we're more popular than all of them. So Mom tells Kimmy to go and get changed as fast as she can, otherwise she'll never be on our videos again, and that'll be just too bad for her, no one will love her anymore.

Tom Brindisi was fifteen years old, the only child of a couple who were florists, with a shop located in the center of Sceaux. He was taken in for questioning the minute he got out of bed, after his mother had just left for the shop, and driven to the rue du Bastion with his father, where he was immediately interviewed by Cédric Berger, with the assistance of a female investigator from the Child Protection Squad. An initial version of the report, written up by the female investigator, was already available on the server.

The previous evening, at around seven o'clock, intrigued by the numerous comings and goings in the garden, the teenager found out that Kimmy Diore had gone missing. He didn't take the matter very seriously—he was convinced the little girl was hiding somewhere—and came up with the idea of frightening Kimmy's mother and making her believe the child had been kidnapped. In no time at all, he opened an Instagram account and sent her the message *Kid missing, deal coming.* He'd had no notion of the gravity of his act, and in the light of ensuing events, he acknowledged that it had been a really bad joke. Once he'd understood that the little girl really could not be found, it kept him awake all night.

While his remorse was genuine, the adolescent didn't hide his contempt for Mélanie Claux. In the transcript of the interview, he said things like, "she's been manipulating them from the start," or even "she exploits her kids to make money, I'm not the only one who says so." A few months earlier, in order to expose the shame and humiliation (those were his words) that Mélanie Claux subjected her children to, Tom Brindisi had even launched a hashtag on Twitter called *Save Kimmy and Sammy*, which had met with considerable success. His parents, busy at their shop, knew nothing about the controversy that followed on social media, with some defending Kim, Sam, and their mother, while others were indignant about the frequency with which the videos were posted, as well as the amount of advertising content, scarcely concealed. The hashtag had an impact, but some people had stepped into the fray to make fun of the children, Sammy in particular, something Tom Brindisi felt sorry about. He didn't like that woman; he'd wanted to frighten her. According to him, a lot of the posts on YouTube were scathing attacks against Happy Recess and Minibus Team, its main rival. Several times over he made reference to the Knight of the Net, a thirtysomething blogger, with a lot of followers, who had been posting videos for several years to denounce the dangers and excesses of YouTube. In his regular column entitled "YouTube: The Lollipop Generation," the Knight of the Net had, on more than one occasion, attacked the Happy Recess Channel. Tom Brindisi looked upon the Knight as a mentor.

Cédric Berger sent Tom Brindisi home after a few hours at the rue du Bastion and a stern lecture. In light of his age, he was being placed for the moment under house arrest. While a certain number of details might have warranted verification—regarding his whereabouts at certain times, or the contents of his computer hard drive—the team leader ruled out any real implication on his part in Kimmy's disappearance.

Clara spent the day finishing her reports and sending sealed evidence to the various labs. In particular, there was Kimmy's cuddly toy, which she called Dirty Camel, and on which Clara hoped to find a DNA trace not belonging to the family.

She worked mainly on homicides. Reports could take several days. After that, the aim was to find out who'd committed the crime. It could take time, sometimes months or even years. Death was the point of departure for her research. Death was a fact, a given: a tragedy had occurred, a tragedy that must be punished, though it would never be repaired.

This time, they had the power to influence the outcome. *They*, not she. For the first time, she felt powerless. Immobile. Because now that she'd finished with her reports, she was no longer on the front line. She had to wait. To her, waiting seemed impossible. Even if every stage of the investigation, every lead, open or closed, would eventually be transformed into a written form by her hand, after a certain delay, even if nothing could escape her knowledge, Clara hated this feeling of latency.

Every two hours, the briefing in the crisis room was held at the far end of the corridor, without her now.

Luckily, she and Cédric occupied the same office, and he'd gotten into the habit of sharing everything with her. He liked to get her opinion, hear her reaction, and he readily trusted her intuition.

And so, whenever he came back from the crisis room, he told her what he'd heard.

As the hours went by, things became clearer.

The woman who'd said she heard cries turned out to be hard of hearing. It was patently clear that the usual volume of her television would have prevented her from hearing any sounds from outside. However, among the statements they'd taken, there were two accounts in which people claimed to have seen a red car leave the parking lot at around 6 P.M.: one resident from building A who was looking out the window, waiting for his son to come home, had noticed the vehicle because the driver had hesitated before turning, while a teacher from building C said he'd been on his way back home from the high school where he taught, and had yielded right-of-way to a little red car. According to the first witness, a man was driving and was alone in the car. According to the second, a woman was driving and a child was strapped in the back in a child's car seat. "You have to be a cop to understand how fragile witness statements can be," Cédric concluded, something he liked to say even at the risk of repeating himself. His words didn't offer any sort of perspective, but he found comfort in their universal tone.

Analysis of the video surveillance tapes covering the pedestrian exit had been quickly completed. One thing was clear: the little girl hadn't gone out that way. Unless she was being held or was hiding somewhere in the residence (something that had not yet been ruled out, since not all the apartments had been visited), the theory of her abduction by car remained the most plausible.

That afternoon, after yet another briefing, Cédric came back to the office looking somewhat less exhausted. The neighborhood door-to-door was beginning to bear fruit. Opinions about the Diore family varied widely, and rumors were spreading like wildfire.

"You'll love this one, I'm sure," he said.

Clara raised her eyebrows to show her impatience.

"Apparently the Diores keep to themselves—let's say they don't mingle much with the others. In the beginning they would join in when there were block parties or drinks in the evening, or any community events, but gradually as they became successful, they stopped taking part. Most of the people in the complex bought their apartments in the 90s while it was still only a plan on paper, and the real estate project was seen as being fairly upmarket. Two or three years ago the Diores bought the studio apartment next door to them to turn it into a film studio. Some people say they won't be staying. Mélanie has turned into a snob and Châtenay-Malabry isn't chic enough for her anymore.

Apparently they've bought a house in the South of France, with the intention to move there someday. There was also mention of an apartment in the mountains. I must say, people seem pretty well-informed. In the last two years Kim and Sam have almost never played with the other kids from the residence. Their mother doesn't like them mixing with the others but most of all, according to what people were saying, they spend all their free time making those famous videos. A few months ago there were some rumors, both on the Internet and in the neighborhood, claiming Sammy had been bullied. Kids were making fun of him, and shoving him, it was even rumored that he was bullied into giving some of the kids money. Apparently Mélanie denied this on a video on her channel. But the neighbors say that's why he changed schools. The fact is that since last year both children have been attending a private school in Sceaux. Mélanie drives them there and back every day. Some people said it's the little girl who's the star of the channel. She was two and a half years old when it all started, and subscribers have watched her grow up; they're crazy about her. Apparently she signs more photographs than her brother does when they have signings, and there are more fans wanting to take selfies with her than with him. But from there to go imagining he might want to get rid of his sister—an accident . . . at eight years old, if you see what I mean—that's what some people went so far as to insinuate. One thing's for sure: everyone in the residence knows exactly who the Diore family are and how much money they make."

Clara left the rue du Bastion at around eight o'clock that evening. She walked home, as she often did: an hour's walk that she liked better than the packed number 13 bus. She needed to get some air.

She was striding quickly ahead, gaze lowered, going over all the recent information from the crisis room, when a man coming the opposite direction stopped to let her go by.

"How old are you?" he called out, as if he were talking to a little girl.

This was something she'd experienced more than once: you could suddenly hear strange, outlandish things like this in the street, some of which could be meaningful. Words with an impact, an echo you had to take in. Another time a man with a hazy, disoriented gaze, who seemed to be suffering from some sort of psychiatric disorder, had stopped her on her way and said, "But where are your parents?" And another time, a woman she'd allowed to go ahead of her in a check-out line had said to her, in a tone that made it clear she wasn't joking, "You can see through people."

In moments like this, she always wondered if there was something about her that invited these intrusions or comments, or whether this sort of thing happened to everyone, and had happened to her repeatedly merely by chance.

In the dark, from a distance, people thought she was a teenager. Or a child. Closer up, they would realize she was an adult woman with a worried gaze.

At thirty-three, she felt caught between two worlds. Neither young nor old. Kimmy Diore was six. At the age of six you're a very little girl. So little and so vulnerable. On the photographs her parents had provided, you could see her even, smooth face, with her huge eyes like those of a manga character. Her disappearance was stifling the department. The air was full of feverishness, a particular kind of tension. Maybe because most of her colleagues were parents. And all of them had thought, at least once: "Could this happen to me?"

They'd been walking side-by-side, back in the days when he still lived in Paris, when Thomas asked her if she thought she'd have a family life one day. Those were the words he used, and coming from a man whose apparent freedom—freedom of speech, of movement, of last-minute changes of plan—so impressed her, the expression made her smile. He'd repeated his question and Clara eventually came up with a way to say no, she didn't want any children. In this world where she thought she could see every trap, every dead end, every imminent disaster, that was a weakness, a form of recklessness she'd decided to live without. Moreover, children died, the way parents died. She knew it all too well, and she didn't want ever again, in her life, to be personally involved in any business of the sort. They had just made love at his place, in that apartment under the eaves where she felt so strong, so relaxed, so desirable, and for a split second a thought had clouded Thomas's gaze. It wasn't a reproach, not even disappointment, maybe just the beginning of a distancing.

Clara continued on her way without speaking to the man who had called out to her.

When she got close to her house, she stopped in a convenience store to buy something to eat—*a can, a plastic container*, she thought, *anything where all you have to do is take the lid off*—aware that she was giving in to two stereotypes: the solitary cop (but she wasn't divorced) and the unmarried citydweller (but under more *normal* circumstances, she would make dinner).

The minute she got home she took a shower, got changed, and switched on her laptop. She had a whole night ahead of her and she wanted to understand.

MISSING CHILD KIMMY DIORE

Subject:
Description (by type) of the videos on the Happy Recess channel, available on YouTube.

UNBOXING

(Up to twenty million views.)

Brother and sister, generally seated side by side, open "surprise" packages as if they had fallen from the sky.

Mélanie's voice is lively and energetic, and she guides them step by step as they unwrap the packages: "Go on, we can open it all the way!" "What's inside?" "Oh, I see something else in there . . ." "What's that little green box?" "Now we're going to put the batteries in!", "Oh, you can play with both joysticks, how amazing is that!"

The children are ecstatic, and express their joy: "Oh my God, look at the huge box!" "That's mega cool!" "Wow!".

Once they've finished unwrapping, Kim and Sam try out gadgets, board games, or consoles.

One of Sammy's catchphrases: "This is really bananas!"

One of Kimmy's catchphrases: "I can't believe it!"

B oredom took on strange, hidden forms. Boredom was concealed and refused to be called by its name. After Sammy's birth, once the nightly interruptions for breast-feeding or the baby's nocturnal wakefulness had waned, once she'd changed her hairstyle, lost a few pounds, and seemed to be in good physical shape—in short, once her life seemed to have reached a sort of cruising speed—Mélanie Claux started getting crying jags. They often came on in the morning, a few minutes after her husband had left for work. Her life, she concluded, was taking a predictable path. On the whole this reassured her, but there were days when it brought on a sort of dizziness, or nausea. At eight in the morning Bruno would play with the baby, at five or ten minutes past eight he would look at his watch and say, Oh my God I'd better get going, and after kissing her goodbye he would reach for his raincoat or overcoat and slam the door behind him. That's when she felt like her body was hovering at the edge of a void, about to fall. Not a great void, rather a sort of dismal hole, hidden inside her apartment. She in turn would try to entertain her son (he had developed a passion for finger puppets), then she'd put him in his baby bed for his morning nap. After that, Mélanie went back to the kitchen, cleared the breakfast things from the table, wiped the surfaces, started the dishwasher, and collapsed into a chair where for twenty minutes or more she would weep. Later that day, there were moments when she stood still, just like that, in the living room, her arms loose at her side. While the baby was sleeping or playing on his own in his recliner or his play-pen, she stood there, unmoving, by the window, not looking out, not looking at anything, or maybe she was looking at the dreary, flat expanse inside herself. She could stay like that for several minutes, impervious to the noise from outside, or the telephone ringing, or Sammy's cries when he was trying to get her attention. Within this absence there was a gentle sensation, an impression of floating, almost of well-being, and she found it increasingly difficult to rouse herself from that state. Sometimes she went with Sammy toward the public gardens, but once she was standing at the metal gate, she gave up on the idea of going in. She didn't have the strength to speak to the other women, women like her who didn't work, or nannies who got together every day at the same time by the old sandbox. She didn't feel like blending into the scenery, let alone into a group of any sort. So she went on walking, faster and faster, propelling the baby carriage in front of her, cleaving through the air like the blind prow of a lost ship. On those days she went straight to the park in Sceaux, where she would walk up and down the lanes until nightfall, searching for an intoxication that might fill that name-less void.

Mélanie Claux had spent part of her pregnancy watching *The Angels of Reality TV*. The first season, broadcast in the winter of 2011 on a TNT channel, had met with considerable success. Former reality TV contestants were selected for this new program; among them she immediately recognized Steevy, one of the emblematic participants from the first *Loft*. He was no longer the twenty-year-old boy with peroxide hair she'd seen laughing and crying; he had survived but he'd also gotten older. The other participants had been chosen for their notorious per-formances in *Secret Story* or *Temptation Island*, all programs that had left their mark on Mélanie's youth; she'd never missed an episode. Marlène, Cindy, Diana, John-David: she knew them all. They'd been lucky a first time, audiences had seen and loved them, and now they were being given a second chance, a second departure, the opportunity to pursue their career or enhance it. As for Mélanie, however, the Mélanie from *Meet You in the Dark*, whose appearance had been too brief to leave the slightest impression, no one had come looking for her. No one had invited her to go to that magnificent villa in Beverly Hills "in order to make her dream come true and become famous." Because that is what *The Angels* promised. No one had thought about her, because everyone had forgotten her.

She'd had her chance and she'd failed. When she thought back on that episode (that was the term she used, which was perfectly suited to the idea she had of her own life, a life she would have liked to have divided up into seasons, in the televisual sense of the word, and which in turn would be segmented into episodes, despite an undeniable monotony), she came to the conclusion that she had failed. It had never crossed her mind that other reasons, related to the economy or the demands of the system into which she was hoping to integrate, might explain her failure. No. She had only herself to blame. She had missed the boat.

Not long after Sammy's first birthday, Mélanie took Bruno's advice—advice he had given because she seemed a bit down to him—and opened a Facebook account. Bruno had insisted: Facebook was booming, not just in France but all over the world, and it was time she got onboard. Even though she didn't have many friends, it would help her to make some new ones, and to renew ties with people she'd lost touch with. She'd been devoting so much of her time to her home and her son; now it was time to open up to the outside world.

Before long, Mélanie no longer had any morning crying jags, and she didn't sit at home staring into space anymore. Nor did she wander aimlessly along the lanes in the park. Every one of her son's naps, every break meant she could connect to her account. She had new connections, she posted photographs and comments, she 'liked' pictures and the comments that others posted, she watched people living their lives and let them see her at her best in return. For several months this was enough to make up for the sensation of something missing. She would discuss things with other mothers, exchange advice or recipes, and she established ties with an association who were actively campaigning for maternal breast-feeding. She felt as if she'd found a place in the world, somewhere she could exist.

One morning she was *nominated* by one of her virtual friends to take part in the Motherhood Challenge, a campaign that had come from the United States and that was devoted to the joys of mothering. The principle was simple: she had to post four photographs on the social media platform illustrating what it was that "made her proud to be a mom," and then tag the women in her entourage she viewed as good mothers. Sammy was a fine baby, round-faced and alert, and Mélanie thought it was a terrific idea. Besides, she genuinely deserved to be branded a supermom, given how hard she'd worked to follow the sometimes contradictory instructions in the baby care magazines that she'd subscribed to very soon after she got married. She found four pictures on her computer that seemed to highlight the ways motherhood had made her blossom: one picture Bruno had taken during her pregnancy, on the beach in a beautiful light at the end of the day; one of Sammy in a gorgeous little cotton bonnet, taken a few hours after his birth; another picture where she was wearing the baby carrier across her belly and Sammy had fallen asleep with his mouth open, and finally, a more recent photograph of all three of them, serene and smiling, sitting like the royal family on the sofa in the living room. She'd made sure the colors went well together, that the photographs constituted a harmonious tableau overall, in tones of brown and mauve. She received lots of praise.

From then on, Mélanie regularly posted pictures of Sammy on her Facebook page, photos that garnered an increasing number of likes and comments full of praise, as she came up with more and more little sketches or innovative settings to show off her son in his best light. She was happy. Her lack of sexual desire for her husband was something they never talked about. She loved him, but no longer felt like making love with him. She'd read on various forums any number of personal accounts from women who'd gone through similar phases: apparently, it could be explained by the drop in hormones, by the wearing effect on the couple of conjugal life, by an overinvestment in her role as mother that worked against her role as wife, the monotony of everyday life, and so on. Depending on the nature of the problem, different solutions were proposed, always substantiated by personal examples: spend a weekend just the two of you on your own, wear sexy lingerie, allot more time for sexual relations, book sessions with a sexologist, take a lover.

Each of the various suggestions was accompanied by the reminder "Appetite comes with eating."

When she fell pregnant for the second time, Mélanie had to stay in bed for several weeks in order to avoid a premature birth. The number of contractions she was having had alarmed her gynecologist. She preferred not to mention this setback on her Facebook page, because it did not seem to comply with the image she had of herself as a supermom. A supermom's pregnancy went without a hitch; a supermom redecorated the nursery herself and hung the curtains, perched on a step ladder three days before her due date, arms spread wide. Mélanie continued nevertheless to communicate on social media, seeking advice on how to help the first child welcome his little brother or sister, inquiring about the best brands of car seat, and what consequences prolonged use of a pacifier might have on a baby's teeth, or other subjects, she conceded, of varying and fluctuating interest. The days went by so quickly. She occasionally joined in conversations about breast-feeding or the various childcare options available, but she was disheartened by the increasingly confrontational behavior she'd observed on social media. Mélanie could not stand conflict. She dreamed of a world of solidarity and exchange. A world where she would be queen.

A few months earlier her father had retired and Mélanie's parents moved from the center of town to a house on the outskirts, a few kilometers from La Roche-sur-Yon. The house was not very big, but the fact that the previous owners had dug a swimming pool in the middle of the garden was a major motivating factor for the purchase. Sandra, Mélanie's sister, had married a young man from the region, the son of an insurance broker who was himself a broker, and very good-looking. Mélanie's mother rarely came to the Paris region, even less often now that Sandra had given birth to three children in less than two years: twin boys first, then, fourteen months later, a little girl. Mélanie's parents were overjoyed to be grandparents, and they posted multiple photographs of their grandchildren on Facebook. Cheerful, colorful images taken by the swimming pool, at the mini-golf, the skating rink, or in the woods. Judging from these accounts, they were dream grandparents: active, available, involved in their grandchildren's lives. Unfortunately, they never offered to take Sammy, on the grounds that he fought with Killian, one of Sandra's twins. In fact, Killian was a sly, bullying child. Mélanie, however, refused to interpret the situation in such a cut-and-dried manner. In three years, her parents had only invited her son once, for a long weekend, and they'd complained afterwards that Sammy was a fussy eater and didn't seem very happy. They never offered again. As usual, her sister had won. On every front, in every domain, Sandra always fulfilled their mother's expectations. She was the one who got to dance in the front line at the school's end-of-year performance, she was the one who kept an eye on the class when the teacher had to step out, she was the one who got to tend a booth at the school fair, she was the one who smiled politely to guests; she'd even found a husband who could get along with their father, which was, if not a miracle, no mean feat. Her sister was clever, most definitely, when it came to sewing, making pastries, and interior decorating. It seemed that everything Sandra set out to do was perfectly accomplished. Moreover, she'd always stayed in her place, there by her parents. *She'd not gotten full of herself.* At Easter or at Christmas, when they had family get-togethers, Mélanie's mother always seemed happier to see Sandra. Sometimes it was something imperceptible, or her voice rising an octave higher, or her movements becoming quicker, more spontaneous—but Mélanie could not ignore the difference in treatment, the additional dose of enthusiasm and warmth her sister received. And now, seeing these almost daily photographs of her sister's children that her mother posted on Facebook was becoming a source of real anguish. There were even times Mélanie would burst into tears at her computer. But not knowing, not seeing what was going on would be even worse.

Mélanie decided not to tell her mother anything about her difficulties toward the end of her pregnancy. Her mother would have found a pretext not to have to come and help, and she would not have failed to draw a comparison between Mélanie and Sandra, whose pregnancies had been active and radiant.

Lying in bed, Mélanie went on looking at Facebook on her cell phone. This activity, which only a few years earlier had seemed like an oasis of sharing and consolation, now seemed to be the source of a confused melancholy.

Mélanie discovered YouTube several weeks after Kimmy's birth, while she was searching online for information about the difficult after-effects of episiotomies. Moms like herself shared their experiences on video. With their cell phones or little cameras they filmed themselves facing the lens, speaking intimately the way they would have in the confession box of *Loft Story* or any other reality TV show. Mélanie subscribed to a few channels. These moms were like her: they were the same age and had the same concerns. They were pretty and took good care of themselves. To see these young women, tastefully made up, their nails polished, their hair smooth and shiny, gave her both a simple, immediate pleasure, and a sort of comfort. Some of them shared their recipes or beauty tips. Mélanie enjoyed 'liking' their posts, and congratulating them with various emoticons: the bravo emoticon, the thank you one, flowers, flowers, flowers, heart, heart, heart. To her, these women were valiant and inspiring. They gave her the courage to face her day. The platform's algorithm directed Mélanie toward other channels and videos. She liked everything that was *real*, everything that was about lives like hers, that could make her feel less alone. The algorithm had figured that much out. She gradually abandoned Facebook in favor of YouTube, which seemed more open and creative.

YouTube was a world unto itself. A generous, providential world, accessible to all.

Sammy had just started kindergarten, and Kimmy was a good, docile baby, who slept a great deal. The computer was on from morning to night; Mélanie would sit at the screen several times a day, often with no precise goal in mind. She drifted on the platform, passing from one suggestion to another, and she always ended up finding some information, an image, or a story that interested her.

Shortly after Kimmy's second birthday, Mélanie happened upon Minibus Team. The father of two little girls, apparently no longer with their mother, had created a channel devoted to his daughters, and the number of subscribers was climbing with each passing day. Everything had begun with a video of the older girl unwrapping and tasting multicolored candies and other goodies from the same manufacturer, and this had instantly led to thousands of views. Then the younger sister had joined the older girl, and their daddy had increased the number of gifts to be unwrapped as the number of subscribers soared. Judging by these images the girls, who were getting more and more spoiled, seemed to be really enjoying themselves.

For a few months Mélanie merely observed how the dad filmed his daughters—how often, what type of stories he concocted. What worked and what didn't work. What children liked so much that they would watch the same video ten times over, and what they liked less. She continued her research with a survey of what existed elsewhere, particularly in the United States and other English-speaking countries, where there was already a plethora of children's channels.

Kimmy was not yet three years old when Mélanie posted her first video on YouTube. She came up with her own strategy. She would move slowly, create attachment and identification before introducing any brands or products. So she began by filming Kimmy wearing a beautiful lilac dress, seated like a grown-up on the sofa singing a nursery rhyme that Mélanie had taught her. The little girl did a perfect job of combining words and gestures: the rabbit and his huge ears, the cruel hunter with his rifle. She was adorable. The fifty-second sequence was little more than a shared family moment, private and touching. Mélanie posted the video along with a short comment: "Little girl singing and doing the actions to *The Rabbit and the Hunter.*" The video racked up a few thousand views. Encouraged, Mélanie went on filming her daughter singing: *Twinkle, Twinkle Little Star, Frère Jacques, Alouette.* Kimmy spoke and sang very well for her age. The words were perfectly articulated, and she accompanied the songs with irresistible expressions and gestures. Then Mélanie came up with a clever idea: give Kimmy some cuddly toys—teddy bears, dogs, rabbits—to illustrate the nursery rhymes she was singing for the camera. Kimmy played with the stuffed animals, gave them parts to play, made them speak. Mélanie waited until they gained over 20,000 subscribers before introducing the first toy unboxing: Kinder Surprise eggs, Chupa Chups lollipops, Play-Doh modeling clay. A little later Sammy began appearing in the videos, and the channel, originally called *Kimmy Sings*, in English, became *Kim and Sam in Happy Recess*.

Brother and sister were a terrific team. Sammy proved himself to be attentive and protective, helping Kimmy open boxes and remove lids, explaining the games to her, the gestures, the rhymes. Kimmy tried to act more grown-up, imitating her brother and laughing at his jokes. Judging from the comments, the pair were as touching as could be. After that, everything happened very quickly: the number of subscribers and views continued to climb, and YouTube addressed a personal message to Mélanie, to explain the principles of monetization. Brands started getting in touch with her for product placements, parcels began swamping the apartment, and Bruno quit his job. Subsequently they were able to buy the adjacent apartment, in order to have more space and devote an entire room to filming and editing the videos. Having a home studio gave them better production options. To stay on top, they had to constantly renew themselves.

Boredom was no more than a bad memory.

MISSING CHILD KIMMY DIORE

Subject:
Description (by type) of videos on the Happy Recess channel available on YouTube.

BATTLES
(*Between two and six million views.*)

Brand or sub-brand
Seated side by side facing the camera and blindfolded, Kim and Sam are tasting a series of products (cream cheese, chips, soda, iced tea, sandwich spread, various cookies).

For each of these products they test two samples: a "real" one and a "fake" one. Then they have to guess which one belongs to the original brand and which is an imitation (sub-brand or distributor's brand).

Taste and guess
This time they are blindfolded and have to identify the different types and flavors of a same product. The most popular videos are those for Oreo cookies and their various flavors (original, vanilla, white chocolate, Golden, peanut, etc.).

They are given the same challenge with a number of other products (cocktail crackers, dessert creams, chips) and a great variety of brands.

C lara was standing opposite Cédric, upright, serious, eager to pass on all the information she'd gathered. Although she'd slept for only two hours, the fatigue hadn't kicked in. She'd begun by watching the Happy Recess videos, then she'd done some additional research in order to situate them in a broader context and understand the ways in which the phenomenon was perceived by its audience. While Cédric often made fun of her formal language, her predilection for conjunctive adverbs, and her tendency to dissect everything, this time he listened and his attention was sincere.

"In the majority of cases it's the parents who film their children and post videos several times a week. The phenomenon began in the United States and has spread virtually everywhere over the last three years, because it's turned out to be a very lucrative activity. This year the YouTuber who made the most money worldwide is an eight-year-old American boy. His name is Ryan and his parents have been filming him twice a week since he was four years old. In 2019 alone, Forbes magazine estimated his income at no less than $26 million. In France, the first ventures date from 2014-2015. Now there are lots of channels. From a financial point of view, a dozen or so dominate the market. Happy Recess was not the first, but it is far and away the most popular."

"And what do the kids do?"

"They started with unboxing. They open the boxes and parcels, and inside they find toys or candy or costumes and all kinds of products specifically targeted at their age group. The kids are elated, and they try out the products on camera, sharing their delight."

"You can't be serious?"

"I most certainly am. The parents film them, mother or father, it depends. In the Diore family, it's the mother who interacts with the children. Over time, to keep their subscribers loyal, they've diversified their formats. She might set them a challenge or invent little scenarios. For example, the children have to taste food items that are all orange or green exclusively, or they might have to guess the price of items in a supermarket, or compare different brands of sandwich spread blindfolded. For a while now they've also been performing pranks. They play practical jokes or hoaxes, mostly copied from American channels."

Cédric let a short silence settle before he went on.

"You mean this is how they make so much money? Are you sure?"

Clara couldn't help but smile. This was familiar territory. This incredulity.

"Yes, I'm sure. Beyond a certain number of views, YouTube inserts advertising in the videos and pays the YouTubers accordingly. The money also comes from the brands who pay to appear in the videos. Not only do they supply the material— Lego, Disney figurines, or Kinder Surprise Eggs—some even pay to be on display or have their product prominently placed. At this point a contract will be drawn up to govern their collaboration. The Diores have set up several companies. If you go onto the website of the trademark office, you can see they've registered and protected every brand name imaginable that might possibly seem related to their children's first names. The father, who had a good position at an IT firm, quit his job. Now he's the one who does the filming and editing."

"And . . . do they make a lot of these videos?"

"When it comes to Happy Recess, I'd say between two and four a week. They have to maintain a prominent position."

Cédric Berger listened to Clara extremely attentively, nodding from time to time to signal his assent. He gave a slight wave of his hand to encourage her to continue.

"That's not all. They're branching out when it comes to merchandizing. The Diores recently created their own brand of stationery—lined notebooks, sketchbooks, and pens—which they promote themselves. Minibus Team, their main rival, has started a quarterly magazine, which is selling like hotcakes. And the Cuddly Toy Gang has just launched their own brand of toys. Spin-offs account for an important percentage of their turnover, and they all intend to keep on developing these products. The Diore family's annual income largely 'exceeds' one million euros. Not to mention all the benefits in kind."

Cédric had taken a few notes in his little black book, a classic Moleskine he always had on him. He was the only one who could decipher its illegible contents. He underlined something and looked back up at Clara.

"Where does that money go?"

"The parents get it. They can do what they want with it."

"It's not regulated?"

Clara had wondered the same thing a few hours earlier. This is what came of being a cop, she thought, this ability to put your finger on the problem right away.

"Children who are models, actors, or singers, are supervised, because their activity is viewed as work. Their schedules are regulated and until the children are of age, the parents have to place most of their income in an account that is frozen, with the Deposits and Consignments Fund. For kids who are YouTubers, there are no restrictions. You could call it a gap in the law. For the time being, their work is viewed as a private leisure activity and is not subjected to any sort of regulation."

"That's crazy . . ."

"Still, as Tom Brindisi said, they are not universally liked. Already in 2016 the Knight of the Net, the famous YouTuber he told us about, posted several videos denouncing the most active family channels. His advocacy criticizes the frequency with which the children were subjected to filming, and questions whether they had any choice in the matter. He was one of the very first whistleblowers. At the time, 40,000 people signed the online petition he launched, and his attacks were shared by other YouTubers. But in actual fact, nothing came of it. When I say nothing, I mean nothing. It didn't prevent increasing numbers of parents from entering the fray, with younger children getting involved each time. In 2017, the Observatory of Parenthood and Digitalization, an association that had already alerted public authorities, referred the matter to the National Child Protection Council to demand that these minors be granted—at the very least—the same status as child models or actors. After four years with absolutely no regulation of any kind, it appears that a draft bill is under review for imminent submission to the National Assembly. The aim is to regulate any commercial exploitation of children by their parents, and to classify the activity as work."

Clara fell silent for a moment and Cédric took the time to write all this down before asking for more. Clearly, he was completely baffled.

"And the media didn't pick up the story?"

"They did, a little, but it's all still fairly unclear. If the law is passed, France will be an international pioneer. The law could shed light on an entire ecosystem which for the moment is not on the radar. However, detractors say that it won't change anything. Some parents, like Mélanie, have already started secondary channels or opened Instagram accounts in their own name, the point being, according to these detractors, to circumvent the law, even though it hasn't been voted on yet."

Cédric held out his hand to stop Clara.

He needed silence to put it all into perspective. Clara had been telling him about an abstract world, beyond reach. She could tell the mood Cédric was in from the expression on his face, his doubts, and the slightest vexation. As he walked toward her, she knew his back must be hurting him again. Ever since he'd had an operation a few months earlier for a slipped disc, it had been coming back to haunt him whenever he reached a certain level of stress.

Cédric took a breath, then a few seconds later resumed the discussion.

"And what does Mélanie Claux have to say about all this?"

"She's aware of the criticism. She's made a few videos on the topic. She responds to the attacks looking straight at the camera. She says she's putting money aside for her children, that she didn't wait for all the controversy to start thinking about their future. She says that Kim and Sam dreamt of being YouTubers, that they love it, that they're happy to be stars. According to her, they're very lucky. It's the best thing that could have happened to them."

The pain was spreading into his ribs, and Cédric reached for a chair to sit down. When she saw her boss's expression, Clara hurried to finish.

"There's one more thing I have to tell you. This morning I went back onto Mélanie's Instagram account, Mélanie Dream. In addition to her famous 'stories,' she regularly posts pictures of the children or the family. Roughly two months ago she posted a picture of an enormous parcel she'd just received from a cosmetics company. On the box you could see their last name, their address, and even the number of the building. In other words, the entire planet now knows where they live."

CRIME SQUAD – 2019

MISSING CHILD KIMMY DIORE

Subject:
Description (by type) of the videos from the Happy Recess
channel available on YouTube.

THE BUY EVERYTHING SERIES
(*Between two and twenty million views.*)

"WE BUY EVERYTHING THAT STARTS WITH AN 'F'"

At the supermarket, Kimmy and Sammy, taking turns, have
ten minutes each to buy whatever they want, regardless of price
or usefulness, provided the name of the item begins with a letter
drawn at random (the letter F, for example).

The aim of the game is to buy as many products as possible
in the time allotted. The winner is whoever places the greatest
number of items in Mélanie's shopping cart.

Then all the purchases are brought home (fettucine, fennel,
figs, a French flag, a frying pan, a farm (Playmobil brand), fudge,
flowers), regardless of whether the family already has similar
products or items, and whether they are useful or not.

Variations: I buy everything that's yellow, I buy whatever you
write down, I buy whatever you draw, if you guess it you buy it.

When she used to explain her job to people, Clara would say, "First blood, then words." Because most often, it all began with blood. Blood from the body, blood from clothing, blood splattered on the ground or on the walls, visible or wiped away, blood that had to be dried, put into evidence bags and sealed, a particular blood whose trace had to be found, blood sent to the lab, blood from an autopsy, collected in plastic buckets. Then came the written procedure, and the use of precise vocabulary to describe what she'd seen.

This time there was no blood. That wasn't enough to reassure her. In close to ten years Clara had already had the opportunity to observe that barbarity could manage very well without hemoglobin. On one of her first cases she went to the bedside of an old woman in the hospital who was in an advanced state of dehydration and undernourishment, her knees covered with bruises. What the woman said, although it was confused and incoherent on the surface, had prompted the prosecutor's office to open an investigation. A fortysomething couple were suspected of having locked her up for several months in order to collect her pension. Clara had taken part in the search conducted in a modest apartment that was a bit shabby, the grime not immediately apparent, hidden in corners. There were no traces of violence. Merely a plastic bowl placed on the tiled floor in the kitchen, which, given the absence of any pets, Clara had noticed at once. It turned out the old woman's torturers had been making her eat from that bowl, on her knees, every evening before they went off and left her to sleep on a straw mat.

Clara enjoyed the atmosphere of a case in its early hours. The lack of sleep, sandwiches gobbled down in haste, the telephone welded to her palm, her eyes glued to screens. The effervescence of it, the feverishness. Sometimes a few hours were enough to come up with a lead: a witness, a video tape, a telephone signal picked up at the right spot. With a little know-how, all they had to do was pull on a thread. Take a suspect in for questioning in the early morning, search the premises, and the case was wrapped up. But more often than not the squad was in it for the long haul. They had to tough it out. The excitement of the early hours was transformed then into a sort of nervous impulse, steady and continuous. An energy that came from deeper within, from a more private place—from the gut, as some of them put it—and consequently, had no limit.

Thirty-six hours after Kimmy Diore went missing, Clara knew they'd entered the second phase, with no immediate prospects of an outcome. They had to admit that they'd come up empty-handed. Analysis of telephone records had yielded nothing, and the neighborhood investigation got no further than malicious gossip. An exceptional dispensation had allowed them to visit all the apartments in the residence. A dozen investigators had carried out a thorough inspection, but found nothing. Any involvement on the part of Tom Brindisi, whether on his own or with partners, had been ruled out once and for all. For his bad joke the adolescent would no doubt be let off with a simple warning.

Witness statements from the other children and their parents had corroborated Sammy's testimony, and this made it possible to establish a precise timetable of events: at 17:55, a new game of hide-and-seek had begun. The little girl had hesitated, going around in circles, before running off in the direction of the waste room. From there she could get into the parking lot without being seen. Once she was in the underground parking lot, of her own will or by force, in a conscious or unconscious state, she had in all likelihood gotten into someone's car. A red car, perhaps. Or one of any other color.

This child who was on display from morning to night, the child you could see clad in a tracksuit, shorts, dress, pajamas, or disguised as a princess, mermaid, or fairy, the child whose image had been reproduced unlimited times, had vanished into thin air.

She'd vanished from that world saturated with brand names and logos that she'd grown up in, as if an invisible hand had suddenly snatched her away from all possibility of a gaze.

The night Kimmy Diore went missing, when they asked Mélanie Claux who might bear a grudge against her family, she'd evoked two possibilities: the Knight of the Net, and the father of the two Minibus Team sisters, Happy Recess's main rival channel. They'd both been called in for questioning at the premises of the rue du Bastion. In addition, the Diore couple's immediate family (Mélanie's in La Roche-sur-Yon, Bruno's in the inner suburbs of Paris) were being closely watched. Their comings and goings and telephone activity were the subject of exhaustive monitoring. The case known as the Petit Grégory affair, a major judicial fiasco in the 80s, had had repercussions that could still be felt.

During her internship at 36 Quai des Orfèvres, Clara had worked with police captain G., one of the most senior figures in the Squad. After more than forty years working on criminal investigations, and now only a few months from his retirement, the man was still an inexhaustible source of advice and anecdotes. He remembered the era when there was no DNA, no cell phones, no CCTV monitors. An era when investigation was based on psychology, intuition, and experience. And he loved to tell stories about it. Their tools were less scientific, and a confession constituted proof. "You know, in order to investigate," he would say, "you have to return to the scene of the crime. Relentlessly. Back to where the deed took place. Where it happened, where it all began. Go back there, over and over, back to the scene of the tragedy. Even after the sealed evidence has been collected, even once it's all been cleared away, even years later."

Go back. Breathe. Look. Clara had committed the lesson to memory.

And so, on the evening of November 11, she took a squad car and went back, alone, to Châtenay-Malabry.

Above the little buildings in the residence, the moon cast a pale light across the sky. The police tape that had been used to mark off the search area was drooping from its posts. It was very dark; a few streetlamps sketched out the pathways. Access to the underground parking lot was still prohibited. There was a little circle of trees where benches seemed to have been placed at random, at varying distances from each other. Clara sat down on one of them. Around her, dozens of windows were lit. From this spot in the garden, she could see inside those apartments where the curtains had not been drawn. Everywhere the same modern, functional homes with their well-equipped kitchens, two- or three-seater couches, flat-screen television sets.

The way the buildings were laid out reminded her of the residence she had grown up in. Not far from there, in another suburb, she'd lived in a nearly identical place. It was certainly less affluent, but it, too, had felt like it was sheltered from the world.

Often, all it might take was an image, a smell, or a word,

for Clara to think of her parents. Sometimes one, sometimes both. As if their deaths, coming one after the other in such a short period of time, had reunited them forever. She missed them. She would have liked to tell them about herself, about her job. She would have liked for them to get acquainted with the woman she had become. A cop, yes, but a cop who would have been deserving of their attention, and perhaps even their respect.

At her age it was probably unusual, or even worrying, to be thinking about her parents so often. It was a void, an absence, a source of regret, and she was not sure she wanted to fill that emptiness. Their conversation had been interrupted before they ran out of things to say. And because she hadn't become a mother herself, perhaps she'd remained a daughter more than anything.

Sitting on the bench, the way she used to of an evening when she was a child, she spent a moment observing people: a woman motionless at her stove, a man talking with a teenager, a young boy brushing his teeth. Then she closed her eyes to listen to the ambient noise; in the distance, the murmur of a radio, and closer to her, the continuous rustling of dead leaves along the ground.

What did it mean to be six years old?

When she was six, she could stay like that, sitting in the garden in her housing complex, watching people live their lives. She didn't imagine anything, she didn't let herself make things up. She was content to simply notice people's habits, the way they spent their time, their prolonged absences. She tried to guess how people were connected to each other, what they were feeling. When she went back up to her apartment, with her feet frozen and the tip of her nose bright red, her mother would spread her arms and pull her close to her hip, then in one breath she would murmur, "My nosy little girl." When she was six, Clara started her first year of elementary school in Madame Vedel's class. When she was six, she lost her grandpa, Eddie, who died of lung cancer. When she was six, she learned to recite *The Dunce* by heart, a poem by Jacques Prévert. When she was six, she leaned over the railing of the balcony to grab a scrunchie that had caught on the other side of the wire mesh. And she fell. From the third floor. She landed on the grass, and luckily her fall had been broken by some branches. The babysitter passed out, a neighbor called the fire department. At the Antoine-Béclère hospital, where they kept her under observation, Clara slept for twenty-four hours. It was the fear, said the doctors. She was unscathed. Years later, when they'd had to accept the fact that her growth was stunted, the main factor they took into consideration, above all else, was her fall. When she was six, Clara stopped growing. It didn't take long for the nicknames to abound. Pipsqueak, Runt, Shrimp . . . and yet, there was something about her, a gravity, or an apparent serenity, that discouraged mockery. When she started secondary school, she began to grow again. But she never made up for the lost time.

Lost in her memories, Clara had been sitting there for several minutes, her back straight, her hands lying flat on the seat of the bench, when Bruno Diore came over to her.

"Can I help you?"

She wasn't startled, didn't recoil. She merely gave him a smile.

Coming from a man whose child had gone missing, the question seemed somehow ludicrous. Once she'd gotten over her initial confusion, she tried to explain why she was there.

"I came to check on a few things."

Bruno looked around him as if he expected some detail that had gone unnoticed to suddenly make itself known, then his tired eyes cast their gaze on her once again.

"You look frozen, would you like to come up for a few minutes and get warm?"

Clara hesitated for a second.

The night Kimmy went missing, she'd stayed outside in order to oversee the work of the forensic teams at the crime scene,
and hadn't gone up to the apartment. She might not get another
chance.

"That's very kind of you," she said, getting to her feet.

Bruno Diore crushed his cigarette butt on the ground,
picked it up, then clumsily gestured to her to follow him.

S ammy was sitting on the sofa in the living room, his face glued to his tablet. When the door closed behind them, the boy raised his head, leapt to his feet, and ran over to his father. In his terrycloth pajamas with their Super Mario print, he looked like any little eight-year-old boy, lively and curious. Because he was staring at Clara, she introduced herself.

"Hello, Sammy. My name's Clara, I'm working with the other police officers to try and find your little sister."

He gave her the automatic smile he had on the videos, but when he came closer to her she could see the imprint of anxiety on his face. There were purplish shadows under his eyes, and his skin was so transparent that Clara could see the outline of his veins. She noticed how long his eyelashes were.

As if desensitized by hours of waiting, the apartment seemed to be plunged in a thick, overheated torpor. Sammy stood facing her, his gaze shifting from his father to Clara, then back again, in the hopes of some information or a revelation. She'd come from outside, she'd come from the rue du Bastion, maybe she had news for them.

Mélanie went over to her son, and with a gesture that was either comforting or protective, took him by the shoulders. Clara glanced quickly around her, looking for her colleague from research and intervention.

Bruno anticipated her question.

"My wife is finding it very difficult to deal with the negotiator's presence. It's nothing personal, it's just really awkward to have someone constantly here in our home, you know . . . at a time like this. So your colleague is keeping to himself, but if we get the slightest sign from outside—"

Just then, as if to prove that he was on the ball, Éric Paulin came into the living room to say hello to Clara. She knew him; he'd provided backup several times for her team in crisis situations, or when they'd had to take someone in for questioning that might prove tricky. They exchanged a few words, then he went off again.

Beyond a doubt, the Diore couple looked like parents who were sick with fear. *There are certain types of suffering that cannot be simulated*, thought Clara, but in the moment that followed, she was consumed by a jarring thought: any cop who worked in criminal investigation knew how deceptive appearances could be. Alexia Daval's husband came to mind: he appeared on every televised news program, the image of a man devastated by sorrow, sobbing profusely as he stood next to his parents-in-law. When he found himself forced into a corner a few months later, he confessed to killing his wife and burning her body.

Bruno invited Clara to sit down, then went off to make some tea. Sammy immediately went right up to her, and in a strange tone of voice, that seemed to be laden with implication, he said, "Do you want to come and see Kimmy's bedroom?"

Without waiting for her reply, he went and stood by the entrance to the corridor.

Clara had never seen so many stuffed animals, dolls, board games, arts and crafts supplies, make-believe scenery or sporting equipment in one child's bedroom. The space was as packed as a toy store. Sammy stood in the middle of the room like a young real estate agent, following her gaze, anticipating her reaction, ready to provide the necessary explanation. The smell of vanilla perfume pervaded the room. Until she saw the perfume bottles crowded on the shelves, Clara could not help but think that this was Kimmy's smell, a sugary imprint that persisted despite her absence.

After a first overview, she took a closer look. Behind the curtain by the window there was a mountain of items wrapped in cellophane—games, boxes, sets—which had never been opened. Sammy explained that there was no more room to store them, and, as if to illustrate what he'd said, he opened the cupboards. In the hanging closet Clara saw a profusion of perfectly folded garments piled one on top of the other, most of which looked unworn. At the bottom there were twenty or more pairs of brand-new sneakers in a pile. Then Sammy closed the sliding doors and Clara let her gaze wander around the room in search of some empty space.

"You see, we have a lot of stuff," he concluded with a sigh.

On Kimmy's desk there were several boxes of felt tip pens, colored pencils, and at least three paint boxes piled one on top of the other. Clara noticed on one side the drawings the little girl had made, which her colleagues had already photographed. On top of the pile was a red-haired fairy driving a tractor.

By the bed, in a sort of large tub, dozens of new cuddly toys lay in a heap.

For a few minutes Clara tried to imagine Kimmy in the middle of this room overflowing with things that were easily in duplicate or triplicate.

What can children who have everything desire?

What sort of children live buried under an avalanche of toys they didn't even have time to want?

Sammy was watching her, his expression grave. She gave him a smile.

What sort of adults will they become?

"And your room, can you show me your room?"

He nodded, apparently delighted that she was interested in him, and he led her into the next room, where Clara saw a similar and equally tidy profusion of things. And just as Kimmy's room reflected all the stereotypical aspects of a little girl's room (color pink, abundance of dolls, jewelry, and perfume bottles), Sammy's room focused on their male counterparts (dark colors, trucks and motorcycles, plastic superheroes, all sorts of soldiers, etc.).

When the boy sat on his bed, Clara picked up the conversation.

"So you're not going to school at the moment?"

"Uh, no, we're off for the Feast of All Saints. Usually we go to a theme park, like Disneyland or somewhere, but this time we can't . . . because Kimmy's not here."

His voice began to tremble; he was on the verge of tears. Then very quickly, with the demeanor of the good pupil he often adopted, he regained his self-control.

"Do you want me to show you my drawings?"

"Sure, that would be nice."

Sammy went over to his desk, opened the drawer, and took out a few A4 sheets of paper.

"Do you like drawing?"

"No. I like gaming better. Yesterday I was drawing because the policemen took my tablet to check things, so I was bored. Afterwards they gave it back to me. I kind of don't know what to do without Kimmy."

He handed her the drawings, then stayed close to her, and she became aware of his attentive, steady breathing.

On the first sheet of paper, Sammy had drawn a manga character. On the second, a motorcycle and a racing car. The last drawing depicted a family (father, mother, and two little children) sitting in a restaurant or a brasserie. Judging by the cups and cakes that were featured, they were having midafternoon tea. Under the table, very close to their legs but not touching them, was a tall adolescent, with shoulder-length hair gathered into a ponytail, lying curled up in a ball.

Clara looked at Sammy. She had no idea how to question a

child of that age, but she couldn't let the opportunity go by. She pointed to the figure under the table.

"This is a boy, right?"

Sammy smiled. He looked pleased.

"They didn't invite him to have something to eat?"

He thought for a moment, as if he were wondering the same thing.

Then he rushed out of the room and ran along the corridor to join his parents. Just as quickly, Clara reached in her pocket for her phone and took a picture of the drawing.

In the living room, equally cluttered with things, Clara sipped on the tea that Bruno Diore had just poured for her and listened as he explained the relationship between the Happy Recess channel and their advertisers. As soon as the channel had acquired more than ten thousand subscribers, the gifts had started coming. Now that they were at five million, they received dozens of parcels every week. With a view to getting "free" publicity, brands of toys, clothing, food—"a bit of everything," he summed up, his hand gesturing around the apartment—sent them their flagship products or latest items. Bombarded with such an avalanche, they couldn't keep everything. It wasn't possible. Given all the things they received for Kim and Sam, but also for Mélanie and for the house, they had to sort through them. Two or three times a year they "had a clean out." Kim and Sam chose the toys they wanted to keep, and everything else went to fill enormous cardboard boxes to be sent to underprivileged or sick children. Mélanie even filmed this sorting job for a new video for the channel, in order to increase her subscribers' awareness of the charitable work being carried out by the associations involved. Unfortunately, in comparison with the shopping or gift-unboxing videos, their charity videos did not elicit much interest on the part of subscribers.

Mélanie was nodding silently next to her husband.

Listening to Bruno Diore, Clara thought about "Dirty Camel." At that very moment, the little cloth camel was being run through the touch DNA analysis along with a few other items they'd picked up the night before—a source of precious hope.

She turned to Mélanie.

"And . . . what about 'Dirty Camel,' where does the name come from?"

A fleeting expression, a mixture of something gentle and sad, passed over the young woman's face.

"Kimmy gave it that name. It's her favorite toy. The one she never wants to be without. It was a friend in the residence who gave it to her, when she was very little. A friend who's gone now. And yet she's got so many cuddly toys, you saw that yourself. In the beginning they called it cami-camel. She never wanted to wash it, and I was constantly telling her, 'He's dirty, he smells bad, we have to wash him!' So she started calling him 'Dirty Camel.'"

Mélanie's voice broke.

"At her age she doesn't care that much about cuddly toys. But she's gone on sleeping with that one. She takes it everywhere. The few times I managed to put it in the washing machine she threw such a tantrum . . . So you can imagine, just knowing she lost it, that she doesn't even have it with her, it makes me—"

Mélanie broke off for a few seconds, the time she needed to stifle a sob.

Clara didn't know her well enough to make a comforting gesture, and the words that came to her seemed indecently banal.

Making a clear effort to control her voice, Mélanie turned back to Clara.

"Do you have children?"

"No."

Clara gave her a smile. She'd learned to answer this

question with a single word, without going into explanations or self-justification. And if she added a certain firmness of tone, most people didn't dare take it further. Mélanie seemed impressed, but continued all the same.

"You don't think you'll regret it?"

Coming from someone else, Clara might have reacted poorly. Mélanie seemed to work on the assumption that this was Clara's choice, and not that there might be something preventing her, as if all it took was one look at Clara to understand as much.

"No," said Clara, "I don't think so."

Mélanie was lost in thought for a few moments, a crumpled tissue between her fingers.

"I don't regret any of it, you know, I love my children more than anything. But sometimes I tell myself that nothing will ever happen to me anymore. That makes me sad, I don't know why. When I'm tired."

"Darling, what are you talking about?" Bruno interrupted, going over to her. "Would you like a cup of tea?"

Mélanie didn't answer and went on speaking to Clara.

"Don't you ever get that feeling, too, that the best is behind you and the rest isn't worth it?"

Bruno looked intently at his wife, both moved and astonished.

"Don't say things like that, my love. You're exhausted."

Mélanie was looking at her husband now. It was as if she were drunk.

"But, darling, you never notice evil. You never notice anything, neither self-interest nor lies."

She turned again to Clara.

"Do you remember Loana?"

After a moment's hesitation, Clara nodded.

"She came through it all, in the end. She tried several times to commit suicide. She was seriously depressed, and yet she survived. So you could say that she came through, couldn't you? She showed a lot of courage, you know."

Bruno interrupted again.

"What are you talking about, darling? You should go to the bedroom and get some rest."

"She looked so confident. Do you remember? She was so beautiful. So perfect. She felt different from the others because she was different. She wasn't cut out for this world."

She sighed, and added, "Are you going to find my little girl?"

Once she was outside, Clara took a deep breath, then walked through the garden.

For a moment, the image of Kimmy's body buried under a pile of gravel tried to imprint itself onto her brain. Clara stumbled, caught herself, then continued on her way.

Clara had to look Mélanie Claux in the eye and answer her question. She said, "We're doing everything we can to find your child." She said, "Please believe we're doing everything in our power to find her." But she couldn't say, "Yes, Madame Diore, we're going to find your little girl," the way some of her colleagues might have. She hadn't known how to make this woman feel better. "There are some disasters you can't do anything about," Cédric Berger had said, another one of those sentences that came out of nowhere and which he repeated, no doubt, to make himself feel better.

Clara left the residence. One thing was certain: until the investigation was over, all her mental space would remain occupied by a little six-year-old girl, who'd chosen Dirty Camel from among a multitude of shiny, brand-new toys.

MISSING CHILD KIMMY DIORE

Subject:
Description (by type) of the videos from the Happy Recess channel available on YouTube.

THE FAST FOOD AND HAPPY SERIES
(Between three and six million views.)

"ORDERING BLINDFOLDED"

At McDonald's, Kim and Sam, blindfolded, are ordering from the menu board. Taking turns, each of them must pick out ten items, without seeing what they've tapped on the tactile screen.

Back at home, their purchases (hamburgers, French fries, milkshakes, wraps, drinks) are taken out of the bag and displayed to the camera in detail.

Obviously, it's far more than they can eat.

Variations: they eat food from McDonald's for 24 hours, Sammy opens a drive-in at home, Sammy and Kimmy open a fast-food restaurant.

These formats exist for other brands (hot dogs, soft drinks, or pizzas).

Clara Roussel had left, and the Diores stayed there, locked in their apartment, with that rumpled man who showed his face the minute one of their telephones rang. Bruno spoke with him, their voices muffled, offered him coffee or tea, but Mélanie wouldn't. She couldn't. She could not speak to him. She would rather act as if he weren't there. To accept the presence of that man in her home was to acknowledge that something very serious had happened, and that their life had come to a halt.

For twenty minutes Sammy had been sitting at the table toying with his food, poking his fork at his peas as they rolled from one side of the plate to the other, his face so pale that he seemed to be in pain. The night before, he had hardly eaten a thing. For the first time, Mélanie felt helpless in her child's presence. She didn't know what to say to him, how to speak. She was too busy trying to tame her own fear, to contain it, to deal with her son's. She didn't have the strength to say, "Eat your peas," or "Don't worry." She wished Bruno would join her in the kitchen instead of entering into endless discussions with that man. She wished he would tell his son to finish his dinner and go to bed. But she was alone with Sammy, who was waiting for her to give in.

"Get yourself some dessert," she said, in one breath.

He got up and stood facing her for a few seconds.

Her son was observing her, looking at his mother's face for some indication, an answer, a sign that would betray her mood. He'd always been like that. Looking at her, scrutinizing her, to detect the slightest inflection in her voice. In a few seconds Sammy could sense her fear or anxiety. Sometimes even before she was aware of it herself. Maybe it was something all older children had, this capacity to tune in to their parents' mood like that? Sometimes it unsettled her.

He opened the fridge, reached for a vanilla yogurt, and stood facing her again, waiting for her approval.

When had he become such a docile little boy, so conciliatory? Maybe he'd always been that way. Always so well-behaved, so reasonable. Suddenly she felt like shouting, "What are you waiting for?"

Anticipating her mood once again, he sat back down.

Only once had her son confronted her. It was in the early days, when the channel was just taking off, when she was acquiring several hundred subscribers every day. It was a stressful period for Mélanie, exhausting even. People didn't realize, but she worked a lot. Planning and organizing the filming, negotiating contracts with agencies, with brands, keeping the social media up to date, it was a huge job that no one seemed to take any notice of. She spent entire days and evenings on it—all her time. That day, Bruno had gone to a seminar on graphical revamping and she had just set up the studio for a shoot. She'd specifically told the children: "I'm putting the camera in this corner to try a new angle, be careful not to trip on the cable." A few minutes later, sure enough, Kimmy caught her feet in the cable and the camera came crashing to the floor with a terrible clatter. So Mélanie had begun screaming at her daughter, hand raised and ready to come down on the girl's cheek. Kimmy looked at her, her chin trembling, her eyes wide open, as she held back the sob that would explode soon enough, and Mélanie went on screaming as if nothing else mattered beyond the accumulated tension that had found an outlet at last. A stream of rebukes, anger, and exhaustion poured from her lips, then suddenly Sammy stood between the two of them, protecting his sister and confronting his mother—acting as a barrier in fact; she had never seen him so dark, so determined. Then his shouts came, even louder than hers: "What's the matter with you! She's your daughter!" Outraged, he added, "You like your videos better than your own daughter!" Or something to that effect. How old was he then? Six? Seven? He had managed to stop her in her tracks. A silence fell, then Kimmy burst into tears. So Mélanie got to her knees to hold both of them in her arms, saying over and over, "There, there, everything's okay," until her little world was calm again.

In the kitchen, staring into space, she relived the episode with terrifying clarity. And again she saw her son's face, suddenly so hard and impenetrable.

She had long been haunted by that moment. She wasn't in the habit of screaming at her children, let alone of raising her hand to them. Under pressure, she'd felt herself suddenly lapse into a state she'd never known. She'd shouted at Kimmy as if their whole life depended on that camera, as if it were the end of the world. Sammy was right. She was out of line. Subsequently, for a few weeks that followed, she'd relived that horrible moment several times a day, and she was ashamed. She had no one to talk to about it. Élise, her only friend in the residence, was gone. She could have told Élise what she felt, the impression she had that she was losing her grip. She could have explained the pressure, all those projects she was trying to accomplish all at the same time. Élise was a gentle sort, she wouldn't have judged her. She would have offered to take the children to her place for an evening, the way she sometimes did, so that Mélanie could have a breather. The children loved going to Élise's place. And yet, before Élise moved away, a distance had formed between the two women. Just like that. There'd been no argument, no particular reason. Other than the fact that Mélanie was now spending all her time on Happy Recess. No one could possibly understand how much it took out of her. The solitude she had to accept. The ransom of success.

Naturally she had her husband. He was by her side. With Bruno she could discuss the videos, choose the brands to partner with, go over the contracts. With him she could plan the weekends ahead, and check the children's performance at school. Talk about their plans, in the short- or medium-term. But what she'd felt that particular day, the bitter aftertaste that had stayed with her, was not something she could talk about with him.

Sammy had intervened that day.

And then once again he became that good little boy, thoughtful and focused, never complaining.

By the time Mélanie managed to emerge from her thoughts, Sammy was still sitting at the table. He had finished his yogurt and was looking at her. She tried to smile at him. He got down from his chair and opened the trash can with his toe to toss the empty container in, and he put his little spoon in the dishwasher. Then without saying a word he went over to her.

And for a split second she thought she could read on his face the words he would never say: "It's your fault. All of this is your fault."

MISSING CHILD KIMMY DIORE

Subject:
Transcript of interview with Loïc Serment.
Recorded on November 12, 2019, by Cédric Berger, police captain serving in the Paris Crime Squad.

Monsieur Serment was informed that he was being heard as a witness and that he could call off the interview at any time.

Regarding his identity
My name is Loïc Serment.
I was born on May 8, 1988 in Villeurbanne.
I live at 12, rue de la Truelle, in Lyon (Rhône).
I live in a domestic partnership.
I'm responsible for the Knight of the Net's channel.

Regarding the facts (excerpt):
My channel was founded to interpret trends on YouTube. I created it in 2014, and I now have over one million subscribers. I speak about the excesses of the Internet, and YouTube in particular. I'm known as the Internet's upholder of justice, but I see myself rather as a whistleblower. I was one of the first people to denounce the commercial exploitation of children on YouTube.

I've published several videos on the subject: *The Shocking World of Child Influencers* in 2016, *Spotlight On: Family Channels* and *Yes, Pedophiles Have Access to your Personal Pictures* in 2017. But regarding this subject, the video that generated the most buzz is the one I posted last year: *The Little Slaves of YouTube.* I'm the one who launched the first petition against these channels. It caught the attention of the media. And so, obviously, all these parents don't exactly hold me dear to their hearts. For a long time no one paid much attention. Sure, the parents make a lot of money, but so does YouTube, if you see what I mean . . . [. . .]

Yes, there is a war on between certain channels. Kimmy and Sammy have five million subscribers now, whereas Minibus Team has reached a plateau of two million, even though Fabrice Perrot started before Happy Recess did. He's furious. He invested in high tech equipment, he's been trying in every way possible to increase his viewership. If you watch the videos, his daughters often look exhausted and blasé, he's the only one who's pretending to have a good time. The girls have been making these videos at an unacceptable pace. Just do the math. It takes time to make a video. Let me tell you, they probably don't have time to do much else, except sleep, and that's provided he doesn't wake them up at three in the morning to play a prank. He and Mélanie Claux are settling scores through videos and rumors. The way I see it, it's six of one and a half a dozen of the other: child slavery and a Stakhanovite work ethic. Because YouTube is one thing, but when they understood it wouldn't last forever, they diversified their positions: they created secondary channels using the parents' names and opened Instagram accounts for everyone. Their aim is clear: dominate the market. Everything is already set up so that they can get around any future legislation. Now some families are even doing live broadcasts. Yes, live, can you imagine? [. . .] Well this means that when the kids are at the swimming pool, or the supermarket, or the school field day, everything is broadcast live via their Instagram account. Subscribers can react or ask questions. Sure to be a success. [. . .]

In my opinion, these children are victims of violence between families. This will come up again, trust me. I'll bet you anything. The parents claim this is a leisure activity—that earns them millions; I call it clandestine labor. Tedious, tiring work, and it's dangerous, whatever they say. Work that is isolating minors and exposing them to terrible things. [. . .]

Privacy is a word that is not in the vocabulary of these people. Look at the way they film their kids, the minute they're out of bed, sitting at the breakfast table, if not in the bathtub, I'm not making this up. You only have to look at the images to realize that this is abuse. Yes, abuse of authority. Of power. Good little soldiers repeating the same sentences they've learned by heart, *Hello Minibus friends*, *Hey there happy fans* (in English, of course), *Hi, my adorable cuddly toys*, they give *hugs and kisses*, or just *oodles of cuddles*, and, *whatever you do*, *don't forget to subscribe*, and *give us a little thumbs up to show us you "like" us*. They've learned to smile the way a savant monkey learns its schtick. Do you think they can say, "No, I've had enough, I quit," when the entire family lives off the income from these videos? [. . .]

Personally I don't believe a three-year-old child dreams of being a star on YouTube. They've been indoctrinated from a very young age—like in a sect—with a simple message that's permanently fixed in their heads: I am a YouTuber, therefore I am happy. I call this a totalitarian regime. Mélanie Claux may have told you that I was her enemy. It's true. And I'm the enemy of any parent who exploits their children. [. . .]

My videos had a lot of comments and support, including from young people. That said, don't go thinking that all young people buy into the system. Many are shocked. Because the real problem is that this doesn't stop with the two or three channels people talk about the most. There are dozens that have a thousand, or ten thousand, thirty thousand, a hundred thousand subscribers, run by parents who dream of making that kind of money. At the moment nothing is stopping these parents from filming their children all day long, and making money off them. [. . .]

There is another discussion to be had, one day, about the children who watch this stuff every day. About the ads they ingest by the ton without anyone realizing. It's not just a few dozen, there must be hundreds of thousands. Eating McDonald's, gorging themselves on Haribo candy, drinking Coke and Fanta . . . That's the ideal they're being fed. An ideal life—really? Take two hours of your time to have a look and you'll see what I'm talking about. You'll see the damage that's being done . . .

Yes, of course, I'll talk about Mélanie Claux. I have nothing against this woman. I met her once at a trade fair. She was the one who came up to me. She acted friendly. She's a woman who expresses herself well, always very polite. At the time I'd made one or two videos on the topic, and she wanted to convince me that I was wrong. She wanted me to know that she was a good mother who cared about her children's welfare, how they were doing at school, a mother who was always there for them, attentive, all the things she shows on camera. I didn't want to get into a discussion, I must admit. I told myself, "We're not on the same side." [. . .]

I know that her daughter is missing. I know because I have contacts here and there who keep up with what's happening on the Internet. You're lucky the media haven't let the cat out of the bag yet, but there are always leaks. People are connected, news travels fast. Very fast. The silence won't last. [. . .]

No, I don't know Tom Brindisi. [. . .] He left comments on my YouTube page? A million people follow me, you know. Especially young people. No, I've never met him, never spoken to him. [. . .]

I feel really sorry for them, I hope with all my heart that the little girl is all right and that she'll be home soon. But I'm not that surprised. When you talk about how you spend your day from morning to night, when you show people your beautiful house, your beautiful children, and all the presents that accumulate until you don't know what to do with them anymore, no matter how often you call people *my sweetie*, or send them *hugs and kisses* or *oodles of cuddles*, no matter how you try and make them believe that by subscribing they'll become part of your family, a time will come when something will get in your way. A time when you have to realize that what you are doing is not right.

There will come a time when someone somewhere will lose their temper and come to rap you on the knuckles.

On the third day after Kimmy Diore went missing, Clara, her eyes stinging and her neck aching, attentively reread the interview transcripts her colleagues had left in her basket. Then she'd sorted the initial findings that had come back from the various labs.

She could hear all around her the silence or buzz of the ongoing investigation. Her colleagues now met for briefings every four hours in the crisis room at the far end of the corridor.

The caretaker, his wife, and all the neighbors from the residence had been interviewed. Testimonies had been cross-checked, and the comings and goings in the parking lot had been listed and timed, but the red car, spotted between 17:55 and 18:05, had still not been identified.

Three more investigators had come to reinforce the Internet team, which continued to search through all the IP addresses that connected regularly to Happy Recess. As expected, children did not make up the only group of loyal viewers. It had been proven countless times that pedophile networks made use of private images. Yet this did not stop thousands of parents from posting photographs of their offspring online on a daily basis. A few profiles, already known to the Child Protection Squad, had been rapidly identified. Now they had to be summoned, questioned, and their whereabouts at the time of the disappearance verified.

With every passing hour, the theory of a kidnapping for

ransom was fading, giving way to darker hypotheses. From among the multitude of children on exhibit in their underwear, a tutu, a leotard, or a swimsuit, maybe a psychopath had chosen Kimmy.

In the afternoon Cédric Berger had wasted a ridiculous amount of time trying to obtain the file listing the former owners or tenants who'd had access to the parking lot. The property manager was supposed to keep a record of all the remotes handed out to residents, most of which, predictably, were not returned when they moved. But in 2017, the residence had changed management. The former manager couldn't be reached over the weekend, but he had finally answered his phone that morning. As he often did, Cédric turned on the loudspeaker so that Clara, immersed in her transcripts, would not miss any of the conversation. In an obsequious tone, the former manager explained to Cédric that the archives had just been transferred to a storage facility located in Bagnolet. If, by chance, the records had been preserved—for nothing could be less certain—they would have to fill out a form to request an excerpt, which had to be approved by the director. And as the director had taken a few days off, the answer might not be immediately forthcoming.

Initially firm, but nevertheless polite, Cédric had eventually turned threatening: he was authorized to obtain a search warrant. At which point the manager had replied, using the same contrite tone, that he would transmit his message to the appropriate party and that someone would definitely get back to him.

After screaming, "a child's life is at stake!" Cédric hung up. For a split second Clara was afraid he might tip his desk over, something he'd already done twice since they had been sharing an office space (a sign of helplessness more than a loss of control), but the memory of his slipped disc was, no doubt, too fresh.

"What can we do about these bastards, Clara? These stupid bastards?"

He thought for a moment, then concluded: "I'll go over there with Sylvain. Believe me, they'd better find their fucking archives if they don't want us to turn their new premises upside-down."

On that note, he put his coat on and vanished.

By six that evening, Cédric still wasn't back, but Clara had received the results of the DNA tests she'd urgently requested. Two touch DNA samples had been identified on Dirty Camel: Kimmy's own, and her mother's. The tissues and cigarette butts found outside and in the parking lot had yielded a dozen or so different results; unfortunately, there were no matches in the national database.

At around half past six Clara learned that Mélanie Claux had just dismissed the negotiator from research and intervention, because she couldn't stand his presence anymore. The psychologist had tried to see her, but she refused to come out of her bedroom.

Later, Cédric called Clara. He'd come away from the property manager's offices empty-handed. He had, however, been able to obtain a guarantee that the stored archives would be returned the next morning.

It had been a long day, littered with multiple vexations, so Clara decided to go home.

When she opened the door to her apartment, she felt her body relax, and as her tight muscles finally expanded, she realized how contracted they had actually been. To be on the alert for hours on end, with no signs of progression, was easily the thing that exhausted her the most. She'd had ample opportunity to experience this. She ran a bath, careful to keep her telephone within reach, then she checked the contents of her fridge. A little bit of taramasalata, some leftover shredded carrot salad (hadn't she read somewhere that you shouldn't ever keep raw shredded carrots for more than twenty-four hours?) and a few slices of bread she could put in the toaster: that would do nicely.

For the first time in ages she could feel a familiar melancholy spreading all through her torso. She thought about calling Thomas. It was with him that she needed to share what she'd been through over the last few hours. With him and no one else. She wanted to tell him about the waiting, the anxiety, the life of a little girl at the heart of an investigation where there were no tangible elements. In close to ten years, she'd seen all sorts of incidents and injuries and tragedies close up. But she'd never been on a missing child case before. And for the first time, sitting there surrounded by her stacks of files, she felt out of her depth.

After they'd split up, Thomas asked for a transfer. He wanted to be away from her, from Paris, to give himself the chance to live a different life. After he'd gone, she was the one who had taken the initiative to write to him. He wasn't the first man she'd broken up with in that way—brutally, unfairly—but he was the only one she'd wanted to stay in touch with. Because once he was gone, she had to face facts: she could not bear the silence. She couldn't bring herself to live without news from him. She wanted to know how he was doing, if he liked his new job, if he'd gotten used to the city, if he'd met people. Thomas didn't answer her first messages. Unwaveringly, she had gone on writing to him and telling him things: their move to the rue du Bastion, the re-configuration of the teams, how hard it was to find parking, and the endless construction around their building. Minor and major stories. Doubts and victories. For a long time, she got no replies to her emails. She didn't know whether Thomas even read them. And yet, aware that she was acting out of a certain selfishness, she had gone on writing. And then one day, finally, he'd answered. In the beginning it was all factual, laconic, but gradually he too yielded to the story he was telling. His role at the police officers' training center, the values he had always tried to pass on, his new life. He'd found a place to live a few kilometers from Saint-Cyr-au-Mont-d'Or, in a pretty village, and only rarely did he go into Lyon. He seemed happy. Clara cherished their long-distance connection, and dreaded the day when he would inform her that he'd met someone. Because then, she was sure of it, the connection would be broken. Over the last few weeks, they'd been writing less often. He was taking longer to answer. She tried to respect the same frequency in her own emails.

This evening, she felt like writing to him, talking to him, more than anything. She would have given anything for him to be there.

When she stopped drawing the bath, she realized it was much too hot. She hastily put together a dinner tray and sat down at her computer screen. In a few clicks she opened YouTube on the Happy Recess channel homepage. Fifty or more thumbnails appeared, corresponding to the most popular videos. Captions under each one gave the number of views, updated in real time. As she nibbled her food, Clara began to watch a few videos. The previous day she'd discovered that she could sort them by date (from the oldest to the most recent, or vice versa). There were hundreds of them.

Start at the beginning, go back to the origins . . .

When she looked up again, three hours had gone by. She stretched to get the kinks out of her back and joints. The bathwater had gone cold. She pulled out the plug to empty the tub and switched off the light.

Even though she was very tired, going to bed did not seem like an option.

She sat back down at the computer, returned to the file she'd been using to take notes since the first evening, trying to come up with a theory.

She had to give names to the images, describe them, put them in order.

She had to remove them from this infinite, shapeless space, where they were both hidden and overexposed. From this space where they generated millions of views, unbeknownst to the rest of the world. From that space where, paradoxically, they escaped from any form of control.

They had to be brought into the real world.

To help her do that, words were her only weapon.

So that others could get an idea of what she had seen—people who hadn't watched and never would watch these images, people who were unaware of their very existence—she had to go on putting them in writing.

Describing them, in black and white.

Yes, that was what she had to do, even if it was a paradox, even if it didn't make any sense.

Even if it was pointless.

Because, for three hours, while she stared at the screen, she kept saying to herself, out loud, over and over relentlessly: "You have to see this to believe it."

MISSING CHILD KIMMY DIORE

Subject:

Summary written by Clara Roussel, regarding the videos on the Happy Recess channel available on YouTube.

At the rate of two to three videos a week, the children have filmed between 500 and 700 videos since the creation of their channel.

These videos have been seen over 500 million times.

The channel currently has 5 million subscribers.

In addition to the traditional unboxing (opening parcels, with toys or things to eat), the most popular videos are the ones featuring games or challenges, filmed at home.

Consumer fulfillment is at the heart of most of the scenarios. Shopping, unwrapping, and eating are the children's principal activities.

Outside the home, supermarkets, amusement parks, and video arcades are the secondary settings subscribers like best.

Before 2017, Mélanie Claux had not yet appeared on screen. Her voice, off-camera, guided the children and commented on their activities.

From 2017 on, she began to appear on screen. Worthy of note thereafter are the rapid changes in her hairstyle and makeup. The more she has been featured on screen, the more distinctive her look has become: she generally wears something in pink or white and likes satin and sequins. Her appearance is clearly a nod to the female characters in Walt Disney movies. Nevertheless, the children remain the primary focus of the videos.

Over time, the formats, editing, and graphic effects have become more professional. The children sometimes play written parts which, visibly, they have learned by heart. Still, the aim is to preserve the impression of an amateur film and of immersion into the family, so that the viewer will feel maximum identification.

As they've grown older, the children's attitude has changed.

In the very beginning, Kimmy paid no attention to the camera. Only her games and her mother's approval mattered to her. Brother and sister both looked to their mother, who was off screen.

Gradually, as the décor began to change (particularly with the creation of the family studio), the children learned to master looking at the lens.

Similarly, over time, their outfits have changed. In the beginning Kimmy and Sammy wore neutral clothing. From 2017 on, every video has featured them wearing a different outfit: T-shirts or sweatshirts with the logos featuring the names of the channel's various brand partners, or with the image of one of their main heroes. Never wear the same outfit twice.

Since the end of 2016, grammar and language have become more specific. Kim and Sam systematically repeat the same phrases at the beginning and end of each video, urging viewers to subscribe to their channel and to "like" their videos.

The initial catchphrase: "Hey, *happy fans*, we hope you're all doing great. We're all doing really really awesome!" Then Mélanie's voice usually takes over to confirm that everyone really is doing great, and to ask her children what the day's challenge will be (a game or gift unboxing), implying that they've decided for themselves and she is finding out at the same time as the viewers.

The catchphrase for the end (Kim and Sam speaking in turn, or in unison): "Bye-bye, *happy fans*! If you like this video, be sure to share it. We're sending you oodles of cuddles, and we love you. Don't forget the little thumbs up, and make sure you subscribe!"

In 2017, in response to attacks the channel received, Sammy filmed a video with his sister. Facing the camera, his smile a bit tense, he explains that he's always dreamed of becoming a YouTuber, and that his dream has finally come true. The text was obviously written in advance and recited. Next to him, her hands flat on her lap, Kimmy is nodding silently. Sammy stands up and takes a sort of dance step, then he thanks "from the bottom of [his] heart" all those who have been supporting them and who love them. He concludes with the words: "We have to set an example for other children who have dreams, and show them that you must always believe in yourself."

Over recent months, Kimmy's enthusiasm seems to have been fading. In spite of the stunning editing and increasingly efficient effects, the little girl's reticence, or her fatigue — which she is less adept than her brother at hiding — are occasionally visible.

In a few recently filmed episodes, her gaze slips away sometimes, as if none of this has anything to do with her. She loses interest, no longer listens, doesn't look at the camera anymore, and generally has to be called back to order by her mother.

Then she forces herself to smile, like a good little soldier.

* * *

Some of the Happy Recess videos have now had 25 million views.

The food challenge is the channel's biggest hit. Where at a time when organic and vegan diets are trending, 80% of the products Kimmy and Sammy present could be categorized as junk food (soft drinks, industrial fast food, candy and snacks).

Use of English vocabulary for the titles of the games is systematic, clearly inspired by the English-speaking channels. As a rule, the Happy Recess videos resemble those of the Minibus Team, or the Cuddly Toy Gang, and other rival channels, who all borrow ideas from each other.

All these videos use the same plot device: instant gratification of desire. Kimmy and Sammy are living every child's dream: to buy everything, right now.

Kim and Sam are regularly called on to promote amusement parks and video arcades. Nearly every weekend involves a trip or a visit.

At least once a year, Kim and Sam meet their fans during a "meet-up." These encounters are held at amusement parks, where they are filmed and become in turn the subject of a new video. Kim and Sam are greeted like stars. Kept behind barriers, their fans stand in line and after a long wait (averaging two hours), they go away again with a signed photograph. The luckiest ones get to take selfies with the children.

Some of the videos aim to promote the spin-offs created by the family (pens, notebooks, pocket calendars, board games).

A few days before Kimmy's disappearance, Mélanie Claux posted a video entitled *The Truth about Happy Recess*, where she appears on her own. For the first time, she's not there to start a game or promote a product. Her tone is grave. She's appearing in response to the various attacks that are increasingly being posted on social media.

Mélanie Claux refers to the draft bill currently under consideration with a view to regulating the activity of children on YouTube, and which she says she supports. She and her family already respect all the rules that will be implemented. A few allusions to "less scrupulous" rival channels come up several times during her talk. She also mentions a number of rumors about the family (the children being taken out of school, the bullying Sammy is alleged to have suffered from), rumors she firmly denies. Several times over she repeats that everything is going "really really great" for everyone, and at the end she concludes: "We are a very united family. Our children are very happy they have a mom who really takes care of them, and I'm sure that is what is causing so much envy. We are stronger than all this gossip. We know you are there, and that you love us. Everything that has happened to us is thanks to you. We love you very very much, too, and we thank you from the bottom of our hearts: thank you, thank you, thank you."

The morning of the fourth day after their daughter went missing, Mélanie Claux and Bruno Diore received a white, standard-size bubble envelope. A childish hand had written Mélanie's name (hers alone) and their complete address, including the building and floor. A very young child—maybe Kimmy—had copied the words. Bruno stared at the careful writing and broke into a cold sweat. Despite the imperious instructions they'd received from the police many times over, when she realized what this must be, Mélanie grabbed the envelope and tore it open.

"Don't do that!" shouted Bruno.

She ignored her husband's cry of protest and slipped her hand into the envelope. From it she took a polaroid photograph, and saw it was a picture of Kimmy—a close-up shot, showing the little girl sitting on the floor, her back against a white wall. When she saw the picture, Mélanie had to stop herself from screaming. Deeper in the envelope she found a sort of tiny parcel. On closer inspection, the parcel seemed to consist of a sheet of tissue paper folded several times over and held closed with scotch tape. There was a note with it, written on a plain card. Mélanie read the message and the trembling in her hands spread instantly throughout her entire body.

Bruno grabbed the card and read the text in turn.

IF YOU WANT TO SEE YOUR DAUGHTER AGAIN,
DO EXACTLY AS I TELL YOU.

FILM YOURSELF AS YOU OPEN THE PACKAGE.
THEN *PUBLISH THE VIDEO.*

He stood up straighter.

"Don't touch anything else!"

Mélanie was frozen, the little parcel held tight in her fist.

"We have to notify Cédric Berger. There will be fingerprints on the envelope, we'll screw everything up. They told us a dozen times, Mel, that if the kidnappers contacted us or we received anything, we have to call them right away."

His tone had suddenly become very firm. He went over to her and tried to pry her fingers open.

"No, no," she begged, "listen to me! First, we do what they say and then we call the police. I promise."

For a few seconds, they looked defiantly at each other.

Bruno had never seen his wife in such a state. The color had drained from her lips, and her eyes were like a madwoman's.

He went into to the kitchen and came back with a pack of latex gloves, which she occasionally used for cleaning. He took out a pair and handed it to her.

Without saying a word she went over to the table and, after hesitating a moment, decided to sit down. Bruno went and got the camera, set it up on a tripod, and switched it on. He looked through the viewfinder to make sure Mélanie was properly centered, then stood ready to start recording.

She pulled on the gloves, took a deep breath, and started opening the little bundle.

He was filming.

When she saw what the paper contained—from where he stood, it looked like it was something tiny, barely visible—she let out a scream.

She burst into tears, and he stopped filming.

Bruno went closer. His legs would hardly carry him. They were wobbling, as if disconnected from each other, unable to fully obey the instructions from his brain.

Before looking at what his wife had seen, he also took the time to sit down, aware that he was trying to delay the sight of something that could completely break him.

Then he leaned over the pink paper, and saw a child's fingernail, smooth and clean. Torn from the index or middle finger, judging by its size.

He stopped himself from ramming his fist in the wall, picked up his cell phone, and dialed Cédric Berger's number.

In cases where minors have gone missing, suspects are generally referred to as "he": with the exception of cases involving the family, homicide and child rape are, in 98.7% of cases, committed by men. When there is a kidnapping for ransom, the plural pronoun must be used: the kidnappers will waste no time in coming forward with "their" demands. The language matches the statistics.

And yet, even once they'd received the envelope containing Kimmy Diore's photo and its strange request, the investigators went on using the singular pronoun. For no apparent reason, subconsciously the squad imagined a man acting alone. The morning after the kidnapping, therefore, *he* had sent this letter from a mailbox somewhere in the 10th arrondissement in Paris. The letter bore a green stamp—second-class mail—and had taken two days to reach Mélanie Claux. The kidnapper was in no hurry. The little girl's clothes and shoes in the Polaroid were indeed the ones she'd been wearing the day of her disappearance. Kimmy was looking at the camera lens, serious, focused, and no traces of duress or injury were visible. The instructions accompanying the little parcel had been handwritten, in capital letters. But Clara very quickly discovered a second message, scribbled in pencil on the tissue paper covering the fingernail: "Don't forget the video, otherwise next time you'll get a finger."

Two messages, handwritten. Was it amateur, or improvised? Perhaps it was meant to throw them off, a sort of trompe-l'oeil.

"Or an underhand stratagem," concluded Lionel Théry.

The boss didn't hide his obvious bewilderment from his teams.

Right from the start, the Crime Squad had been expecting a ransom note. This assumption, along with the child's high profile, was what had led the prosecutor to refer the case to the Crime Squad. For the moment, the kidnapper had asked for only one thing. For Mélanie to post a video.

"But this is no random video," Clara pointed out. "It's an *unboxing* video, like the ones her children have been making by the hundred."

After a short pause she added, "But this time it's Mélanie who's opening the box."

According to experts, the photograph had been taken the day after the disappearance. The fingernail they'd received was indeed that of a six-year-old child, but it had been cleaned, which made any hopes of a more precise analysis unlikely.

Now the squad had to make a decision: to agree to the kidnapper's demand, or not. In ransom cases, the general strategy consisted in trying to play for time. For the moment the kidnapper wasn't asking for money. He hadn't indicated a time to meet. He wasn't asking for anything, other than a video; invisible among the multitude of fans or curious viewers, who were sure to watch it over and over, he could see it from home or any cybercafé. Then there was the algorithm: by virtue of the video's viral nature, it would probably go on being promoted for a long time to come. Should they give in, hoping that the kidnapper would then specify his demands, or should they wait, at the risk of receiving further proof of his determination? Opinions were divided. Following a very tense debate, Lionel Théry was the one who settled the matter. They had to take a step in *his* direction. Make him come out with his intentions, establish contact, send a new message.

So, Mélanie Claux would have to comply with his demands.

They had yet another discussion, to determine which media should broadcast the video, and Clara was categorical: YouTube was where *unboxing* took place.

At around seven in the evening, at the police premises on the rue du Bastion, where the police still had possession of her confiscated computer, Mélanie Claux went ahead and posted the video her husband had filmed to the Happy Recess channel. The only title was the day's date. The video lasted little more than forty seconds, and there was no commentary. It showed Mélanie as she opened the little parcel, cried out, then hid her face in her hands. Silent, short, and enigmatic, these images nevertheless evoked real dramatic tension. Anyone who saw them for the first time, even without any context or explanation, would understand that this was not a hoax or a staged event. The video, short as it was, invited the viewer to a tragedy. Mélanie's pain became a spectacle, and the video's implicit violence was a sure guarantee of its potential to successfully go viral.

Maybe that was precisely the desired effect.

And sure enough, as soon as the video was online, the rumors that had been more or less contained until then spread in a few seconds to every social network: Kimmy Diore had been kidnapped. Pictures of Mélanie Claux were duplicated and commented on ad infinitum. Most of the speculation came to the same conclusion: the mother had been sent one of the child's fingertips.

C lara had just turned thirteen when her parents finally agreed to buy a television. After years of fruitless discussions and repeated refusals, she'd had to bring out the big guns: kitchen and living room walls covered in campaign posters, the creation of an *in situ* protest movement, petitions and daily pamphlet distribution. An action committee that included her dog Mystic and her cousins Elvira and Mario was quickly assembled. A first sit-in below the windows of the apartment had shaken her parents' convictions, a second one outside the concierge's lodge—aimed at recruiting new sympathizers—had broken their determination. In the end Clara had won her case. She would at last be able to talk with her friends about *Charmed*, *Friends*, and *Doctor Quinn*. She had to wait until Christmas for her victory to materialize. At the home appliances store, Réjane and Philippe picked out a medium-sized TV set, and now they had to find a place for it in the living room. A few months later Philippe was regularly watching cultural and media analysis programs, while Réjane didn't miss a single episode of *E.R.* And although the time Clara could spend in front of the television remained officially regulated, her parents' numerous outside activities left her with a considerable margin of transgression; Réjane and Philippe turned a blind eye.

In the evening when all three of them were at home, Philippe liked to sit next to Clara and analyze the images on screen. He had gradually taught her how to decrypt the manufacture of media broadcasts: the use of the conditional tense to make up for the absence of hard facts, the shortcuts taken by the evening news program, the use of dramatic effect in reportage or economic bulletins, and the utter fiction of reality TV programs. Philippe was particularly interested in the first 24-hour news channels—their grammar, their vocabulary, and their fantastic aptitude for padding out senseless rubbish. He and Clara had come up with a skit they called, "The-Special-Correspondent-Live-from-Great-Nonsense," and they never missed an opportunity to perform it for each other.

Once she was grown up, and her parents were no longer there, Clara understood that she had been the cherished only child of two activists who were very much in love. Réjane and Philippe were the first among their circle of friends to have a child. They were very young when Clara was born, and they took her everywhere. Clara went to all the parties, all the picnics, all the meetings. There was an anecdote, one of her favorites, told hundreds of times, about one particular party they'd gone to after a protest, Clara's first, when she was a few months old. Réjane and Philippe were among the first to arrive at the party that evening, and they had left the Moses basket in which she was sleeping on the bed in their hosts' bedroom. Then other friends and people had arrived. Crammed into the tiny living room, they drank and talked. Two hours later, Réjane found the Moses basket buried under a pile of scarves and coats. And in it, impassive, was Clara, still sleeping soundly. Their retroactive fright entered family legend, and Philippe had concluded that it meant his daughter had the guts for just about anything.

She grew up surrounded by adult conversation, was lulled by words like *reproduction, domination, violence, insubordination, struggle,* and many others. As a child, Clara had an acute awareness of poverty in the world and of her own privilege, of having been born in the right place. When she stopped growing at the age of six, her fall was not the only theory put forward to explain why she wasn't developing. For several months Clara went to a psychologist, who worried about her maturity, and her level of lucidity, which he found preoccupying for her age. He firmly advised her parents to keep her well away from certain types of discussion.

Her education had left her with an expectation of rigor and a spirit of resistance. She tried to engage with things, while never ceasing to question her approach. And so she brought the same outlook to her work. She often recalled her parents' mutual affection. It had been a source of stability in her life. And of strength, undeniably.

But now, at the heart of this mythology that nothing could modulate or contradict, that affection had become an inaccessible model.

Certain cases brought back memories, trauma. She and her colleagues sometimes talked about it, reluctantly, but they would rarely admit they felt empathy, or hatred, or that one case resonated more deeply than another. They had to show they were strong. That they kept their cool. No emotions. She recalled how one evening Cédric had broken the silence. He told her how cases of spousal homicide kept him awake at night. His father was violent toward his mother, and several times he had nearly killed her. And whenever he was confronted with this in the execution of his duties, he felt a change in his metabolism. All it took was a few words, a few images, and his blood would flow with a rush of fear, something he'd had to learn to resist.

Clara had left the rue du Bastion an hour earlier. At first, she was just putting off taking the metro, then once again she decided to walk home. With a woolen beanie and warm gloves, she was now walking along the Avenue de Saint-Mandé, conscious of the fact that Kimmy Diore's disappearance was, strangely enough, taking her back to the little girl she'd once been.

And, no doubt, to the little girl she would never have.

Like her colleagues, Clara preferred working in silence, and out of the light. "In the dark and without glory": at a certain point in time, this had been the Crime Squad investigators' actual or implied motto.

The reprieve was over, and she knew it. A bomb had just exploded in the media and on the social networks. From now on, the spotlight would be on them—parents, family, cops, neighbors—and no one would be able to fly under the radar.

One hour after the video had been posted, a dozen journalists were already hanging around impatiently outside the Bastion. Others had besieged the Poisson Bleu residence, still others had descended on the local shops. The Special-Correspondents-Live-from-Great-Nonsense were at work. Their noses red with cold, microphone in hand, they would stay there until the end, in search of anecdotes, theories, and comments.

When Mélanie swiped her smartphone screen to the right, it lit up with a selection of recent news. Notifications whose spectacular, sensational or scandalous nature was perfectly obvious: that was without doubt the reason she was glued to her screen—in the morning when she woke up, during the day when she gave herself a few minutes off, in the bathroom, in line at the supermarket, in the evening just before she went to bed. If she were asked to guess how many times a day she made that gesture, she would have come up with a figure far short of reality. Because that gesture, a simple swipe of the thumb, had become for her and for so many people a way of being connected to the world, or rather to the world's propensity to create drama.

And so at around ten o'clock that evening, for the twentieth time, Mélanie read the notifications that had popped up on the screen of her iPhone.

lci.fr
LIVE: Little Kimmy, the YouTube star, has been missing for four days.

bfmtv.com
THE VIDEO FROM HELL: Kidnapper demands video from Kimmy Diore's mother.

ouest-france.fr

TOMATO VIRUS: Contamination confirmed at a farm in the Finistère.

leparisien.fr

UNEMPLOYMENT BENEFITS: What's in store for 2020.

Weather
Châtenay-Malabry
Sunny
Chance of rain

Under normal circumstances she would have paused at the first notification and, given her natural curiosity when it came to human interest news stories, she would have delved deeper into it, despite a vague feeling of guilt. "How awful," she would have thought, and her body would have felt genuine emotion, a mixture of fear and sorrow, a sort of surge of compassion conjugated with relief that she wasn't involved. Because she well knew: you need a glimpse of disaster to appreciate the extent of your own peace of mind. When you know that a life can change dramatically and irreversibly in the blink of an eye, peace becomes that much more precious.

Except that this time, it was not *a* little girl who had gone missing. It was *her* little girl.

During the evening, Mélanie Claux and her husband had been transferred under a false name to the TimTravel, a relatively new hotel located a hundred meters or so from the Bastion. A light, spacious junior suite had been placed at their disposal. Bruno's parents, comfortably settled at home since the day before, had managed thus far to protect Sammy from photographers and to stop him from watching television.

Mélanie had published the video, and from that moment on, the views started racking up.

Before going to bed, she walked around restlessly for a few minutes, hesitated, then couldn't help but look at the dashboard of her channel. YouTube produced the statistics automatically.

In pride of place, her new video appeared on the first page, along with the following comment.

"Your latest video has been performing exceptionally well!"

Given the circumstances, Mélanie was perfectly aware of the absurdity and violence of this machine-generated comment, but she couldn't stop looking at it.

Undeniably, Happy Recess's other videos had been given a boost by the sudden spotlight on her site. The light had turned green for all her data: in the last twenty-four hours, the audience had grown by 24%, viewing time by 23%, and income by 30%.

In bold capital letters, the platform sent its compliments: "Great job! Your channel has had 32 million views over the last 28 days. Congratulations!"

Mélanie reread the comments several times. She felt flattered. Rewarded.

Once she realized what this meant, she was overcome with disgust. Yes, she was disgusted with herself.

She thought about the pleasure a person could sometimes get, smelling their own body odors. Smells of sweat, of fluids, of dirty hair. As a child, when she took her socks off, she used to hold them up to her nostrils to smell them.

That was exactly what she was doing now.

On the morning of the fifth day after her daughter went missing, Mélanie got up just before six. The tranquilizers had given her three hours' sleep. That didn't seem so bad.

As soon as she awoke, the fear was there. An acid fluid spread all through her body relentlessly, making it hard to breathe. At times it was all she could do to keep from screaming and rolling on the floor; at other times all she wanted was to find a place where she could curl up in a ball. She dreamt of burying her head inside something soft and losing consciousness. Visions of Kimmy—her smile, her adorable little face, her girlish gestures—constantly assailed her. Sometimes, in the silence, she could hear her daughter calling for help. Never, in the past, could she have imagined such suffering, or the effort it would take just to keep going.

Their life had come to a halt, and yet time continued to go by, at the same pace, perhaps a bit more slowly, yes, perhaps in slow motion, but she wasn't altogether sure. She wasn't sure about anything. It was as if part of her primary, vital senses had been amputated. There were moments when she no longer knew the time of day, or where she was.

And yet the letter she'd received the day before had given her hope. Kimmy was alive.

She went over to the window. For a while she looked out at the waking city: the first deliveries, the first pedestrians coming out of the metro station, the ballet of the city hall's little green street sweeping vehicles. On the Internet, it was impossible to get away from the news. On every single search site: *Missing, dead, kidnapped, ransom, severed finger*, were the keywords most often associated with Kimmy Diore. Speculation was rife. Some people, claiming reliable sources, maintained that the ransom was as high as a million euros; others pointed out the inconsistencies in the story, the fact it had only just been made public, and they favored the hypothesis of a fake kidnapping staged by the family to gain publicity.

The day before, Mélanie's mother had called her. Sobbing down the line, she reproached her daughter for not keeping her informed. She too had the right to know. Bruno's parents were not the only ones who were worried. It was bad enough to have to put up with all these questions, and insinuations, and inspections, but now that word had gotten out, her telephone hadn't stopped ringing. Not saying a word, Mélanie listened as her mother bemoaned her own fate ("You won't tell us anything, you don't care about us, you just don't realize"). At no time did her mother inquire how she, Mélanie, was feeling, nor did she ask for news of Sammy, or express any compassion for Kimmy, or for anyone else. Her mother complained about all the people tramping through the house or harassing them on the telephone to find out whatever they could about the investigation—both at their place and at Sandra's, actually, so much of it that her sister'd had to take her children out of school. It was all very hard on her, all those nosy remarks, the media pressure, particularly when it was on the Internet that she found out about each new twist in the case. That was the word she had used, *twist*, and Mélanie had hung up.

As if anesthetized by the humming of the air conditioner, Mélanie felt a wave of immense despondency come over her. Her mother had tried to call her back, given that she couldn't possibly conceive that the interruption in the conversation might have been deliberate, but as soon as she heard the first ring Mélanie declined the call. She had to keep it together. She had to resist. She wasn't alone. She had a community. A chosen family. Because, on her Instagram account, she had received hundreds of messages. Messages of support, compassion. An avalanche of little red hearts, and hearts of every color, emoticons overflowing with love.

Her mother hadn't jumped on a train to come and be by her side. Her mother had stayed at home to field her neighbors' questions. This was a fact Mélanie could not get around. But her subscribers, the ones who had followed and loved her for a long time, they were there. With her. Standing by her. They told her to take heart, and showed her their support.

Under the effects of the sleeping tablet he too had eventually taken, late in the night, Bruno was still asleep. For the first time in four days Mélanie was hungry. She thought about calling room service and ordering breakfast, then decided to wait until her husband woke up.

She looked out the window again. It was getting light; the city streets were busier. The traffic was heavier, men and women in ever greater numbers pouring out of the metro station. Seen from high up, the figures seemed to be gliding through the drizzle. Just outside the building a tram went by at regular intervals, allowing waves of passengers to get on and off. People who were in a hurry, some worn out, but faithful to their routine. People whose lives had not foundered in an ocean of fear. Mélanie stayed like that for a moment, her nose against the windowpane. Then she went back to the bedroom and observed her sleeping husband. Bruno was lying on his back, one arm along his side, the other one flung out at a right angle on top of the comforter. His brow, eyelids, and lashes were twitching infinitesimally. In thrall to visions, impressions, or dreams he would probably not remember at all—like hundreds of tiny electric shocks—his face could not find rest. Mélanie leaned so close to him she could feel his breath. Bruno's skin was smooth. He was handsome. He had a healthy diet, didn't smoke, practiced various sports. He was the man she'd always dreamt of. A man you could count on. Bruno had always gone along with her. Without hesitating, he had left his work to join her in this virtual conquest, which she'd led right to the summit. He had given up on a fine career as a computer scientist, he'd taken courses in cinematography, editing, accounting, and special effects. He had believed in her, in her capabilities, in her power to change their life. Bruno was loyal, he would never betray her. He admired her. How many times had she heard him say about their family, in jest, "It's my wife who gives the orders," or, "You need to check with my wife, she's the boss." Bruno was a modern man. A good man. And pragmatic. He didn't need to be in charge or act the boss to assert his virility. He was a man a woman could lean on.

In the half-light she watched his chest rising and falling to the rhythm of his breathing. From time to time, in the silence of this room that was perfectly insulated from outside noise, her husband let out a little moan. She suddenly felt like stroking his hair, kissing him, but then decided not to, for fear of waking him.

Mélanie got undressed in front of the mirror in the bedroom and stood naked facing her reflection. She went closer, until her breath left a trace of mist on the smooth surface of the mirror. It would only take a quick head-butt to split her forehead and send the blood spilling onto her face. The vision passed through her mind. Then she turned away and went to shut herself in the bathroom for her shower.

While the hot water was streaming over her skin, she took the time to look at herself. Her thighs, her belly, her breasts. She had long dreamt of having a different body. A body that would be desirable at first glance. An explicit, obvious body.

A body made for sex, like Nabilla's, or Savane's, or Vanessa's. She had dreamt of long legs like theirs, and their round, muscular buttocks. Her body was not particularly attractive. It wasn't perfectible like those women's bodies, which they could go on transforming to make them even more desirable. Mélanie had an ordinary body, no more beautiful or ugly than average. She'd had two children, and over time her figure had filled out a little. Her skin was not as taut as it used to be. But her breasts were intact. Full and dense, as if reaching out to the Other.

She closed her eyes and a vision went through her mind: hands caressing her breasts, or rather, her breasts cupped in a pair of hands. Wide, eager hands. That didn't belong to her husband.

When she came out of the shower, Mélanie made a decision.

She was going to get dressed, go out, and walk all the way to number 36, rue du Bastion. At the reception she would ask to speak to Clara Roussel, and she would tell her everything.

On the morning of the fifth day after Kimmy Diore went missing, the moment she arrived in her department, Clara ran into Cédric Berger, who was gesticulating in the corridor, in the middle of a serious conversation on his cell phone. With a jerk of his head he motioned to her to join him in their office, and she followed close behind him.

Now that she was standing opposite him, she could study him at leisure. His features were drawn, his skin was pale. "He hasn't slept in four days," thought Clara, smiling at him. Cédric sat down while he was wrapping up his conversation, and indicated for her to do likewise. On listening to the end of the conversation she understood he was on the phone with the Research and Intervention Squad.

Their initial acquaintance had not been easy. Before working with her, Cédric Berger had gotten wind of her reputation. She was said to be finicky, nitpicking, cerebral. She was the daughter of two teachers, and during a previous posting she'd had a passionate love affair with a captain: two indelible pieces of information that would follow her from then on, wherever she went. He had met her two or three times before she was assigned to his team, and had been impressed by her youthful appearance and her figure, like that of a ballet dancer who's suddenly switched to running marathons. At first he'd been wary of the strange authority she emanated, despite her small stature, and he'd taken her on, making no effort to hide his reservations. To her credit, she had a reputation for being able to work for hours on end without even a glass of water, and for never giving up. He was in the habit of forming his own opinions. As for Clara, she had informed him that she wanted to go by the title "evidence custodian" and not "evidence manager." Cédric didn't see anything wrong with that, but he couldn't resist pointing out to her that the word custodian went nicely together with shrew and busybody. To which she replied that that was perfectly fine by her. For the first time they shared a laugh. Later on, Cédric was surprised by her instinct, her open mind, and her physical endurance. Clara might express herself like a young woman from the 60s who you'd find in the sound archives of a historical museum, but she knew how to laugh at herself. And like any good hunter he knew how to adjust to his focal distance and his angle of observation. It didn't take him long to realize that she was an excellent investigator, and that she would be a driving force within his team. After a few months had gone by, when she began harassing the team with her demands regarding grammar and spelling, making all of them (Cédric included) rewrite their reports—on the slightly exaggerated grounds that the image of the Squad was at stake— he had baptized her "the Professor."

The nickname had stuck.

After a few minutes, he hung up.

"You'll never guess what I just found out."

"What?"

"My daughters are fans of Happy Recess! And of Mélanie. They're crazy about all that. Both of them. Apparently this has been going on for a while, because they gave me a rundown of everything that has happened to the family over the last two years. I'm half tempted to summon them for an interview. The youngest adores Kimmy, and the eldest prefers Sammy. As soon as she got her smartphone, she also subscribed to Mélanie Dream on Instagram. She's obsessed. She thinks Mélanie is 'so beautiful, so kind, she's like a fairy.' Basically, they've been watching this thing nonstop for months, and neither my wife nor I ever realized. We must have heard it playing in the background, but the music is cool, there are kids playing, so we weren't particularly on our guard. As long as they're not watching porn, you know, we figure everything's okay. Not for an instant did we think about the amount of ads they might be consuming, as if it were the most normal thing in the world . . . You know, I'm sure it's the same with most parents. From a distance they can't see that there's any harm in it. Their kids are watching other kids having fun, at worst it's a bit cheesy but it's not dangerous. But now that I've read your report, I have to admit I'm a bit more worried. I have a better understanding now of why my youngest threw a real tantrum the other day at Carrefour trying to get me to buy some Disney figurines that had just come out. And her sudden passion for Oreo cookies."

"Well, as long as they're not begging you to go to Europa-Park every weekend . . ."

"Well it's funny you should say that, Clara! Not even a month ago, my eldest asked why we never go to theme parks. Implying that we're poor wretches who never have any fun, that we're poverty-stricken and have nothing to do."

They both laughed. They had to let off steam. He continued his story.

"Last night I took the time to look at a few videos. I'll be honest, Clara, I'd never have thought something like this could exist. You have to see it to believe it, don't you think? It's insane . . . Seriously, do people even know this exists?"

"People, I don't know. But hundreds of thousands of children and young adolescents dream of a life like Sammy and Kimmy's . . . A life of plenty."

"What does the Professor say?"

"Actually, I wanted to talk to you about something. Mélanie uses the word 'share' all the time. She says, 'I'll share this in a little while,' or 'We have a lot of great news to share.' I think the way she uses it comes from globalized English, but in French it's plain wrong. Because we'd say share something *with* someone in a case like this."

"So in fact they're not really sharing much at all, if I've understood correctly."

Cédric paused for a moment then continued, more gravely.

"With all the money she's made, she's not altogether wrong when she says she has enemies."

For a moment he was lost in thought, then went on.

"By the way, for Halloween, the guy from Minibus Team went on vacation with his daughters to a Club Hotel, all expenses paid, and he'll be coming home today. He'll be here this afternoon. We looked into his whereabouts and how he'd spent his time, as well as his telephone records. Everything checks out, but I'm interested all the same in hearing what he has to say. So anyway . . ."

He might have been looking for one of those pat sentences he liked to end with, but nothing came to him. Clara began to feel she knew her team leader well. He might be acting boastful, but he seemed put out. Sometimes a sensation, an impression, someone's behavior he didn't understand could spoil his day. She was about to ask him what was wrong when he decided to come out with it himself.

"You know, Clara, by the time I'd seen the third video, I wanted to make her shut up, Mélanie Claux. I wanted to say to her: leave your kids alone, dammit! Let them live. In fact, as far as I'm concerned, Happy Recess doesn't make me happy at all. It could actually make me fairly depressed. Do you see what I mean?"

Clara knew very well what he meant. The excessive cheerfulness of tone, the ever-increasing numbers of stupid or even demeaning games, the unreserved and undiscerning embrace of consumption or of the act of purchasing, the ecstatic welcome given to junk food, the same phrases repeated ad nauseam—it all inspired a confused malaise in her adult self.

Just as Clara was about to reply, Cédric's telephone rang again. He picked up, listened without saying a word, his face turned toward Clara, then he hung up.

"Mélanie Claux is here. She asked to see you. Just you."

KIDNAPPING AND CONFINEMENT
OF CHILD KIMMY DIORE

Subject:

Transcript of Mélanie Claux's second questioning.

Completed at the request of the interested party on November 15, 2019, by Clara Roussel.

(Excerpt)

I know I should have said something, I just didn't think it was really relevant. I mean I kept saying to myself all the time, this doesn't have anything to do with what's happened. This morning I saw things differently. I told myself that I had to let you know. You have to believe that I love my husband, Bruno. We're a close-knit family. I didn't want to run the risk of destroying everything we've built together. [. . .]

After Sammy was born, my husband and I went through a rough patch. It happens to a lot of couples. Tiredness, obligations, routine . . . Life suddenly revolving around the baby, realizing that's all there is: the baby carriage, the car seat, the baby carrier, the recliner, the folding crib for when you go to a friend's place, all that equipment, you know, you have to unfold it, fold it back up, all the instruction manuals, and then all the measurements you have to stick to when you're making the baby bottles, and then you start with the vegetables. It's ridiculous, because in reality it's so simple, but back then sometimes it seemed so complicated. So gradually a sort of distance came between us and kept getting wider without us noticing. We slept together less and less often, and after a few weeks we stopped altogether. In fact, I couldn't stand my husband anymore. I couldn't stand him wanting to get close to me. I liked it when he took me in his arms, or held me around the waist or the shoulder, or when he caressed my cheek, but the minute I sensed his desire I tensed up. I couldn't stand for my husband to touch me. There. I said it. I'm sorry to tell you this . . . I'm aware that it's personal. You're a woman; I was hoping maybe you would understand. [. . .]

Everything else was going fine, we never argued, never got angry, not a single fly in the ointment. I read the confessions of other young mothers on forums. There are lots of them, you know, and it's really reassuring to find out that other women have been through this too, before you. Things kind of settled, came to a standstill, even, and the more time went by, the harder it got to do anything about it. My husband eventually accepted the fact that I wasn't interested. He didn't try to get close to me anymore. No more caresses, no more proper kisses. He kept his distance. One evening I went out to the restaurant with a friend, I'd known her in my lycée years in Vendée, and we'd met up again a few months earlier through Facebook. She'd just moved to the Paris region. It's crazy how many people you can find again thanks to social media. It's really amazing, don't you think? She wanted to get back in touch. Sammy had just turned two and in all that time I hadn't made love. Not once.

We had dinner at a brasserie in the fourteenth arrondissement. I didn't go out much in Paris in those days. During the entire meal, at the table next to us, a man kept looking at me. He was facing me, having dinner with another man, whom I could only see from behind. When they'd finished, he parted with his friend and moved to the bar counter on his own. He was waiting for me. I understood that right away. His face looked familiar, like someone I might have known many years ago, at another time in my life. And yet I simply could not remember where I might have met him. I took my time and finished dinner. I knew I would go and join that man at the bar. I knew he desired me. This had never happened to me before, this absolute certainty of an encounter. It was entirely up to me. After the meal, I walked my friend to her car, and I pretended I'd forgotten my scarf. She drove away and I went back the way we'd come and entered the brasserie. He didn't look surprised. He gave me a smile. Only then did I recognize him. [. . .]

His name is Greg. You may have seen him, he was in one of the very first seasons of *Koh-Lanta*. I didn't know him personally, but like everyone, I'd seen him on television. On the red team. That doesn't ring a bell? His nickname was Rahan because he had long blond hair and was very muscular. He'd changed a lot. I went over to him, we had a first drink, then a second one, I think he was touched and flattered that I recognized him after all that time, over ten years. I think it made him happy. He hadn't won the game, but he had been one of the finalists. He told me he thought I was beautiful. He asked me if he could slip his hand under my sweater and I said yes. He lived just next door to the restaurant, I went up to his place and we lay down on his bed. Before my husband, I'd only slept with one man. But I'd never made love like that. I mean I've never felt so free, and it's never happened again since. I went back to my car, I felt good, as if my body had suddenly come back to life, started working again. As if it had all been just some mechanical glitch: a circuit, a belt had jammed and someone with some skill had just got the machine going again. [. . .]

From then on, and this will probably seem strange to you, I was able to make love with my husband again. That very evening, to tell you the truth. Yes, that very evening. [. . .]

One week later I knew I was pregnant. It was still early days, but I could tell. [. . .]

I didn't see Greg again, we hadn't even exchanged phone numbers. I thought about him, sometimes, with gratitude, the way you think about someone who's helped you get out of a predicament. I put the story away in a box, a beautiful box, but a box that I could double-lock. You know, women have learned to do this, to lock away the memories it's better not to revisit, because they'd do more harm than good. Women know how to do that. A few weeks later I bought a pregnancy test and it was positive. I could see that Bruno was a little disappointed when I told him I was pregnant. We had only just begun to have a sex life again, but given the way we'd both been brought up, abortion was out of the question. [. . .]

And so I decided the baby was his. I decided, as if it depended on my will and nothing else. [. . .]

Kimmy was born and everything seemed simpler to me. She was so cute. She started speaking very early. She was so lively; everyone adored her. I started making the videos because I wanted to share those wonderful moments with others. I saw some families in the US were making it work, and I figured, why not us? It took me a few months to reach a hundred thousand subscribers. And then suddenly things started moving faster, and Sammy began taking part in the videos, too, and the rest you already know. [. . .]

Not long after Kim's fourth birthday Greg got in touch with me. I had just opened my Mélanie Dream account on Instagram in addition to our YouTube channel, and he sent me a private message. He wanted to see me. It was like a blow to the heart, you cannot imagine. I'd forgotten he existed. Yes, I'd forgotten him. Wiped him from my memory, as they say. I agreed to see him in Paris. I was afraid. Afraid he'd wreck everything. We met in a café not far from the brasserie where we'd met the first time. He didn't even wait for them to bring the drinks. He asked me if Kimmy was his daughter. He'd been thinking about it for a long time, he thought she looked like him, he'd worked out the dates. I said no, she was the spitting image of my husband, whose hair had gone darker with age, but he'd been blond, too, as a child. Greg took some pictures out of his wallet of when he was a child, and even though I said, "Oh, could be, maybe," trying to sound nonchalant—I didn't want to ruffle his feathers—it was like a punch in the gut, because Kimmy did look like Bruno. Looked like him, *too*. Because she really looks like Bruno, everyone says as much. I felt kind of dizzy. I thought that my life was about to go to pieces. Everything was ruined. Everything I've been working for—our family, our success, the waking dream we'd been having for those last few months—it was all going to be blown to smithereens. I thought Greg had asked me to meet so that he could blackmail me. The newspapers were beginning to talk about how much money we made, there had already been one or two features on television. As for Greg, he'd been on the cover of *Télé Star* and *Télé 7 jours*. He'd had his hour of glory, but after *Koh-Lanta* it had all faded away. He pictured himself as a TV presenter or a sports reporter. But in reality he was still a supervisor in a private secondary school. Once I'd regained my composure, I asked him how much he wanted. He gave me a very sad look. He was calm. He didn't want money. He wanted to see her, just once, one time only, he thought that would be enough for him to make up his own mind. That's all he asked. And then I would never hear from him again. He repeated that there was nothing else he wanted. Just to know. In any case, he had nothing to give her. He was alone, and worn out. There was nothing she could learn from someone like him. I remember him saying, "I fucked up, big-time. What would I do with a kid?" I felt sorry for him. We spoke for a little while, I told him I would think about it and plan a meeting, then left. Once I was in the car, I wondered whether he might commit suicide. He looked so depressed, and I have to confess, for a moment

I wished he would. I wished he would go home and swallow the entire contents of his medicine cabinet; it would have made things so much simpler. I'm ashamed of myself for thinking that, but I was so afraid of losing everything.

I arranged a meeting with Kimmy, one Wednesday afternoon, in a *salon de thé* in Paris. He was the one who knew the place. I brought both children. There was no other way without making it seem suspicious. I told them I had to meet an old friend from my school days. We drank hot chocolate, both of them were very well behaved. Normally Kimmy fidgets all the time, but this time she sat there quietly. Straight as an arrow. The perfect little girl. She was very taken with Greg, I could tell. He was taken with her, too. He would steal glances at her, too emotional to look her in the eye. They only said a few words to each other. She ordered a Napoleon, her favorite cake; she hardly touched it.

In the car on the way home Sammy asked me if he could tell his dad they'd seen Greg. It's crazy how children can sense things. Terrifying. I said "Yeah, sure." I'd even told their dad that I was going to see a long-lost friend. We went home, Kimmy took Dirty Camel and then went and lay down for a while. We never mentioned it again.

That's it. I thought he would get back in touch. That he'd eventually ask for money. But I never heard a thing. I kept track of him on his Facebook account. A few months after our meeting, I saw he went to live in Australia. For two years he hasn't posted a thing. Nothing at all. Sometimes I go on Google and type: Greg, *Koh-Lanta*, to see if anything comes up. Sometimes I even add the word *death*. Just in case. [. . .]

I should have told you about this earlier, I know. You told me several times: every possible lead must be examined. The slightest detail, the slightest memory, even the most anecdotal in appearance. I'm really sorry . . . [. . .]

You know, I'm convinced Kimmy isn't his daughter. You might

have noticed, as she grows her hair has been getting darker, and she looks more and more like my husband. But this morning I thought I should tell you all the same. You never know, right? I'd rather my husband didn't find out about any of this, as you can imagine. Do you think that's possible?

They'd had no trouble finding Grégoire Larondo's name and address. He'd spent only one year in Australia, where he had several jobs as a farm worker, then as a *chef de rang* in a French restaurant in Melbourne. When his visa expired, he went back to France. A quick neighborhood investigation confirmed that he'd gone to live with his mother in a three-room apartment in the fourteenth arrondissement. The signal from his telephone corresponded to the address. Earlier information painted the portrait of a solitary, uncommunicative man. He'd been unemployed since his return, and in all probability his mother was making sure he was fed.

It took the Crime Squad only a few hours to identify his IP address and track his activity on YouTube. Grégoire Larondo connected regularly to the Happy Recess Channel, and over the last month had spent roughly fifteen hours watching Kim and Sam's videos. And all it would have taken was to follow Mélanie's stories on Mélanie Dream for him to find out the family's exact schedule: when they expected to be home after shopping at Vélizy 2, the start of the game of hide-and-seek at 17:15. From the fourteenth arrondissement he had just enough time to get there with his mother's car, an old red Twingo, according to the registration information on file.

Cédric Berger had decided to carry out a morning search. The team had arranged to meet at the Bastion, just long enough to get their gear and have a quick briefing. They did not rule out the possibility that Kimmy Diore might be there in the apartment. Clara had asked to go with them, she was sick of going around in circles in her office.

At five o'clock the Berger team members drank a quick coffee then each put on a bulletproof vest. Clara loved this last-minute preparation: the feverishness, barely contained, the clatter of their service weapons being engaged, the metal locker doors impatiently slamming shut.

There were five of them, and they took two cars from the parking lot: Cédric and Sylvain took the first one, Clara, Maxime, and Tristan the second. At this hour the streets were still deserted.

As they drove silently toward this man who, in the space of a few hours, had become their prime suspect, Clara thought about Mélanie Claux. Or rather, about the way the woman expressed herself: clearly, fluently, slightly self-conscious. A strange mixture of very personal confessions and empty, stereotypical phrases. Mélanie said things like, "we're a very close-knit family," "I didn't want to run the risk of destroying what we had built," or even "I'm a real mother hen, you know." Expressions she seemed to reproduce as if she were parroting someone deliberately or unconsciously. Where did these words come from? The Internet? The TV series? Clara had listened to her without interrupting; she had let the story unfold. That was what she'd been trained to do. Let them talk first. If need be, she could go back and question every one of those sentences. Sometimes, a suspect would be sitting opposite her and she would know they were lying. She could interpret their body language. But that was not what she felt sitting opposite Mélanie Claux. This woman had come to her to tell her a secret, a secret she had risked keeping silent until then. Clara had felt compassion for her. There was something touching about Mélanie Claux, her worry and distress, yet at the same time, something else inside her—some form of denial, or blind spot—was unbearable.

Mélanie Claux brandished her maternal status like a banner. Her main identity had become that of the perfect, irreproachable mother. Her finest role. Her life and Clara's did not have much in common. Clara had always lived alone, she knew nothing about the way couples can tire of each other, nor about the transformation wrought by motherhood. But that didn't mean just a difference of perspective. This woman's very language was beyond Clara's grasp.

Shortly before 6 A.M. Cédric and Sylvain turned into the rue Mouton-Duvernet. They found a parking space near their target, while the other three parked in the next street over. Thanks to their access cards, they were able to enter the building together and go up the staircase in silence. At six o'clock on the dot they rang the doorbell.

After a few minutes they heard the shuffle of footsteps coming nearer, then a female voice asking who was there. Cédric Berger introduced himself, waving his badge in front of the peephole. The door opened on a little woman in her sixties. She let them come in, visibly stunned. Cédric stood next to her, while the other team members silently began to fan out through the apartment.

"Good morning, madame, is your son here?"

"Yes . . . he's asleep in his room."

"Is he alone?"

"Yes . . ."

"Well, if you don't mind, we're going to wake him up."

Cédric Berger was known for the polite way he treated people, even in the most critical situations, sometimes to the point of absurdity. The woman motioned toward the corridor. The first door was open on an empty room, the second was closed. Cédric signaled to his men to open it without knocking.

Grégoire Larondo sat up in his bed with a start, dazed.

Wearing only a pair of briefs, he asked if he could get dressed. The clumsiness of his gestures betrayed his confusion. He managed nevertheless to hastily pull on a T-shirt and a pair of jeans, then went out to join his mother in the living room, sitting next to her. When Clara saw him like that, huddled over on the sofa, she immediately recalled Sammy's drawing. Beyond a doubt. This tall adolescent with long hair, the clandestine guest the child had depicted, sitting under the table like dust that's been swept under the carpet: it could be no one else.

Mother and son were informed that the apartment would be the subject of a search, to begin immediately. Neither one of them raised any objection.

Three hours later, the team had to admit defeat: the search had yielded nothing. Not a trace of Kimmy Diore, not a single element found to indicate she might have been there. Moreover, Grégoire Larondo's mother had lent her red Twingo to her daughter the previous year, and had never taken the time to change the registration papers. This had enabled her to free up her parking space so she could rent it.

At the end of the morning, mother and son agreed without a fuss to accompany the investigators so they could be interviewed at Squad headquarters. A few items, including Greg's computer and cell phone, were confiscated.

Despite their siren, they were blocked in an inextricable tangle of cars and trucks for a good half hour around Porte de Clichy. At the intersection, the road works were never-ending.

Back in her office Clara felt exhausted. She needed caffeine. Above all, she had to admit she was disappointed. Granted, the scenario of the biological father thinking he'd found his daughter on YouTube was a bit romantic, but she had fallen for it. Whether Greg Larondo was the little girl's father or not, the lead was unraveling. In a few hours they'd be back to the drawing board.

All she could do now was get back to work.

Reading and rereading the same documents a dozen times over, sorting them, going over the photographs, the statements, searching for a clue she might have missed, memorizing time-tables, facts, blind spots: that was her profession. Sometimes a motif, a tiny detail emerged from the procedure, that mass of paper that grew before her eyes as if under the effect of an ineluctable multiplication, the detail that would suddenly shed light on the whole. Or else, at some point during an exhausting night spent going over everything again, all it might take was a word, an association of ideas, for a path to open.

But for now, no such path had appeared. Quite the opposite: any possible way out seemed to have closed again now.

KIDNAPPING AND CONFINEMENT
OF CHILD KIMMY DIORE

Subject:

Transcript of Fabrice Perrot's interview.

Completed on November 16, 2019, by Sylvain S., Brigadier Chief of Police, on duty at the Paris Crime Squad.

Monsieur Perrot was informed that he was being heard as a witness, and that he could stop the interview at any time.

Regarding his identity:

My name is Fabrice Perrot.

I was born on 3/15/1972 in Pantin.

I live at 15 rue de la Cheminerie in Bobigny (Seine-Saint-Denis).

I am divorced.

I have custody of my two daughters, Mélys (7) and Fantasia (13).

I run the Minibus Team channel.

Regarding the events (excerpts):

Of course I heard what happened, that's all anyone is talking about. The girls are afraid to go out in the street now. Above all the youngest, she's terrified at the thought she might be kidnapped. But the way I see it, there's no smoke without fire. [. . .]

It's sad about the little girl, what's happening to them. Very sad. You know, Mélanie Claux has made herself a lot of enemies. You must've heard about a few fairly heated conversations I had with her. I imagine that's why I'm here, but believe me, there're a lot of people who think she's been going too far. And what's more, she thinks she can lecture other people. She claims to have been inspired by American channels. But actually, right from the start she's been sponging off me. Without wishing to brag, I was first, in France. You can check. Mélanie Claux didn't come up with anything new. All the challenges, and games, all the ideas, you know where she got them? From Minibus Team! Granted, I keep up with what's going on in the US, but I adapt, I improve, I make up new things. She just steals other people's ideas, left and right, especially mine, and then reproduces them. All you have to do is compare the dates. If I put up a new video with the girls, like *Daddy says yes to everything for 24 hrs*, it goes viral, and a week later she comes out with *Mommy says yes to everything for a whole day*. Look at the archive in YouTube, the dates speak for themselves. I started with nothing. In the beginning I bought them myself, the products—the Kinder Eggs, the Lego, the Barbie dolls. I invested. And after that the brands began to contact me. Mélanie Claux got her start playing a two-faced game, like "I'm filming my little girl singing a nursery rhyme, I'm not here to do business at all," but in no time her goal became obvious.

Question: That may be so, but you aren't the only ones. There are other family channels, aren't there?

Answer: Yeah, sure, now there are loads of them. There are three with over a million subscribers: Happy Recess, the Cuddly Toy Gang, and us. The others, such as Toy Club, Funny Toy, all those, they came after. Well okay, some of them are doing quite well, because they're plugging into niche markets. Felicity, for example, you know that one? The mother of the little girl they named the channel after is a former Miss Côte d'Azur. It's going down well with the very girly fans. In fact, we all know each other, more or less. There are clans . . . Me and my daughters, we get along well with Liam and Tiago, from the Cuddly Toy Gang. They live in Normandy. We've even done link-up videos with them for our subscribers. We stick together. Mélanie Claux has always done it alone. Right from the start. She doesn't give a damn about others, she's got no morals, all she wants is to make money. Have you seen the house they're building? Ah! She didn't mention it to you? And all the merchandising, the diaries, the notebooks, wait and see, before long she'll be launching her own clothing line for children, with cosmetics for mommy. I'll bet you anything.

[. . .]

Question: Have you ever met Mélanie Claux and her children in person?

Answer: Yeah, sure, we've seen them several times. At meet-ups at Aquapark or Europa-Park, I can't remember which. Several family channels were invited. We also ran into each other at Paris Game Week last year or the year before, I can't remember which. That's when we clashed. That woman never says hello. She acts as if she doesn't recognize us. I'm not the type to be intimidated, so I went straight up to her and said that I was fed up with her insinuations. There were witnesses; it created plenty of buzz on the Internet. Because in several interviews she said that *she* was the one who respected the rules. Every time, she can't help but add that this isn't true for everyone. I'm the one she's targeting. But have you seen how many videos she makes a week? And those short clips she's started posting? I can tell you, that takes a hell of a lot of time: you have to rehearse, start over . . . There's the set-up, the staging. Her kids have to be constantly ready for action like everyone else. And so what? Why not admit it? My daughters love it. They're the ones who ask to do it. They'd get bored otherwise. But when Mélanie Claux has the nerve to insinuate that I film more than she does, that I don't respect my girls' time off, or that I spend all their money . . . that drives me crazy.

Question: She said that?

Answer: She never says our name. She's too clever for that. You've seen that video of Sammy where he sticks up for his mother, explaining that he's not exploited? He's like a hostage! Poor kid . . . Not to mention all the insults he got on social media: *Mommy's boy, little fag, top-notch brown-nose*, and those aren't even the worst ones.

Question: As it stands, the Happy Recess channel has significantly overtaken you, how do you explain that?

Answer: I just told you, she's sponging off everyone. Frankly, I don't envy them. I must admit, it was a blow for my daughters when Kim and Sam overtook us. Until then they were the queens. They were proud of being on top. That's normal. And so of course they felt down. Particularly Mélys, the youngest. I was afraid she might get really depressed on me. She didn't understand why people liked Kim and Sam better. She felt as if nobody loved her and her sister anymore. So I explained it to them. What's important isn't being first. What's important is all those children who still watch us and who are counting on us. Because the wheel turns, right? So yes, Mélanie Claux may have overtaken us, I can't argue otherwise. But the way things stand, and I don't mean to boast, I'd rather be in my shoes than in hers.

It was customary for the Crime Squad team leaders to share their office with their assistant, but Cédric Berger had had his office to himself for a long time. A moody man, known to swing between long periods of complete silence and sudden fits of rage, he was not exactly swamped with applicants. When Clara joined his team, to everyone's surprise he'd offered her the vacant desk next to his. He wanted to keep an eye on her. She'd agreed without hesitating. She was used to sharing spaces with difficult people, and her ability to concentrate was such that she would have been able to work in the middle of a hard rock concert. The bets were on that she wouldn't last two weeks but, against all expectation, she went on sharing a relatively small space with Cédric for several years, without a hitch. It was going so well that, a few months earlier, she had turned down the offer of an office to herself, with his approval.

Clara was sitting at her computer reading the last of the transcripts of the two interviews that she'd found in her basket that morning when she got a call from the lab. She listened for forty seconds or so, then hung up. She immediately turned to Cédric to pass on the information: there was no trace of DNA on the fingernail Mélanie Claux had received. If there had been any blood, it had been thoroughly washed away.

Cédric thought for a moment.

"What I don't get, Clara, is why the guy still hasn't gotten in touch since the video was put online. He knows we're waiting for his instructions. Either he's leading us up the garden path, or else he's trying to work out the surest way to get the money he'll eventually demand. The little girl's photo has been issued to all the police stations, both parents' phone lines are being tapped, and we have three teams doing the rounds nonstop in the tenth arrondissement."

Clara tried to change the subject slightly.

"Do you have any news from the Internet team?"

"Nothing great. On YouTube, over the last few months all the comments have been turned off under videos featuring children, because of the tendentious or sometimes even pedophilic content that was creeping in. Some advertisers threatened to withdraw their advertising budgets. On Instagram, Mélanie Claux said she spends a certain amount of time every day removing negative or aggressive comments. As for IP addresses, given that the kids watch the videos nonstop, it's not easy to locate suspicious users. Having said that, they've managed to find a link with the database, and they've identified four men who already had criminal records or had been brought in for questioning for having downloaded child pornography, and who regularly watch Happy Recess, with a preference for summertime videos, where the two children are either not wearing much or are in their swimsuits. Two of them were in the Paris region at the time of the events. Their alibis have been checked, along with the signals left by their cell phones on the day of the kidnapping. It would appear that both of them are in the clear. In any case, since the beginning of this investigation, there's not a single lead that's managed to hold up for more than three hours."

"And Grégoire Larondo?"

"Larondo and his mother were both at home the night of the kidnapping. She made a thirty-minute call from her landline, and he came back from his daily walk at around 6:30 P.M. He always takes the same route, along the Avenue du Général-Leclerc,

Avenue René-Coty, and rue Bezout. The neighbors saw him go out and come back. I'm waiting for the CCTV results, but it's unlikely he deviated from his usual ritual. He's depressed, and his life is as regular as clockwork. I can't really imagine what he would've done with the little girl, either, given that we didn't find anything in the apartment, and there's nothing to support the theory of an accomplice. So it looks like we're back to square one."

"The kidnapper is bound to come forward again."

"He'll wear down the parents' psychological resistance, he'll test us, and then he'll present the bill."

"Do you think he'll ask for money?"

"I hope so, Clara. Otherwise, it will mean he's really twisted, and that wouldn't be good news. How are you getting on?"

"I'm up to date with everything. I passed on the information you asked for to the judge in the Clerc case, I completed my report on the Rocher case . . . and I went over the most recent interviews in the Diore case."

She hesitated to say more, but Cédric was beginning to know her well, too.

"What is it you want?"

She smiled before coming out with it.

"I'd like to see all the Instagram stories. All the ones Mélanie Claux posted over the last two months on her account, and which are still in her archives. I'd like to have them on my computer to look at them one by one, at my own pace."

"That's not very orthodox . . ."

"It's only a little software program and some data to copy. We have departments that can easily do that . . ."

She waited a few seconds before adding, "I want to understand."

Mélanie Claux begin each Instagram story by speaking straight to the camera. She had recently changed her hairstyle, again (a more layered cut, which emphasized her curls), as well as the way she dressed (since her finances and her sponsors had enabled her to expand her wardrobe, she seemed to have confirmed her penchant for flowers).

Over time, Mélanie Claux had become Mélanie Dream. Glamorous, magical, and domestic all at the same time; her image skillfully combined the codes.

But Mélanie Dream remained, first and foremost, the mother of Kim and Sam. A fairy-mother, who orchestrated their happiness. From morning to night, in a permanent to-and-fro between herself and her children—so they could not be parted from her, nor she from them—she described how they'd spent the day and, in this way, had created a sort of self-produced family reality TV show, with sponsors who were more or less subtly integrated. The main aim was to give each subscriber the feeling that they belonged to the clan.

Clara began by looking at the oldest stories (the archives allowed her to go back to 2016), then she skipped to the previous winter. From there on, she'd let the program run the images in chronological order.

The days followed in succession, an unchanging repetition, every day beginning and ending with the same words: *Hello, little bears, I hope you're all doing really well / That's all for today, my angels, I wish you a very good night and send you oodles of cuddles!*

Clara gradually allowed herself to be sucked in. As she listened to Mélanie's ever-confidential tone, where every inflection could be easily varied for effect, Clara became aware that Mélanie Claux's voice was beginning to put her into a sort of trance, somewhere between fascination and repulsion. There was no denying the addictive potential of these images.

After an hour, Clara put the computer on standby. She needed to take stock.

Mélanie had upped her pace over recent months. Capturing their daily life began the moment they woke up, and there were more and more opportunities. The slightest activity, the most insignificant event, the most ordinary errand became fodder for a story.

In their beds, in their rooms, in the kitchen, the living room, on the way home from school, in front of the television, hunched over their homework or their tablets, in the street, at the supermarket, in the car, in the woods, at the swimming pool, Kim and Sam's mother filmed them. She would appear without warning, cell phone in hand, and she would comment on the images.

Not a single moment, not a single place (with the exception of the toilet and the shower) eluded the eye of the camera. School notebooks, report cards, drawings, unmade beds—everything was filmed. And when there was something she couldn't show, Mélanie would describe it. Like a special correspondent at the heart of her own house, she would report on everything. If, by some misfortune, she'd been sick or tired or spent a few hours without showing up for any other reason, she apologized to her subscribers.

As with the YouTube videos, a viewer could merely observe these images from a distance (in which case, they would likely appear harmless), or decide to take a closer look.

It was undeniable, the malaise came from the repetition.

In this succession of images one thing stood out clearly. Over the last weeks Kimmy's attitude had changed. Sometimes it was no more than a detail: an expression on the child's face, a recoiling motion, a gesture interrupted as she attempted to dodge the camera. But at other times the little girl's unease was flagrant. More than once, Clara felt like putting her arms around her. To get her out of the image. To get her out of there.

More and more often, while Sammy went on trying to put on a brave face—an instinctive smile, thumbs up in approval—Kimmy would hide behind her hood or turn her back. She seemed to be trying to disappear.

Confronted with these images, Clara feel like saying: cut! And switching everything off.

She started up the program, and once again Mélanie's voice filled the room. Clara observed the little girl on the screen, never taking her eyes off her.

In a story dating from the end of the summer, shot at an optician's called Optic Future, Mélanie had her subscribers vote on the choice of frames for Sammy. She asked Kimmy for her opinion, too, but the little girl, sitting in a chair and visibly exhausted, wouldn't answer anymore.

As soon as they were out of the shop, Mélanie announced the results of the vote: thanks to her *sweeties'* advice, the Jacadi frames had won the day!

Sammy smiled at the camera while Kimmy stayed in the background, staring into space. After a few seconds, when she realized she was being filmed, with a tired gesture she hid her face behind her Dirty Camel.

That day, Kimmy seemed to have thrown in the towel, no longer able to play the game, to smile, to pretend.

In another story, dating from one Wednesday in September, brother and sister were filmed by their mother while they were signing the new range of stationary items Happy Recess had launched.

Sitting side by side in the foyer at a major retailer, Sammy and Kimmy looked out at a horde of children and young adolescents, who'd come with their parents from all over the region to meet them. Mélanie was describing the scene, raving about the size of the crowd and the long line of people waiting for signatures. Leaning on one elbow, Kimmy looked worn out.

Once they'd had their diary or their notebook signed, most of the children asked for a little hug or a selfie.

After each hug, Kimmy struggled to hide her disgust, cringing and wiping her shoulders with her hands. And the gesture was immensely sad.

On yet another day, in a hotel room, when the entire family had apparently been invited for the weekend to Fantasia Park, Kimmy got herself locked in the bathroom. The lock had jammed. They'd had to call for a service technician, and the child's rescue had been the subject of several stories. In the end no one had been able to come up with a satisfactory explanation. Once the little girl was set free, the technician asked her which way she had tried to turn the lock. Kimmy was unable to reply. "She's tired," her mother concluded.

Only a few days before Kimmy's disappearance Mélanie had archived a terrible scene. After looking for her daughter all over the apartments, she finally found her all alone in the middle of the recording studio.

Kimmy was sitting on a chair, facing the camera.

As she often did, Mélanie went up to her, filming the scene, cell phone in hand.

"What are you doing here, sweetie, you know the studio is off limits without your parents?"

Kimmy was unable to reply.

"Did you want to film yourself?"

Kimmy eventually nodded.

"What did you want to film, all alone like this in the studio?"

The little girl let out a sob before she could answer.

"I wanted to say goodbye to the *happy fans*."

"Goodbye?"

"Yes, goodbye forever."

Kimmy wasn't looking at the lens, she was looking at her mother.

Her chin trembling, tears in her eyes, she waited for an answer.

So Mélanie turned the camera toward herself and addressed her subscribers, "Well, that was a close call! Kimmy was getting ready for her farewell tour!"

Then, winking knowingly at the camera, still not looking at her daughter, she added, "But you're too young to say goodbye, my darling, just think of all the *happy fans* who love you, and who would be so unhappy!"

Clara was overwhelmed by a terrible melancholy. She was finding it hard to breathe, and had to hit the pause button again. On her screen, transformed by one of those Instagram filters which made her look like a doll—her eyelashes longer, her skin like a peach, her irises blue as night—Mélanie Dream's face was frozen in a TV presenter smile. Her lips, too, seemed shinier and more well-defined.

Clara rolled her chair backwards to distance herself from the image.

"Who is this woman?" she asked suddenly, out loud.

It was impossible to ignore the need for recognition that emanated from these images. Mélanie Claux wanted to be seen, followed, loved. Her family was her work of art, an accomplishment, and her children were a sort of extension of herself.

The stream of emoticons she received every time she posted an image, the compliments on her outfits, her hairstyle, her makeup, must have filled a void, a restlessness. And now, the hearts, likes, and virtual applause had become her mainspring, her reason for living: a sort of emotional and affective return on investment which she could no longer live without.

Clara opened her desk drawer, looking for a cereal bar or a packet of cookies she might have left there. She was starving but couldn't bring herself to go home. She rummaged under the pens and papers, found nothing more than an old stick of chewing gum. She brought her chair closer and stared again at the frozen face.

Or maybe Mélanie Claux was a formidable businesswoman. She'd understood how the algorithm worked, how the different media complemented each other, and how social media had become the requisite window display. She had transformed herself not only into a fairy but also a company boss. She saw to all the planning, filming, editing and communication, and she organized her family's business trips more than six months in advance. Nothing was left to chance. Kimmy and Sammy had to be visible every day. Weekends and school vacations were the time to honor invitations from hotels, fast food restaurants, and amusement parks. So many moments that would become the subject of new videos. They had to distribute love to the people watching them. They had to send them heaps of *hugs and kisses*, and *oodles of cuddles*, and give them the feeling that everything was shared. *Sharing* was an investment. Sharing secrets, brands, anecdotes: that was the recipe for success. From the moment Mélanie had launched her enterprise on the networks, the likes and views had never stopped going up.

Clara sighed and started gathering up her things.

And what if she was barking up the wrong tree . . . She wondered who Mélanie Claux was, but the question made no sense. Mélanie Claux was not an exception. Mélanie Claux was like the others. She was like Fabrice Perrot, like the parents of the Cuddly Toy Gang, like Felicity's mother, like those dozens of adults who'd created channels in the names of their children and for whom the question of exposure or overexposure did not exist. And they were not the only ones.

All anyone had to do was look on the sharing platforms to see that the notion of privacy, as a general rule, had radically evolved. The borders between private and public had disappeared long ago. This staging of the self, of one's family, one's everyday life, the pursuit of "likes": this was not something Mélanie had made up. It had all become a way of life, a way of being in the world. One third of the children who were born already had a digital life at birth. In England, a mother and father had shared with their subscribers the funeral of their son who had died a few days earlier. In the United States, a young woman had accidentally killed her boyfriend while filming a sensationalist video that was meant to go viral. And in every corner of the planet, hundreds of families were sharing their daily lives with thousands of viewers.

A third hypothesis occurred to Clara: this woman was neither a victim nor a torturer; she belonged to her era. An era in which it was normal to be filmed before you were even born. How many ultrasounds were posted every week on Instagram or Facebook? How many family photographs or selfies? What if private life had become an old-fashioned, outdated notion, or worse yet, an illusion? If anyone should know, it would be Clara.

There was no need to show yourself to be seen, followed, identified, classified, archived. Video surveillance, the traceability of means of communication, of travel, payments, the multitude of digital fingerprints left everywhere: they had transformed our relationship with the image and with privacy. All those people seemed to be saying, *What's the point of hiding, since we're so visible.* And what if they were right?

Nowadays anyone could open an account on YouTube or Instagram and try to attract their own viewers, their own audience. Anybody could perform and multiply content in order to satisfy their subscribers, their virtual friends, or any voyeurs who happened to be checking out their page.

Nowadays, anyone could imagine that their life warranted other people's interest, and offer proof of it. Anyone could see themselves as, and behave like, a personality straight out of *People Magazine.*

Basically, YouTube and Instagram were fulfilling every adolescent's dream: to be loved, to be followed, to have fans. And it was never too late to make the most of it.

Mélanie was a woman of her time. It was as simple as that. You had to rack up reviews, likes, and stories if you wanted to exist.

Clara sometimes felt so sad, so out of touch. This wasn't new. But the feeling had grown over the last few years and, although there was no bitterness, it had become painful to her. She had missed a step, an episode, a stage. She'd been given *1984* and *Fahrenheit 451* for her fourteenth birthday, she'd grown up surrounded by adults who were always ready to protest against the excesses of their era (what would Réjane and Philippe have made of the era she lived in?), she came from a world where everything had to be constantly called into question and thought through—and yet she had watched the train pull away and hadn't been able to board. Her parents had got it wrong. They'd believed that Big Brother would be incarnated in an outside power, authoritarian and totalitarian, against which they would have to take up arms. But Big Brother hadn't needed to use force. Big Brother had been welcomed with open arms and a heart starving for likes, and everyone had agreed to become their own torturer. The borders of privacy had moved. Social networks censored images of breasts or bottoms. But all it took was one click, one heart, or one thumbs up, and you could display your children, your family, and the story of your life. Everyone had become the curator of their own exhibition, and that exhibition in turn had become an indispensable part of self-realization.

The question was not to find out who Mélanie Claux was. The question was to find out what the era would tolerate, encourage or even exalt. And it was time for people like Clara, who could no longer move about in that era without feeling astonished or indignant, to admit that they were ill-suited, out of their depth, or even reactionary.

Clara managed at last to turn off the computer. Her spine was in pieces.

She grabbed her things, switched off the lights in the office, and left the Bastion. Outside, the air was cool, and she took the usual way home.

Who, besides her, would screen those videos and those stories to the point of exhaustion? No one.

But maybe that's where the answer lay? In that clash between worlds. Between this virtual world, with its rules and its idols, and her own world, where these images of miraculous plenty and counterfeit joy produced nothing more than anguish and sadness.

She thought about the little girl. All the time.

Her body, recoiling almost imperceptibly. The look on her

face when her mother came in the room, cell phone in hand. That look which, for a split-second, was trying to find a way out.

However Clara would eventually come to perceive Mélanie Claux, she was sure of one thing: there were no laws that could stop her.

Six days after Kimmy Diore went missing, a new letter was delivered to the Poisson Bleu residence. The superintendent immediately notified the Squad and in less than an hour the envelope had been picked up and brought back to the Bastion.

Mélanie and her husband had just arrived at the crime division, escorted by two investigators. Mélanie was paler than ever and seemed to be having trouble standing. Bruno was holding her up, his face tense, impenetrable, less affable than on previous days. He'd lost weight and his features seemed to droop.

When she saw their distress Clara forgot about her questions from the night before. Exhausted, consumed by fear, the Diores had once again become, more than anything, the parents of a missing little girl.

Like the previous time, the address had been written with ballpoint pen in a child's hand, and mailed from the tenth arrondissement. Afraid that she might faint, Cédric invited Mélanie to sit down, then he put on a pair of latex gloves and carefully tore open the envelope. He found a new Polaroid of Kimmy, sitting on a kitchen chair. The picture had been taken close up, carefully framed, the white walls behind her would teach them nothing more. She was staring at the camera lens.

A serious, intense, undecipherable gaze.

Cédric Berger then unfolded the message that had come with the photo, and read it out loud.

*

"I'M BUYING MY DAUGHTER'S FREEDOM."
THAT'S THE TITLE OF YOUR NEXT VIDEO.
MAKE A DONATION OF €500,000
TO THE ASSOCIATION CHILDREN AT RISK.
ANNOUNCE YOUR DONATION ON YOUTUBE
AND SHOW PROOF THE MONEY HAS BEEN TRANSFERRED.
IF YOU DO WHAT I TELL YOU
IN THE NEXT 72 HOURS,
THE LITTLE GIRL WILL BE RELEASED.
INSTAGRAM DOESN'T
CONTROL YOUR DAY. I DO.

There was something else at the bottom of the envelope. The team leader put his hand in and took out a tiny baby tooth. Mélanie began trembling all over. She grabbed the photograph and refused to let go of it. It took several minutes to persuade her to hand it over for forensic analysis, so that samples could be taken of any traces that might have been left by the kidnapper. No prints had been found on the previous photograph, but they'd been able to specify the type of camera, the brand, and the year of manufacture.

Later on, when he was escorting them back to the ground floor, Cédric Berger tried to reassure the parents: their daughter was alive and the kidnapper had set out his demands. Whether they were serious or were merely a scheme to get the money, it was good news. The crisis cell was about to meet urgently and decide on their next move. On top of that, the investigators were still hard at work: round-the-clock surveillance of the residence, special units patrolling the tenth arrondissement, analysis of the video surveillance tapes, verification of all the witness statements recorded on the dedicated phone number.

At eleven o'clock Mélanie and Bruno left the Bastion. It was going to be a long day. They took the underground tunnel to drive out, to avoid the journalists. Once they were on the Boulevard Berthier, Bruno suggested going for a walk before shutting themselves back in the hotel room, but Mélanie just didn't have the strength.

They'd been back in their suite for an hour when Mélanie decided to run a bath. She was chilled to the bone, and couldn't get warm.

Next to her, Bruno was pacing back and forth, too restless to sit down.

Since the night before, they'd hardly said a word to each other. Bruno had helped her all the way to the Crime Squad, and into Cédric Berger's office. She'd been able to lean on him the way she'd been doing for years, but he didn't put his arms around her. He didn't take her hand or hold her close.

Her husband, her dear husband. So reliable and devoted. Her husband whom she'd betrayed.

From where she stood, she could see the tension in his back and thighs, "a bundle of nerves," she thought, not daring to go closer.

The night before she'd come out with everything. She had no choice.

Because once Grégoire Larondo had been interviewed by the investigators, he hadn't stopped phoning her. She didn't know how he'd managed to get her number. The first time, luckily, Bruno hadn't heard anything. Mélanie had gone some distance away to explain what she knew, how the investigation was going, the means they'd put in place. Firmly, she'd told Grégoire not to call her again. But three hours later he got in touch. From his voice she could tell he wouldn't stop there. Something hermetic, which until then had contained his anxiety, had given way. Now he wanted to know the details of the investigation, to take part in the search, he couldn't sit there with his arms crossed while his daughter was in danger. He was losing control.

And so, as Clara Roussel had advised her (it was impossible, she repeated, to guarantee that Bruno would never get wind of Grégoire Larondo's interview), Mélanie decided to speak to her husband. Not going into detail, but not omitting the essential facts either, she told him about that evening six years ago, and Grégoire's request all these years later. Clenching his fists, Bruno listened without interrupting. She could see the muscles in his jaw twitching, just the way they had that day when he'd come to blows with a man in the street who was about to spit at Mélanie.

Then he stood up without saying a thing and shut himself in the bedroom. All that time Mélanie had gone on sitting on the sofa in the living room, perfectly immobile.

When Bruno came back out his eyes were red and he spoke to her in a tone she'd never heard. A tone that left no doubt or room for protest. This man who was normally so gentle, so conciliatory, had returned his verdict. Kimmy was his daughter and he knew it. There would be no further discussion. They had to remain united in their waking nightmare. They had no energy to waste on quarrels or foolish mistakes. They had a far more important battle to fight.

Bruno was looking out of the window now. She could hear him breathing. Hard, too hard. While she waited for the bathtub to fill, Mélanie switched on the television and came upon one of the news channels. She had started putting a few things away when she heard her mother's voice. She crept closer to the screen.

With the microphone below her chin, her mother had a worried expression.

"Yes, this is a terrible trial for my daughter and son-in-law. They're coping, of course, but we're all very worried about our little girl. If we only knew something about the conditions where she's being held . . . You know what sort of state the kids are in, sometimes, by the time they find them . . . The police are at a standstill, that's a fact. There are pedophiles everywhere, Monsieur. You can't help but think about it."

They were filming her close up, a slightly low-angle shot. Her face seemed very red.

"Do you have any news from Mélanie?"

"She's holding up. They're waiting, and so are we. It's hard, very hard."

With a sudden brusque gesture, Mélanie Claux aimed the remote at the television, then collapsed on the sofa. Bruno hadn't moved. She burst into tears. Since her daughter's disappearance she had succumbed to tears, but whenever she risked being overcome by sobs she'd managed to regain her self-control. Several times over she'd felt she was about to go over the edge—to fall, or collapse—and she'd always managed to ride the wave, the current, the dark force that was dragging her down, right to the bottom, where there would be nothing left to cling to, no help, a place from which she wouldn't be able to get back to the surface. She couldn't allow that to happen. She had to keep her strength to resist. To survive.

But this time the onslaught was far more powerful. Her chest was heaving with spasms of unprecedented violence. As if her entire organism were trying to rid itself of a foreign body or a toxic molecule, and an unbearable pain were making it impossible to breathe.

An ancient lament from far away, a lament from her childhood or from every childhood, came from her throat. She'd never expressed anything so horrible. She had never felt so alone. She let herself collapse on the floor. And then she felt as if she were leaving her own body behind. She saw herself there, curled up in a ball in that hotel room, a poor abandoned little girl, and felt immensely sorry for herself. She didn't deserve this.

After a few minutes, Bruno stepped away from the window. He went over to her, helped her to her feet, and took her in his arms.

If I've got this right, a six-year-old kid has been kidnapped in broad daylight by a sicko who tears her nails and teeth out to send them to the mother, and six days later, we're still sitting here like cretins."

Lionel Théry was known for his ability to sum things up neatly. Given the atmosphere, it could be dangerous to go in for too much nuance.

Cédric Berger took the floor.

"Mélanie Claux informed us that Kimmy's two lower teeth had begun to loosen, a few days before she went missing. Dr. Martin confirmed that the tooth found in the envelope was her right central mandibular incisor, Number 81, to be precise. In all likelihood it simply fell out, the way children's baby teeth generally do at that age."

"That is very valuable information."

Clara spoke up.

"That may be more than a mere detail. The kidnapper sent a tooth, he doesn't claim to have pulled it out. He's giving us proof that he's got the girl. On the photograph, Kimmy is wearing leggings and a sweatshirt, but that's not the outfit she had on the day she disappeared. On closer inspection, you can see that these clothes aren't new. So the kidnapper already had clothes that were the right size, that had already been worn, or else he bought them in a secondhand shop. Whatever the case, he made sure to have a clean outfit for the little girl, something which in itself is quite interesting."

Lionel Théry was a good loser.

"Right. And we still don't have anything on that fucking car?"

Cédric Berger spoke up again.

"A Twingo, a Clio, maybe a Peugeot 206, according to the witnesses . . . not exactly unusual makes. I'll remind everyone that none of the people currently authorized to officially use the parking lot have a red car, and that no one lent their garage door remote to anyone on the outside. In terms of former owners or tenants, who might have had access to the parking lot, the former property manager, who was dismissed, can no longer provide us with that information. They either lost or threw out part of their archives."

A silence fell. Clara hesitated, then took over.

"The kidnapper has seen enough television to have known to wear gloves when he sends his correspondence to the mother (and not to both parents). His messages refer to her channel on YouTube. The ransom demands arrive by mail, and are handwritten. Given that nowadays any dealer can buy a disposable cell phone and a prepaid SIM card, there's a kind of old-fashioned side to his approach which I find rather charming. Moreover, the kidnapper is not demanding the ransom for himself, but for a good cause. We may have our doubts, of course, and we should have it verified. He's asking Mélanie Claux to donate half a million to an association that has been around for twenty years: Children at Risk. This might be a message. And it seems all the clearer to me, given that the kidnapper refers explicitly to Happy Recess. Because when he writes, 'Instagram doesn't control your day. I do,' it's more than likely that he's referring to the *Instagram Controls Our Lives* videos, which are phenomenally successful on YouTube."

She fell silent for a moment, hesitating about whether to go on. Lionel Théry encouraged her with a little wave of his hand.

"Let me explain. Roughly once a month, Mélanie Claux spends a whole day sending out surveys to her subscribers.

They're the ones who decide on everything: which cereal Kimmy and Sammy should eat for breakfast, which cartoon they're going to watch, which sweatshirt they're going to wear. She asks the question on her Instagram account and, in the space of a few minutes, gets her results. The day itself is the subject of a new video, edited and enhanced with graphic effects, then posted on YouTube. The most recent ones to date got five or six million views each. Mélanie Claux hasn't invented anything new. It's just that nowadays it's not the fans who control her day, it's her daughter's kidnapper . . . and he's telling her to write a big check."

Lionel Théry listened, tensely. Cédric Berger spoke again.

"The association is an institution, it's hard to imagine it might have any ties with the kidnapper. Nevertheless, we'll be interviewing the president, treasurer, and general secretary here during the day. Obviously, the parents want to pay. I've persuaded them to wait, I'm going to see Bruno Diore in a little while. He seems to have things under control, and he understands where we're coming from."

Lionel Théry cleared his throat.

"They have the money, I imagine?"

"Yes. The funds can rapidly be made available."

Lionel Théry thought for a moment before concluding.

"Granted, it all seems a bit amateurish. It could even look like a nasty hoax, except that the little girl really has been missing for six days. So let me remind you of one thing: amateurism doesn't rule out perversion. And improvisation is not incompatible with barbaric behavior. So, no letting up. We don't move until we're sure the association is legit and that they'll be prepared to return the money if the parents ask them to. And then, if necessary, we'll act as if we're about to give in. If the little girl is released, we'll have to be prepared for discussions about the way we communicate our strategy. But before anything else we have to get the guy to make his intentions clear."

Night had just fallen, and Mélanie was rereading the comments of support and love she'd been receiving on her account since she'd posted the first video and the media had confirmed that her daughter was missing. Her *sweeties* hadn't forgotten her. Just knowing they were there, by her side, was such a comfort. Dozens of moms who said they could cook for her, look after Sammy, or put them up at their place. Dozens of children expressing their concern and their sadness, with flowers, hearts of every color, and adorable emojis.

She had created a community. It wasn't just a word. It was a reality. A community, and she was at the epicenter. In this world that was so cruel and violent, it meant a lot. "It means a lot," Kim Kardashian had once said on her Instagram account, and she was right. From the very first day Mélanie had spoken to her subscribers she had called them *my sweeties*. Because she wanted to say how much she loved them. Because they made her life sweeter.

They had brought her so much.

Everything.

She had so many *sweeties* that she couldn't imagine them individually. Her *sweeties* made up a sort of huge, faceless family. A kind family, united across generations, where both children and adults were represented. She liked this idea of having an audience she had to please and satisfy, an audience whose happiness was her responsibility. She liked the instant gratification, so warm and enthusiastic, that they gave her whenever she appeared online. She needed their attention. Their compliments. They gave her the feeling she was unique, someone who deserved to be noticed. There was no shame in that.

She missed her daughter terribly. The memory was unbearable—that little body snuggled up against her side when she came to cuddle, those skinny arms around her waist. Her beautiful Kimmy. So wild, so independent. She didn't look like the little girl Mélanie had been. She didn't look like any little girl Mélanie knew.

Of course, sometimes she would get into a mood. Or start crying. Recently, Kimmy's mood had been glum. She balked at filming certain videos, not because she didn't like to, but because some of her classmates made fun of her. Madame Chevalier had called Mélanie in to talk about it. The teacher had asked her questions about the filming, what it consisted of, at what time, how often . . . she wanted to know everything. How much time Happy Recess took up every week, and how much time was left for playing and being bored. "Bored? But she's never bored!" Mélanie replied proudly. Happy Recess was their life. That was something this woman could not understand. Madame Chevalier said that Kimmy was beginning to become aware of things, particularly the fact that the videos were seen by a great number of people, people she didn't know. According to the teacher, this was upsetting her. Kimmy seemed tired to her, a little depressed even. "This woman is crazy," Mélanie thought. The woman had no proof of what she was claiming. She was basing her judgment on impressions that reflected nothing other than her own prejudice. But the teacher wouldn't stop. She claimed that out on the playground, whenever another child spoke to her about Happy Recess, Kimmy would clap her hands over her ears. Some older children called her *Dirty Baby* or *Camel Baby*. One day, Kimmy burst into tears because a boy from a class of older children had told her, probably reproducing word for word an unkind remark his parents had made: "Your mother is going to be reported to the family court."

During the appointment, Mélanie had listened politely to the teacher, then she had set the record straight: she would not have her children subjected to such malicious gossip. She'd enrolled them in a private school to avoid this sort of difficulty, so if Kimmy or Sammy were the victims of such mockery or ridicule—fuelled solely by envy—it was up to the teachers and administration to take action.

That was what she had replied to Madame Chevalier, in a firm tone.

In the weeks that followed, Kimmy became more and more reluctant to participate in the videos. So much so that Mélanie wondered if the teacher hadn't put ideas into her daughter's head. They had to beg Kimmy to get her to do anything. She forgot her text, didn't listen to instructions, and acted as if she didn't understand a thing. The primary stumbling block was her clothing. At the age of six, her little girl categorically refused to wear a skirt, dress, pair of tights, or any outfit, for that matter, that was the least bit feminine. She didn't want to have anything to do with the color pink, or lace, or ruffles. Mélanie was beside herself, particularly because the day before the release of *Frozen 2* she had signed an important contract with Disney. The company had provided them with a whole slew of costumes, toys, and merchandise to promote on their YouTube channel and on social networks. Kimmy refused point blank to wear the Elsa gown or coat, and Mélanie'd had to wear the crown herself, as well as the earrings and satin gloves.

Then there was that day Kimmy had managed to lock herself all alone in the hotel bathroom. How could a child have such a twisted idea? It must have come from somewhere. The teacher had a grudge against Mélanie. A personal grudge. That woman was jealous of her success, of her clothes, of her life. It was plain to see. And that manner of hers, the way she looked at Mélanie whenever she came to get her daughter. That half smile. Acting superior. What business was it of hers?

Mélanie had very nearly asked for an appointment with the headmistress to report the teacher, but Bruno had dissuaded her. It could blow up out of all proportion and Mélanie had no proof. She had come round to her husband's point of view. Bruno was less emotional, less sensitive than she was. He managed to calm her down.

She could not help but recall those moments of conflict, and the memory of that time broke her heart. But she knew she couldn't allow herself to be overcome by negative thoughts, or by all those rumors meant to hurt them. She had to stay strong, the way she always had.

Bruno was waiting for the green light from the Crime Squad in order to make the transfer as requested to the association's account. The money didn't matter. She would have given twice that amount if she had to.

When night began to fall, Mélanie opened the curtains to look out at the street. The people walking, talking, coming and going made her feel a little calmer.

Suddenly she realized that she hadn't thanked her *sweeties* for all their messages. For several days she hadn't replied. Not once. She couldn't leave them like that, with no news, without a word.

She reached for her smartphone and wrote:

"Thank you all for your support and for all the love you have given us. You are our stars in the dark night, our horizon amid this ordeal."

She added a dozen prayer emoticons, two joined hands pointing toward the sky, and an emoticon of star-filled eyes.

A few seconds later the first hearts and *kisses* emoticons appeared. In a few minutes she'd already received seven hundred and eighteen likes.

She smiled.

Clara had long wondered if someone could be a cop and lead a normal life. Insofar as she could imagine what a normal life might look like, the answer was no. The truth was that she led the life of a cop, living in a residence for cops, with friends who were cops, having conversations about cops, and the issues that went along with being a cop. Most cops got married to other cops, but not Clara: she'd let the cop of a lifetime get away.

This was the conclusion she came to on evenings when she felt *blue*, as her mother used to call it, when Clara was a child, always asking her to indicate the precise nuance of the color, from palest to darkest blue—the way you'd evaluate your pain on a scale from one to ten. *Blue* evenings, when even her old friend Chloé from university days was not available to go for a drink. On other days, Clara took a slightly more indulgent view of her life.

That evening she would have liked to tell herself that things were going in the right direction. Kimmy Diore was alive and was apparently not being mistreated. Children At Risk had the recognition of a large number of private and public partners, and it offered all the requisite amenities. During the day, they'd been able to rule out the possibility that the association or any of its members were in any way involved in Kimmy Diore's abduction. The president had agreed to comply with the Crime Squad's instructions, including restoring the money if necessary. The wire transfer had been made that evening, and Cédric Berger had convinced the Diores to wait until the following morning to post the proof.

None of the squad members really seemed to believe what was happening. Who would kidnap and confine a child then demand a ransom to be paid for the benefit of an association? They could not exclude the premise of someone with a perverse, disorganized profile, increasing their demands to prolong the pleasure.

As for Clara, she couldn't help but think that the aim was first and foremost to put an end to the system Mélanie Claux had put in place.

And it had worked: over the last few days, Kimmy and Sammy had no longer seemed elated on opening their parcels; they were no longer testing chips or soda then letting out cries of joy, they had stopped buying whatever they felt like at the supermarket, and they no longer mindlessly ordered more hamburgers than they could eat in a week.

Their mother was no longer chronicling their lives by the hour to thousands of strangers.

Someone had said: enough. And the machine had ground to a halt.

At 9 P.M., when she was just about to start writing a letter to Thomas, Clara got a message from Cédric telling her to switch on the TV. On France 2 they were rebroadcasting a reportage on children who were YouTube stars. She did as he said, and curled up on the sofa.

Judging from the age of the children, the program must have been a few years old. Several children's channels were featured, but most of the investigation was focused on Happy Recess. Kimmy must have been around four years old, and Sammy was six. The journalist and cameraman had gone with them to a major shopping center where several hundred children were waiting for them. A delightful doll dressed in pink, Kimmy strode ahead next to her brother, careful to walk in step with him. Like a young bodyguard, Sammy didn't take his eyes off her. The images showed their arrival at the area that had been set up for the event, where they were met with noisy applause, then the time devoted to signing and selfies, lasting several hours. All through it, Mélanie kept an eye on things and orchestrated it all, managing the line of waiting children, checking whose turn it was, attentive to the smaller children and making sure that no one stayed over the allotted time.

Before leaving she agreed to a short interview. Yes, of course, she was pleased with their success, and extended her thanks above all to the *happy fans* for their enthusiasm and loyalty. The journalist asked her if she realized that some people, even very young viewers, might be shocked to see children put on display like that. Mélanie shook her head sadly, as if to say no, she didn't get it, and then she answered, her voice gentle but firm. As a mother she knew very well what was good for her children and what wasn't. And in any case, these were *her* children, she hastened to add, stressing the pronoun. And *her* children were very happy just as they were. The journalist turned to the children then to see what they had to say. In a slow voice, like a doll controlled remotely, whose batteries were starting to drain, Kimmy explained that she thought it was great that she was making her *happy fans* happy and to "see the happiness in their eyes." With a bit more conviction, Sammy asserted that this was his dream and that he wanted to pursue it as a profession.

Radiant, Mélanie added, "You heard it from them. What more can I say?"

And then, beaming with a reassuring smile, she concluded, "You know, in our family, the kids run the show."

On the morning of the eighth day after Kimmy Diore went missing, Clara was one of the first to arrive at the Bastion. She had woken up at five and hadn't managed to get back to sleep. A strange impatience had propelled her out of bed.

She went through the security doors then over to the elevators. From behind his glass window, the agent at reception motioned to her to come over.

"A woman has just arrived. She wants to see someone from your team."

Clara turned toward the waiting rooms, usually empty at this time of day. In room number 4 she saw a woman her age with drawn features, wrapped in a light-colored raincoat. She went over to her.

Then her gaze caught the child sitting next to her.

The little girl looked up and their eyes met.

Clara's pulse suddenly began to beat faster and she could feel her heart pounding in her chest.

She had studied her so much over the last few days that she felt she knew her.

KIDNAPPING AND CONFINEMENT
OF CHILD KIMMY DIORE

Subject:

Transcript of interview of Élise Favart.

Completed on November 18, 2019, by Clara Roussel, criminal investigation officer with the Paris Crime Squad, and Cédric Berger, police captain with the Crime Squad.

Regarding the facts:

Élise Favart came on November 18, 2019, at 8:05 A.M. to the premises of the Crime Squad together with the child Kimmy Diore, who went missing on November 10, 2019. Without waiting for the interview, she explained to the officer from the Criminal Investigation Department, Clara Roussel, that she was the perpetrator of the kidnapping and confinement of Kimmy Diore, and that the child had just spent the last seven days at her home.

Regarding her identity:

My name is Élise Irène Favart.

I was born on September 10, 1985, in Suresnes.

I live at 209 rue Lafayette in Paris, 10th arrondissement.

I am divorced, and the mother of a little boy aged six, born in 2013.

I'm a medical secretary but I stopped working a year ago.

(Excerpts.)

I moved to the Poisson Bleu residence with Norbert S. not long after we got married. My partner was working for a security firm, in charge of recruitment and team management. I met Mélanie Claux when my son, Ilian, was a few months old. We had given birth the same week, and I often ran into her in the residence with her stroller or baby sling. This was her second child, Mélanie knew the town really well, and she gave me a lot of advice regarding pediatricians, how to sign up at day care, and so on. After Ilian was born I went back to work part-time as a secretary in a medical and psychological center in Antony. She and I became friends. We went to the park together, or met in town to go shopping. Mélanie was very friendly. She sometimes seemed a little sad and I occasionally wondered whether she was bored because she didn't work. From a very young age, Kimmy and Ilian got along very well. She loved to play with cars, the electric racetrack, or toy soldiers. She was always a bit of a tomboy, and her mother didn't like that very much. For a few months we met fairly often, I would look after the children when Mélanie had things to do. And Ilian loved going to their place. [. . .]

In 2015 my husband left me. He went to live in Marseille where there was a job opening. I think it was mainly because he'd realized, before I had, that there was something wrong with Ilian. At about the same time, Mélanie started her business with Kimmy on YouTube. She didn't tell me about it, I found out from the neighbors, when it began to take off. It had become the number one topic of conversation at the residence. Back then I wasn't very good with computers and I wasn't interested in what was going on, on the Internet. Mélanie became very busy with her filming and editing. Sometimes she asked me to look after the children because she had to meet with agencies or labels in Paris, and I didn't mind. Her daughter was very articulate, advanced for her age. Kimmy and Ilian were the same age and I could see that he wasn't developing at the same pace. In the beginning I didn't worry because a lot of children come into the center where I was working and I could see how different they all were from each other. I was working three days a week, and it was my mother who looked after Ilian. I eventually asked for the child psychiatrist at the center to see him. My son was two and a half years old. She broke the news very gently, explaining that Ilian was significantly behind in his development and that he'd have to have additional tests. My son had a learning disability, those were the words I would have to learn to live with. When I shared the news with Mélanie she was really sympathetic. She tried to reassure me, and told me never to give up hope. Medical treatments were constantly progressing and Ilian was such a good boy, so easy, so I already had a lot to be thankful for. Which was true. My son is a great source of joy. But Kimmy and Ilian gradually stopped playing together. Mélanie always gave a good excuse. Her daughter was tired, she had to make a new video, she had to go to the hairdresser's, try on new outfits . . . At the time, Happy Recess was really booming. Mélanie was never available. I think she was already in another world. From time to time she gave me some toys—they were beginning to amass quite a collection—and even clothes, but she was always in a hurry. We would run into each other, but that was all. I felt hurt, it's true. I thought we were friends. When Ilian turned three, I found a special-needs school for him. A few months later I moved out of the residence to be closer to his school, where he spent most of his days. I didn't keep in touch with many people at the residence. Disability frightens people, drives them away. There was only Madame Sabourin, who I go to visit once or twice a year for tea. She's retired and she was always very kind to us. [. . .]

On November 10, Madame Sabourin had invited me for tea at her place, and I told her I'd come with Ilian. From time to time we would do things the other way around and she'd come to our place, but since she doesn't have a car, it's more complicated. And I enjoy spending time at the Poisson Bleu. In spite of everything, I'm nostalgic for those days, when Ilian was only a few months old and everything seemed so simple.

When I go to see Madame Sabourin I always park in the parking lot. I forgot to give back the remote when I moved, and then I ended up keeping it. There's a sort of little recess by the entrance to the waste room, where you can leave a small car and it won't be in the way of other cars on their way in or out. I'm not the only one who uses that spot for an hour or two, it's never been a problem. [. . .]

I was parking the car when I saw Kimmy come out of the waste room. Ilian had fallen asleep during the ride. The little girl immediately recognized me. I rolled down the window and asked her what she was doing there, and she asked me if she could hide in my car. I said yes and I went out to open the back door for her. She was all excited at the thought of having found such a good hiding place. She lay down between the front seat and the back without making a sound, she'd noticed that Ilian was asleep. She asked me if I could put some clothes over her to hide her better. She hadn't changed, she was still so lively. I handed her my coat and she was the one who arranged it so that it covered her completely. A few seconds had gone by, she'd curled up so tight that it was impossible to see her from outside. [. . .]

No, I already told you. I didn't go there with that intention. I didn't see Mélanie's Instagram stories saying that the children were outside. I was on my way to Madame Sabourin's, and everything happened just the way I told you. I didn't have anything in mind. [. . .]

I can't say exactly how long it lasted. I don't remember anymore. Maybe two minutes. Then I turned the ignition. The car started and I said to Kimmy, "We're going to hide even better, you'll see. Just don't move." I put the car into reverse, maneuvered, and drove back out. I didn't hurry. My mind was completely blank. I could hear her giggling behind me, she was thrilled to be playing a trick on her brother and her friends. When we left the parking lot, I hesitated for a few seconds. I didn't know which way to go.

I didn't think, "I'm taking Kimmy away with me," or, "What are you doing?" No. It was really weird. My mind was a blank and at the same time it was as if I was obeying something. In the end I took the same route as usual and kept on driving. I remembered the conversation we had in the car, Kimmy asked me if Ilian's teacher was nice, and if he had a lot of friends at his school. Ilian woke up while we were driving, he was overjoyed to see her! I was really glad he recognized her. I parked in a street near my house. I didn't try to hide Kimmy, we went home, calm and normal. I don't have any neighbors. I called Madame Sabourin to apologize for not showing up, I told her something had come up.

Later that evening I told Kimmy that I'd called her mom and she asked if I could keep her here for a while because she had to go to Vendée. I didn't want Kimmy to worry. She seemed to think this was perfectly normal. She just asked me if Mélanie was mad at her because she hadn't been able to film her video. I reassured her: her mom was sending her big hugs and was thinking about her all the time. [. . .]

Those first days she slept a lot. She woke up late in the morning, and sometimes she slept in the afternoon. I wondered if she was sick, but she didn't have any symptoms. For that whole week the children didn't go out, they played all sorts of games. Ilian loves to paint, and so does Kimmy. They made a beautiful mural, with fish and octopuses and seaweed of every color. I called the grocery store just downstairs from my place two or three times to order things, and went down to pick up the shopping. I only left the children alone for a few minutes, and made

up the excuse that Ilian was sick. People know us in the neighborhood. [. . .]

A few weeks ago Ilian had jammed his finger. The nail went all
black and it fell off while Kimmy was there. One day when I was
watching a crime series on television I learned that there is no
DNA in fingernails. Only the fine layer of cells on top of the nails
can reveal it, or traces of blood. So I let Ilian's nail soak in bleach
all night, then I scrubbed it. Then I put it in an envelope with the
Polaroid. Until then I hadn't really thought about doing anything.
What happened after that, I don't know. I let myself go with the
flow . . . I sensed some great danger, but I couldn't stop. [. . .]

I'm the one who wrote those letters. I just asked Kimmy to
copy the address onto the envelope and I made her believe we
were going to send her parents a drawing. It's ridiculous. I can't
explain it. I don't know if I wanted to hurt Mélanie. Maybe. More
than anything I wanted to make her do the one thing she really
didn't want to do. I wanted her to realize what it meant.

I mailed both letters from the mailbox that's on the corner of
my street. I was careful never to switch on the television or the
radio when the children were there. [. . .]

Yes, I do watch the Happy Recess videos, and follow Mélanie
Claux's Instagram page. At first I just wanted to see how the kids
were doing, to find out what they're up to, and Mélanie, too. And
then I got hooked. It sucks you in and at the same time it's terrifying. I didn't want to watch, but I couldn't help myself. It's hard
to explain. Lately, I could see that Kimmy was really fed up, that
she couldn't stand it anymore. That was the only thing I saw. She
wouldn't look at the camera, and when she did look at it, it was
as if she was calling to me for help. As if she was asking me to
come and get her. It happened several times. I told myself I must
be losing my mind. But every time, it made a terrible impression
on me, and it haunted me all day long. It made me feel like I was
one of those people who look away and just keep on walking
when a child is being mistreated right there before their eyes.

Since I could see she was distressed, it made me feel guilty for doing nothing. [. . .]

Once she seemed rested to me, I didn't know what else I should do. I wanted a sign . . . a symbol. I searched on the Internet. The Children at Risk Association deals with all sorts of abuse, even the least visible kind. That's what it says on their homepage. That's all. There was no other reason. So I sent the second message. Not for a moment did I believe that it would work. [. . .]

I don't think Kimmy felt like a prisoner. She did ask for her brother, or her parents, but whenever that happened I think I managed to reassure her. Except last night. Last night she realized that something was going on, something not normal. She was starting to get scared. It was . . . like an electric shock. Suddenly I realized that Kimmy had been at my house for a week and that . . . that I . . . I was the only one who knew . . . It was as if I suddenly regained consciousness, as if . . . I was returning from some parallel reality. I panicked.

So this morning I dropped Ilian off at my mother's, along with a bag with almost all his belongings in it. She asked me what was going on, and I left without telling her. I was afraid I'd go to pieces. I got back in the car and came straight here. I'm really tired. [. . .]

I wanted to help Kimmy. To give her a moment of peace and freedom. It was . . . it happened just the way I told you. I didn't think it through. This morning I realized that it was all pointless. It wouldn't change a thing. I don't know if I'm making sense. To be honest, when I look at those images, it makes me afraid, for the children's sake.

2031

You got the feeling that unimaginable things would appear during your lifetime, things that people would get used to, the way they had so quickly gotten used to cell phones, computers, iPods, and GPS.

—ANNIE ERNAUX,
The Years

Santiago Valdo is a psychiatrist and psychoanalyst of the Freudian school—an endangered species, he adds, whenever he introduces himself. He works part-time at the hospital, and divides the rest of his time between his office practice and writing academic articles or essays for the general public. Known for his work on the impact of the digital revolution on anxiety disorders, he is, notably, the author of two landmark works: *In the Event of Prolonged Exposure* and *Violence on Social Networks*. In recent years he has freed himself from any affiliations, and devotes himself to research incorporating neuroscience, without turning his back on psychoanalysis.

On this May day in 2031, as he's getting ready to go home, Santiago Valdo's watch vibrates, displaying an unfamiliar number. He hesitates, then takes the call. The voice emerges from a remote speaker: a young man inquires whether he's dialed the right number. Then, in a tone devoid of any emotion, as if what he's about to say does not concern him, he continues, "My name is Sammy Diore and I need help."

Santiago Valdo repeats to himself, *Sammy Diore*; it vaguely rings a bell, but at the moment he can't think where he's heard it, particularly as his memory, far from perfect nowadays, has automatically associated the name with a female individual.

"Did someone refer you?"

"An intern at the Sainte-Anne hospital gave me your contact information."

"Were you hospitalized?"

"No. But I saw her in the emergency room and she recommended I call you."

His voice is very young. His intonation still sounds strangely false (the boy seems to be reciting, or reading a text he has in front of him), so much so that Santiago wonders whether this is a joke. His contact information is available on the Internet, and it wouldn't be the first time he'd been targeted with a prank call.

"I'm not taking on any new patients at present," he says, "but I can recommend someone else."

The young man seems to panic, his voice catching, shrill.

"No, no, it has to be you! Please, I beg you . . ."

This time Santiago Valdo glances at his electronic diary, programmed to open automatically on his computer screen whenever he gets a call on his office number.

"Look. I suggest you come and see me at my office tomorrow evening at eight, and we'll have a first discussion. After that I'll send you to a colleague. The most important thing for you is to find help, isn't it?"

"But I can't go out."

"You can't go out of your home?"

"No. Not anymore. Not at all."

"And why is that?"

"They're everywhere . . . in the street, in stores, in taxis. Everywhere."

"Who are you talking about, Monsieur Diore?"

"The cameras. They're hidden, but I see them. They're filming me, all the time, whatever I do. First they hacked the CCTV cameras near my house, and now they have their own system set up wherever I go. And when they can't find me, they send drones."

Santiago can hear him breathing, and he suspects the boy is inhaling through his mouth. Perhaps a sign that he's already undergoing treatment.

"And . . . why would someone be filming you?"

"They sell the images."

"I see. And how long do you think this has been going on?"

"I don't know. In the beginning they sent people, with hidden cameras. I didn't notice them at first. It lasted for a while. Once I realized, they had to come up with other methods that were less visible."

"And consequently, you've stopped going out altogether?"

"Yes."

Torn between a desire to put an end to the exchange (it all seemed a bit obvious) and a fear he might fail to detect genuine distress, Santiago Valdo pauses again for a moment of silence.

He listens to the boy's anxious breathing, then resumes the conversation.

"How do you get your meals?"

"I order through the Internet. I ask the deliveryman to leave the bags outside the door, and I open it once he's gone."

"How old are you, Monsieur Diore?"

"Twenty."

"Do you have anyone close to you? Parents, brothers or sisters, friends?"

"No. Well, there's my mother, but . . . No."

"When was the last time you went out?"

"I don't know . . . three months ago. Maybe four."

"You've just spent four months without ever leaving the house?"

"Yes."

"And no one has come to see you?"

The young man suddenly loses his patience.

"You don't get it! There's no one I can trust—shopkeepers, taxis, my friends—there's not a single place I'm safe. They implanted cameras in the eyes of everyone close to me so they could film me!"

"Monsieur Diore, a doctor or a nurse could easily come and

get you to take you to the hospital. You'd be safe there. We wouldn't allow any visits and we'd make sure that you're safe there."

"No, no, no! They'll be there! They'll send someone!"

Now Santiago can hear the fear in the boy's voice. His terror, even.

"And who are *they?*"

Sammy Diore hesitates for a second before answering.

"That's what I need to know. I have to find out where the images are being used. Who they sell them to, you see? But one thing is for sure: they go for a high price. Very high."

"Sammy—may I call you Sammy?"

"Yes."

"You know what my profession is?"

"Yes."

"If you've called me, maybe it's because you are not quite sure that those people are really there to film you?"

"No. I know they're there. I called you because the intern at Sainte-Anne told me you were a specialist in digital technology and networks. So I figured you could help me find out who's behind all this."

"Sammy, I'm a psychiatrist. And yes, I have specialized in pathologies associated with the development of social networks, virtual reality, and artificial intelligence. But I'm a doctor. So let me suggest something: I'm going to come and see you at your home, to make sure that your living conditions are suitable, and that you're not in any danger. Then we'll decide together how to go about helping you. Do you agree to this?"

The boy's relief is touching.

"Yes, Doctor, thank you. But whatever you do, don't tell anyone you're coming."

It only occurs too late to Santiago Valdo that he should have recorded the conversation. He is sorry, he would have liked to listen to it again. He likes working on his patients' speech after the event—their associations, their intonation. He likes to guess who or what matters to them. Nowadays, for most of his patients, that means gaming and series. As a rule he asks them if he can keep a record of the session. But there are times when he foregoes that courtesy and records them without their knowledge, even though it is against the professional code of ethics.

It's late. He has to get home at a decent hour to have dinner with his partner and read the dissertation project on neuroplasticity that one of his students has sent him, and whose approach is of great interest to him.

As he is getting ready to leave the office, he calls out to his personal assistant, whom he has baptized "Jacques the Shirker" in honor of Jacques Lacan.

"Tell me, Jacques. . ."

The synthetic voice answers immediately.

"Yes, Santiago, how can I help you?"

As always, the same affable tone, a touch obsequious, exasperating. It's been that long, they could have come up with other options. He's tempted to shout, "Go fuck yourself!" even though he readily acknowledges the benefits of vocal assistance, particularly when his hands are busy with other tasks (in this case, putting away the many files piled on his desk), or when he's doing several things at once (a very common failing, something he doesn't even try to fight against anymore), but he keeps silent. At a time when he was trying to test the limits of the tool, he had his fill of absurd and sterile conversations with Jacques, and he knows the voice refuses to respond to insults.

"Who is Sammy Diore?"

The computer boots up and then, in less than two seconds, the screen displays the results of the search. Smooth and learned, Jacques reads out the answer he considers the most relevant:

"Sammy Diore is a French YouTuber. Born in 2011, he became well known thanks to the Happy Recess channel created by his mother, Mélanie Claux. Between 2016 and 2023, the channel broadcast over 1,500 videos on YouTube. Various media estimated the family's income at over €20 million.

"In 2019, Sammy's sister Kimmy, who was six at the time, was kidnapped by Élise Favart. An intense search lasted seven days, until the kidnapper, accompanied by the child, handed herself in to the Crime Squad.

"Between 2019 and 2020, the number of subscribers to the Happy Recess channel went from five to seven million.

"In anticipation of pending legislation on the commercial exploitation of child YouTubers, the Diore family created new channels in the name of each of the children. The Happy Sam channel, devoted to Sammy Diore, immediately met with huge success. On Instagram, in the space of a few months, Sam's official page reached over 1 million subscribers.

"On October 19, 2020, the parliament passed the law regulating the activity of child influencers. Happy Recess and Happy Sam nevertheless continued their activity without letting up.

"On his own channel, Sammy specialized in testing video games.

"In 2023, an investigation led by the newspaper *Le Monde* unveiled the financial strategies and arrangements put in place by the parents of child influencers in order to get around the requirements of the law.

"In 2029, at the age of eighteen, Sammy disappeared with no explanation. He stopped posting to his YouTube channel or any associated social networks. From that date on he no longer appeared in any of his mother's videos. Several journalists tried to find out why he had stopped all activity so abruptly, to no avail.

"All of the Happy Recess and Happy Sam videos are still available on YouTube and still generate traffic and income."

"Thank you, Jacques," says Santiago.

"You're welcome, Santiago. I was very glad to be of assistance."

"Yeah, sure. . ."

Santiago puts a few files away and repeats the name to himself: *Diore* . . . Yes . . . Of course . . . The case had been all over the news. One of his colleagues at the hospital had even been called on to provide an assessment of Élise Favart, the little girl's kidnapper. As he recalls, the young woman did not present any psychiatric disorders. After several evaluations, despite a few signs of depersonalization, she was held criminally responsible for her acts. As a result, she spent at least two years in prison without any medical treatment order.

As he's switching off the lights in his office, the details gradually resurface: the young woman wanted to save the little girl. A sort of Don Quixote in petticoats, tilting at money mills. For a few weeks all the talk in the media was about child influencers and the parents' responsibility. Purely by chronological chance, the bill was passed into law not long after the kidnapping. And then, as always, interest waned.

Santiago slams the office door. The automatic lock kicks in behind him, while the elevator announces its presence with a high-pitched chime.

He raises his head for facial recognition, and the doors open in front of him.

C lara Roussel is forty-five years old. She still lives alone and has no children. In a paradoxical context of declining resources and ever-increasing connectivity, her life, on the surface, has not changed all that much. To her it does seem, however, that she has begun a slow and necessary metamorphosis. To the ever-present barbarity of the cases she investigates, she responds with emotional distance, hard won through demanding self-discipline. The asceticism of her life has become more acute: she'll gladly have a few drinks, but doesn't eat much; she doesn't have many possessions, other than some jewelry that once belonged to her mother, including an old Lip wristwatch that she never takes off. She aspires to a sort of reduction to the essentials, deprivation even, and she is not afraid of isolation: it is one way to remove herself from violence and sorrow. That's how she protects herself. Or thinks she does.

She can count her acquaintances on one hand. Chloé, her friend who's become a lawyer, has two little boys, and Clara regularly looks after them; they adore her. Her neighbors, two police couples whom she's known for fifteen years, invite her to dinner nearly every week. She's the single friend they like to tease—about her conquests, her love life, as if, to them, she is frozen in a sort of eternal adolescence; their children look on her as one of them.

More than ever, she feels as if she is at the service of a Higher Reason, which she is careful not to name. No Gods no masters, but a path. Her own path, undeniably, is a bloody one. While from time to time she does succumb to a nostalgia-tinted daydreaming, she will forfeit nothing to regret. She is where she was always meant to be.

At the Bastion, she is still an evidence custodian, part of the Lasserre team now. According to tradition, each team bears the name of its leader, and Cédric Berger left this squad a few years ago to take up a position as department head at the Child Protection Squad, where he began his career. His farewell party went down in history, not only because of the number of empties they found the next morning: his words to Clara during his farewell speech are now part of the squad's legend. Such a beautiful declaration of professional love had rarely been heard in the Criminal Investigation Department. After Cédric's departure, Clara was offered a position as deputy team leader, but she turned it down. Procedure is what interests her, the more complex and voluminous, the better. She enjoys training younger recruits, and custodians from other teams often come to ask for her advice.

When she's not collecting findings at crime scenes, and autopsies, both of which she must attend, she spends most of her time in her office, writing up official reports and search warrants, classifying sealed evidence and lab results, and conducting or rereading interviews. Reports are at the heart of every procedure, and they remain her key concern. Her primary task is to be sure to eliminate any ambiguity or approximation, and to produce a narrative that keeps as close as possible to the facts. And that is what she wants to pass on to others.

From time to time, when she's fed up with paperwork (which remains ubiquitous in spite of the exhaustive digitalization of documents and data, and the regular arrival of new software), she goes out on patrol with her fellow officers.

A few years ago, when she went along to apprehend some suspects for questioning, a procedure that didn't seem

particularly dangerous at the time—they had no backup—
Clara and two of her colleagues were caught in an ambush. She
was physically immobilized for several minutes, a stranger's arm
wrapped around her neck and a gun pressed to her temple.
She remembers feeling her heartbeat slow, as if her blood had
almost ceased to flow, her entire body focused on her vital func-
tions. Sounds, words, gestures, everything going on around her
seemed to come from a muffled, faraway world, unfolding at an
entirely different speed to her own. She wasn't afraid. One of
her colleagues was wounded in the leg, the other in the shoulder; she got off with whiplash and a few bruises on her neck.
The two suspects eventually got away. They were intercepted
two days later at a highway rest area.

Back at work after a short visit to the hospital, Clara searched
inside herself for a trace of that moment out of time, both unreal and written on her body. Armed men had opened fire in
front of her, one of them had taken aim at her, but she hadn't
felt any fear. This was not a source of pride. It wasn't normal.
That evening, a navy-blue thought came to her: this absence of
fear revealed an absence of love.

She doesn't think that often about her parents anymore. A
sign of age, no doubt, or of time passing. It is as if the memories
she has of them have been covered in a fine sticky film, like
those photographs that turn yellow through prolonged contact
with the air. They belong to another era, which might be called
pre-digital, and which sometimes seems as distant to her as the
prehistoric era she studied so passionately in elementary school.

In this world where every gesture, every move, every conversation leaves a trace, she would like to leave none. She is
well-positioned to know how much smartphones, no matter
the kind (there are many, nowadays), vocal assistants, smart
houses, and social networks are all unscrupulous snitches and
inexhaustible sources of information both for businesses and

the police. Nowadays, in the Crime Squad and elsewhere, a good portion of the investigation relies on *tracking*: video surveillance, facial recognition, live or retroactive monitoring of a suspect's movements, access to their communications records and invoices, hard drives and search histories, and behavior analysis. Nothing can elude control anymore.

The more Clara Roussel uses these tools in the exercise of her profession, the more—as if responding to an inversely proportional urge—she would like to disappear.

If, as people say, contemporary society is divided in two, she is on the recalcitrant side. Those who refuse to be tracked, in the way that everything from battery hens to packages of pasta are rated with scores, those who have rejected, as much as they can, everything that might enable others to find out about their activities, what they like, who their friends are, how they spend their time—people who no longer belong to a network of any kind, or to any online community, and who would rather open a book or a newspaper than a website, with the help of Google. Disconnected. The choice of a minority, but one which is gaining ground. A choice that is hard to maintain, but which shares a common credo: let well enough alone. Because Clara's not naïve: in this day and age it is impossible to vanish completely off the radar. Even just to communicate with her colleagues, she has to use a system of instant messaging, where their data, supposedly encrypted, is preserved by the private company in charge of the task, and that data remains within reach of any hacker with a modicum of skill. But limiting the traces she leaves behind, reducing the halo she produces, and erasing her digital footprint: these are all part of a struggle she refuses to abandon.

In her everyday life she tries to leave as few traces as possible. She doesn't have a car, she goes everywhere on foot or on her bike, she doesn't use any plastic, doesn't travel by plane, doesn't eat meat except when she is invited somewhere. As a rule she consumes very little, buys her clothes in consignment stores, and recycles and reuses everything she can.

The brave new world that was evoked during the Covid pandemic in 2020 never materialized. As a famous writer predicted at the time, the world stayed the same, only worse, blinder than ever to its own destruction.

When the fancy takes her, Clara focuses her attention on an international movement against climate change and ecological collapse. On occasion she has gone to some of their protests and taken part in debates at local gatherings over the course of action to adopt. She's in favor of mobilizing engaged citizens, calling for nonviolent protests, and she's not completely against a degree of civil disobedience. During these gatherings, to everyone's surprise, she's open about her identity as a cop: she's not afraid of debate or confrontation.

Thomas got married to a coroner and is the father of two children. From time to time he sends her a handwritten message on a scrap of paper—archaic, old-fashioned signs that manage to scale the walls of time and distance, and which always start with the words, "Lovely Clara, how are you?"

She is fine. In any case that's what she says, when asked. In fact, she shows no major signs of depression or melancholy, even though she discovered not long ago that she is, regrettably, drawn to the void. On two occasions, the first time while standing on the edge of the cliffs at Étretat, the second on the balcony of a victim's apartment, located on the eleventh floor; her own fall came back to her. A possibility, a call or a memory surfacing from childhood? She could not say.

She would have liked, at least once in her life, to know what it meant to experience *true love*—she likes the expression, no matter how trite it sounds when she hears her young colleagues use it—but that would have required a self-abandonment of a kind she could never have possessed. Perhaps she should have tried lying on a shrink's couch to understand why, but she prefers standing on her feet, come what may. For as long as she can remember, she's always been in a state of tension and vigilance, even wariness, which today seems inseparable from her metabolism. She cannot help but imagine what would have come after *true love*, eventually: the fall, or the betrayal.

She shares, more than ever, the Crime Squad's motto, whose symbol, ever since the department was created, has been the nettle: *Get too close and you'll be stung.*

On this June day in 2031, summer has come a few weeks early, and the heat record from the previous year has just been broken, yet again. Clara has arrived just in time for the briefing her team leader holds every day at the same time, over coffee reputed to be the best in the building; no one is allowed to know where it comes from. Lately, things have been quiet, but starting tonight her team will be on duty for the entire week. Until next Monday, any *bullshit* will be theirs to deal with.

Right after she gets out of the morning meeting, and is on her way back to the office she now occupies on her own, Clara receives a message from reception on her watch: her ten o'clock appointment has arrived. An alarm goes off: the appointment has not been entered into the department's schedule. She swears out loud at the new software which, on the pretext of identifying anyone who has entered the premises, goes berserk over the slightest thing—so much so that her colleagues in the anti-terror departments have baptized it "the fusspot." And it's true, the "fusspot" is short on composure, and is frequently on the verge of setting off the red alarm on the Vigipirate security alert system.

Clara sits at her desk and says a few words to reactivate her computer.

The appointment doesn't appear on her schedule. Consequently, the software views the intruder as dangerous and ill-intentioned, particularly as the facial recognition system was not able to make a positive identification. Fortunately, the visitor does not have a police record. After a few seconds, a young girl's face appears on Clara's screen with the caption: not valid. A pre-recorded voice asks her to identify the *individual* immediately, or else to set off alarm number 1. Exasperated, Clara resorts to a good old method, tried and true, and calls down to the switchboard: *Don't bother sending the helicopters, I'm on my way down.*

While waiting for the elevator she looks again at the young girl's face, which continues to flash up intermittently on her watch. She doesn't know the face, she's sure of that, and yet it is strangely familiar.

Clara steps into the elevator and presses the button for the ground floor.

In the time it takes her to go down, her brain has associated several images and there can no longer be the shadow of a doubt: under the watchful eye of the two cameras in waiting room number four, sitting on the same chair as she was twelve years ago, Kimmy Diore is waiting for her.

Faithful to her morning routine, Mélanie Claux gets up every day at 7:45. Before making herself some fresh fruit juice (thanks to her Juna juicer, the best on the market: the manufacturer provides her with the latest model every year, in exchange for her putting in a few good words on one of her networks), she opens the picture window and looks out at the sea. "We really have an exceptional view," she says out loud, as if congratulating herself; she says this almost as often as "It's a little paradise on earth." She could talk for hours about her house perched on the hills above Sanary, and about the garden full of luxuriant flowers that surrounds it; it costs a fortune to maintain but it's one of the settings her fans like most.

A few years ago, they decided to leave Châtenay-Malabry. They enlarged the original building—a typical Provençal farmhouse—on the basis of a design by Killian Keys, a young architect who has become the darling of real estate thanks to *Houses of the Stars*, one of the latest reality TV programs broadcast on an over-the-air channel.

At the time, Mélanie and Bruno had been chosen among a dozen celebrities to share their incredible adventure with TV viewers. The three episodes devoted to the transformation of their house, shown on Sunday afternoons, broke a historical audience record. Naturally, Killian Keys had become a friend, and the Diores left the Paris region with no regrets.

The pressure that came with their celebrity had become unbearable.

Not that they are less well-known here, in the south, but they can always isolate themselves at their country estate, in their garden, their little "love nest," as Mélanie likes to put it, endlessly, on her networks. They're well away from the lack of privacy they'd had to put up with at the Poisson Bleu residence, where the neighbors seemed to have teamed up against them to spread malicious gossip. In those days, the worst rumors were going around, and not many people had stood up for them.

Kimmy's kidnapping remains a shadow, a fissure in the wonderful edifice she has built. A terrible moment she would like to erase from her memory, from everyone's memory; the repercussions were felt long after Kimmy's return. Now she knows that everything negative that has subsequently happened to them stems from that time, from the madness of that woman. That woman sullied their life. That woman is an indelible stain on the exemplary narrative of her family. What they went through back then, and in the years that followed, the horrible after-effects her little girl suffered, and which they all suffered . . . it doesn't even bear thinking about. It's a period she has forced herself to obliterate and she refuses to speak of it. Because to move on you sometimes have to act as if those things had never existed.

And now, even though her children no longer live with her, Mélanie has over three million followers, if you take into account all her main profiles: New Mélanie (although Instagram is clearly going downhill, and looks dépassé, she renamed her page and is host to a faithful community) and With Mélanie, which she created just two years ago on the rapidly expanding new social network, Back Home. More about *cocooning*, and *staying safe*, Back Home offers her an even larger audience, with whom she shares her recipes, her philosophy, her *routines* and, of course, her every mood or feeling.

Eager to keep up to date, attentive to every new trend, Mélanie was actually one of the first influencers to start her own home reality TV channel, Mel Inside, now available on the paying platform Share the Best. Thanks to this concept, subscribers can spend entire days with their favorite *celebs*. In a sector that is full of promise, Mélanie has met with tremendous success. It has to be said, she gives of herself, unstintingly. She takes her fans with her wherever she goes and promises them they won't miss a thing: doctor's appointments, visits to the hairdresser's, lunch with a fellow vlogger or influencer: everything is *shared*. And more than ever, *sharing* is her reason for living.

Several cosmetics and clothing brands come to her on a regular basis for product placement on her networks, where she invites her *sweeties* to take advantage of promotional codes. The remuneration she receives for these services is commensurate with her unassailable popularity, and her skill at recommendations. Her enthusiasm, her advice, her little secrets have all borne fruit. Moreover, following her appearance on *Celebrity Homes*, a famous furniture and interior decoration manufacturer chose her as their ambassador, and they renew her contract every year. And while her annual income does not attain the summits of the heyday of Happy Recess, her fame ensures her nevertheless of a very comfortable revenue. She refuses to divulge that information in greater detail.

Bruno has remained her most loyal support. He is still the honest, reliable man she married in 2011, over twenty years ago.

Only once, at the time of Élise Favart's trial, was she afraid he might falter. Confronted with this new wave of slander her husband, normally so strong, began to doubt. All of a sudden he no longer seemed sure of anything. "What if we got it wrong?" he murmured one night, just before switching off the light. This man who had always seemed so invincible when it came to envy and hateful content was now beginning to worry about what others were saying about his family on social networks. This man who had always trusted her so much, trusted her judgment. Who had always gone wherever she told him to go.

He had shown a moment of weakness. Or despondency. He was having nightmares.

One evening when they had just come home from the courthouse, Bruno broke down, sobbing. He kept saying, "We have to stop everything we have to stop everything, please," while pacing back and forth in the living room. She'd never seen him in such a state. The following night, Mélanie wondered what he meant by *everything*. Was he talking about the trial or, more generally, about everything they had built?

The very next day her husband had gotten over it. They never spoke about it again, and she was careful not to broach the subject. Once again, her husband had shown her proof of his loyalty.

"Yes," she thinks, "we have to overcome any obstacles and not look back." That is actually what she advises her fans, while tiny little stars sparkle all around her face and a warm light enfolds her like a halo. "We need beauty in our lives, so much," is what she often concludes, facing the camera.

For reasons she cannot comprehend (apparently it was causing psychological issues among certain individuals who had embarked on a quest for recognition and approval, which subsequently led to depression), it is no longer possible to click 'like' on Instagram. But fortunately Back Home has come up with an approval method that is just as gratifying: her followers send her messages, in English, that say *"Yes, I'm in,"* or *"Yes, me too!"* and can leave comments limited to fifty characters that are filtered by the platform through a semantic recognition system. Anything negative or disparaging is automatically deleted.

Every day, Mélanie continues to receive a quantity of love that delights and fulfills her. This must be why she is so happy. Because she *is* happy even though her children are gone. They've grown up. That's life. *Every mother hen on earth must prepare herself for her children's departure* was one of her most viral videos. With tears in her eyes, and her voice trembling slightly, Mélanie filmed Kimmy's and Sammy's bedrooms, the empty cupboards and neatly made beds. That day her mother hen heart was so sad. Her subscribers love it when she confides in them or opens her heart. They want to know everything about her, and go into raptures over it all.

Unlike her rivals, who have opted for short titles in English, Mélanie has become a specialist in poetic titles in French, and she doesn't mind how long they are. Encouraged by her initial success, she followed with *Women over forty have well-hidden secrets* (a video devoted to inner beauty and youth) and *Mother for a day, mother forever. Children stay in our hearts.*

After these videos, she was attacked by Clean Up!, a bashing site that claims to reveal the contradictions of Internet stars. On the pretext that she has gone on using smoothing and filling filters to address her community, they reproach her for the lack of coherence between what she says and what she does. Those people just don't get it. They don't know anything about magic, or wonder, or harmony. "The world needs sweet things, sequins and pastel colors," she replied, immediately deciding to make this the title of her next video. She felt hurt, particularly by the repeated, unfounded insinuations about her current relations with her children. The site asserted that Kimmy and Sammy had broken off all contact. People are prepared to say any old thing to generate clicks, there's nothing new about that, but it has become more widespread. Mélanie dreams of a pink and blue world, where violence and envy no longer exist, a world where everyone can fulfill their dreams, assert their tastes, and be proud of their optimism, without becoming the target of criticism and mockery.

And sometimes she wonders if it's not up to her to create that world.

Kim and Sam haven't been in touch very often lately. They haven't broken off all contact, of course they haven't; however, she often has trouble reaching them. She cannot share this with her subscribers. For a start because she is afraid of malicious gossip, and then because they would no doubt be disappointed to learn that after everything she's done for them, her children have gone away. She was such a devoted mother, really there for them. She worked so hard to secure their future. Thanks to Happy Recess, this empire she created from scratch, not only are Kim and Sam genuine stars, but now they have their own apartments in Paris. And they both live on the money from the account she opened at the Deposits and Consignments Fund and which, as prescribed by law, they were given access to as soon as they were of age. Unfortunately, it's as if the money were burning a hole in their pockets and they'd both agreed to squander it; neither one of them is following the advice she gave them.

They've gone away. It is in the order of things. "Every mother hen on earth must prepare herself for her children's departure." Yes, that's life.

Mélanie calls Sammy at least once a week. Usually her son answers, but he speaks in a hushed voice and hangs up after a few seconds. He's strange. She doesn't know what he's doing, what he lives on. He always seems to be in a hurry. He says he'll explain later. Sammy doesn't tell them anything anymore. So Bruno is worried.

Bruno worries a lot these days. About the children, about a lot of insignificant little things that get blown out of all proportion. He asks himself a lot of questions, he ruminates about the past, he orders e-books about psychology. It's his midlife crisis. Sometimes she wonders if this strange behavior didn't start when they heard on the radio that Grégoire Larondo had died. Greg committed suicide. It's dreadfully sad, of course. She'd had no news from him in years. After Kimmy's return, he stopped calling. In 2025, he attempted a failed comeback in the first (and last) season of *Veterans of Koh-Lanta*. The whole program had been a complete and utter failure.

On the evening when they heard the sad news, Mélanie supposed her husband must be feeling very relieved. They looked at each other in silence. Bruno seemed very upset. She told herself that it must be stirring up a lot of bad memories. But ever since then—maybe it is just a coincidence—he's been worrying about everything.

As for Mélanie, she thinks Sammy is going through a late adolescent crisis. This is what happens with pampered children. Because unlike Kimmy, who gave them hell because of that woman, Sammy never defied them. He always worked hard at school and always managed very well.

Mélanie loves remembering the little boy he used to be, so sweet, so well behaved, always enthusiastic, always smiling, capable of starting the same scenes five or six times over without flinching. In fact, Sammy always agreed to everything. Challenges, jokes, trips. Unlike his sister, he didn't drag his feet, he never questioned anything. Sammy always had his own fans. As a child he adored unwrapping the toys, but when he got older he went wild about pranks, when they became trendy. He wrote his own scripts for videos. When he started his own channel devoted to gaming, it was a huge success. He was able to develop his own community. His smile, his green eyes, that sweet teddy bear look he got from his father, were such a hit. Sammy was the ideal older brother or best friend. Girls dreamed of meeting him, and boys wanted to be like him.

What had happened for him to quit, just like that, from one day to the next, with no explanation, no message for his fans, she never found out.

Seated below a poster for the prevention of digital identity theft, Kimmy Diore is waiting for Clara.

As soon as the young woman sees her, she stands up and walks over to her. She's tall and haughty, with curly hair down to her shoulders. "She looks Swedish," thinks Clara, and suddenly the story about Grégoire Larondo comes back to her, the man's fair features forever in the shadow.

Kimmy Diore introduces herself and holds out her hand. Her restless gaze sweeps the room and Clara has no difficulty seeing the connection between the young woman standing before her and the little girl she spent so many hours staring at, over ten years ago.

"I don't know if you remember me. . ."

"Of course I do, Kimmy. What can I do for you?"

"I'd like to have access to my file. To the interviews. I'd like to know what I said. Everything. The story I told when Élise Favart brought me back. I seem to recall that it was your role to check and archive everything. I imagine there must be some record."

Clara suggests they go up to her office to talk in private. Just as they're going through the turnstile, Kimmy seems to hesitate for a split-second. Clara takes the opportunity to apologize.

"I've been calling you by your first name, forgive me, it's because I knew you as a child."

"You're not the only one. Everyone calls me by my first name."

In the elevator Kimmy observes Clara, not saying a word.

They go out the doors and the young woman follows close behind Clara.

As she listens to the sound of Kimmy's Doc Martens dully pounding the floor, Clara is sure of one thing: Kimmy Diore has not finished settling scores.

Once they're in Clara's office, Kimmy looks around again, apparently curious to find out what kind of place she has ended up in. There are not really many clues. No plants or personal photographs, just a pile of pending files, stacked in a single tower that is more or less stable, and a dozen or so gruesome photographs which Clara carefully moves out of sight.

"Where did you find my name?"

"In my mother's papers, a long time ago. Your face is the only one I remember. Everything else is hazy. The psychologists, the doctors, the other cops, I've erased it all . . . except for you. You came over to me and I remember that you crouched down to speak to me. The tone of your voice made me think, 'It's not so bad.' I was afraid for Élise. I think I understood, despite how calm and gentle she was, that she was probably in for a lot of trouble. I never saw her again, you know. You stayed with me all that morning. I know that excerpts from my interview were produced during the trial, but I didn't have access to those documents, or to anything else from my file. My parents wouldn't show me anything."

"Is there something in particular you wanted to know?"

"Everything."

Clara's mind wanders for a moment, on hearing her speak of that time; it's as if the bitter aftertaste the case had left her with has come back.

"There's a lot available in the press, you know—"

The young woman interrupts her.

"I can't live with the thought that that woman, the only one who understood what we were going through, the only one who tried to put a stop to it, spent two years in prison because of me."

"It wasn't your fault, Kimmy. Élise Favart spent two years in prison because she broke the law. She kidnapped you, and held you captive for several days. Later on it was established that she hadn't used physical coercion, and that she had no sordid intentions. She handed herself in, and the judges took that into account. You have no reason to blame yourself, believe me. On the contrary, your testimony helped to reduce her sentence. She would have been handed a much longer one without it."

"Are you sure?"

"Yes. From what I remember, your testimony and hers tallied perfectly, and that worked in her favor."

"I've read the newspapers. The story about the kidnapping and about my 'captivity,' as they called it . . . But what I can't get over is the fact that no one wondered whether I wasn't relieved to spend a few days shielded from all that. A few days not being filmed from morning to night, without my life being on display hour after hour to my entire class, my school, and to hundreds of thousands of total strangers."

Her anger sets off something like little electric shocks beneath the smooth surface of her face.

"But they did, Kimmy. The question was raised during the trial, particularly because Élise Favart had interpreted a certain number of signs coming from you as proof you were tired, or even in distress, and—"

"But they took me back there, to my house."

"That's true."

"Do you know what happened afterwards?"

Afraid she might interrupt the flow of Kimmy's story, Clara merely shook her head.

"My mother waited. For things to settle down. For the media to turn their attention elsewhere. She let Christmas go by, and all that winter. For a few weeks, a few months, we lived in a sort of interlude. It was strange, you know, to have time. To have time to get bored, time to wonder what we were going to do, time to do nothing at all. My mother had trouble living like that. She was scared to death that she would be forgotten. If she became invisible, that would be like vanishing. Around the month of March, I think it was, she suggested doing a Yes Challenge. Just for fun. Not to have fun among ourselves, in private, the way most families do. No. To have fun and a film it. To make money while we had fun. Before the kidnapping, the last video like that had been seen twenty million times. The kids who watched us loved that sort of thing. Can you imagine seeing your parents say yes to everything for an entire day? Every kid dreams about that. Not to mention the return of the poor little kidnapped girl. It was the perfect scenario, sure to create a buzz. And the minute the video was posted it broke all our records."

She pauses for a moment, as if she wants Clara to imagine the event, then she goes on.

"So we started it all again. First a little story from time to time. To reassure the fans. 'Of course, *sweeties*, Kimmy is doing just fine and she sends you lots of hugs and kisses. Don't you, my little kitten, can you send them tons of hugs and kisses?'"

Kimmy imitates her mother's voice to perfection, that nasal, fake cheeriness, with her clever inflections. Clara smiles, but the young woman doesn't want her smile.

"Then she upped the pace. Élise Favart's trial wouldn't be held for months, the media had already forgotten us. But not the fans. The fans were having withdrawal symptoms. What was I supposed to do? Say to my mother, 'get out of my room with your fucking telephone and your fucking *sweeties*—half of them are probably masturbating while they look at these lovely images you share with the whole world?' No, obviously, children don't talk like that. They don't think that way. But now I'm eighteen years old and I can speak like that. Half the people I meet think they know who I am better than I do. And if, by sheer chance, they've somehow never heard of me before, all it takes is four clicks to find me in my panties or a tutu, or eating French fries—not using my hands but straight off the table, like an animal."

Kimmy's face hardens.

"Do you think a two-year-old, or a four-year-old, or a ten-year-old kid can really *want* all that? That they have any idea what they're doing?"

Clara has stopped moving. She doesn't take her eyes off the young woman.

"How many of you here went on watching Happy Recess once I was back at home? Who saw our fantastic *Lick or Crunch*, or our great *Toilet Paper Battle* during the Covid lockdown? Who saw Sammy handcuffed to the bars of his bed in a ridiculous production that brought him no end of awful mockery? Did anyone have the guts to talk about the fact he was being humiliated?"

Kimmy Diore doesn't wait for an answer.

"I imagine you all had more important things to do. The truth is, the channel had just gained a million new subscribers. So, bit by bit, we started up again. Yes, after a few months: filming, amusement parks, signings, the whole shebang, all over again."

Kimmy hardly takes time to catch her breath.

"How are you supposed to make friends when you don't have the slightest thing in common with their lives, while they're looking at your life through a screen? We were alone. We were apart. Admired or despised, adored or insulted. 'The price of fame,' she said. But that's not the worst of it. The worst is that we weren't safe anywhere. There was nowhere we could go and be beyond her reach."

This time the young woman stops. A fine blue vein throbs at her temple, as she grows increasingly angry.

Clara asks if she'd like a glass of water, and Kimmy says yes, so Clara goes out of the office, relieved to get away for a moment. The young woman's emotion has reawakened the incredulousness Clara had experienced while watching Happy Recess, and that violent feeling of being out of step, maladjusted, that she had experienced at the time.

A feeling which, if she thinks about it, has never really left her.

She'd forgotten Kimmy Diore, it's true. Or, rather, she moved on to other things. Corpses, for the most part. Bodies still warm, or totally cold, bodies that had been tortured, bones scattered and found in the depths of a forest. She did her work. Work that required extreme precision, sharpness and concentration.

But Kimmy's right. She didn't go on watching Happy Recess. When the law was passed, she had assumed that the problem was solved. And like everyone, she closed her eyes again.

Clara comes back into the room with the glass in her hand.

While she was gone, Kimmy stood up, and now she's looking out the window.

The young woman drinks the water all in one go and sits back down. She came here to talk, and she hasn't finished.

"When I was eight or nine, I developed a nervous tic. My eyelids started blinking uncontrollably, you can see it on the videos, when I'm facing the camera. After she'd taken me to several specialists—they all prescribed rest and patience, because most of these tics are just temporary in children—my mother decided that Sammy would continue on his own for the unboxing videos. As for me, I could have a role in other formats, where my problem would be less visible. For a while Sammy opened the parcels and the Kinder Eggs by himself. It was back then that we filmed nearly all the 24-Hour Challenges, because they were doing really well on the other family channels: *24 hours in a box, 24 hours in the shower, 24 hours in a bouncy castle, 24 hours in a canvas cabin* . . . We had a whale of a time. . ."

Clara doesn't dare look at her watch. She has an appointment and she's sure she's already very late, but she has to let the
young woman finish what she has to say.

"And then?"

"When the tic went away I started getting these blotches
on my face. In a few weeks the rash had spread all over. On
my hands, on my neck, my stomach, like crocodile skin, really
scary. My mother tried to cover it with makeup, but any cosmetics she tried only made things worse. So bit by bit, Sammy
became the hero in Happy Recess, and I disappeared from the
channel. When I was thirteen or fourteen, I began smoking
joints and I slept with half the boys at the nearby lycée. The rash
was gone, but there was nothing left of the perfect little girl my
mother liked to put on display. The princess costume was torn
to shreds, and my mood was not at all compatible with my sur-
roundings. I became a teenager, almost the same as any teenager,
bad mannered and rebellious around my parents. To piss them
off I told them I wanted to go and live with Élise, even though I
knew very well that there was a court order preventing her from
seeing me. After we'd had a few arguments, my father agreed to
send me to boarding school, although my mother was against
it. Once I was there I dyed my hair jet black and decided to call
myself Karine. I informed the headmaster and the teachers and
said it was a matter of life and death. When people asked me if I
was Kimmy Diore I said she was my cousin, a real stupid bitch.
My classmates understood soon enough not to press the issue.
Some girls went on making fun of me, they'd whisper about me,
or say stuff on social media. I didn't give a shit. My skin was
clear and I could breathe. Happy Recess came to an end. Of
course my mother kept her Instagram accounts for all her *happy
fans* who wanted news of the family. And she went on telling the
story of her dream life, embellished with filters and showers of
sequins. And then, there was Sammy. He had his own channel,
which was getting more and more successful. After I was gone,

she became his coach, his stylist, his financial manager. Sammy never questioned anything. She told him he had an exceptional, fantastic life, and he believed her."

For a split second, Clara sees the little eight-year-old boy she once met at their place, lively and anxious, and tries to imagine the young adult he's become.

"And what about Sammy, how is he doing?"

Kimmy paused and was silent for a moment before she answered.

"I don't know. I don't know where he is or what he's doing. Back when I was in boarding school, we didn't see each other much. When I came home for the weekend, we would sometimes see each other in passing, but we didn't speak. It's sad to say, but we weren't on the same side. I had declared war, and I got it into my head that he was colluding with the enemy. He was making all those videos for his channel, still controlled by our mother, and she took part as a guest star. The way I saw it, he was fraternizing with the enemy. We grew apart. He had these huge partnerships with various brands, and lots of projects with other influencers, he was really doing well. He went to live in Paris to be where it was all happening. Our mother kept a close eye on his activity, went over his contracts, advised him. She remained present, even from a distance. When I got to Paris, I called Sammy. He told me to meet him at a café. I saw right away that it was over. Between us. It had become so hard to talk to him. I figured he was mad at me for having jumped ship, for having gone in a different direction. I even got the impression he didn't trust me. And yet we'd been so close. You can't imagine. He was my big brother. I adored him, I looked up to him. It made me really sad. I thought that away from our parents we'd be able to reconnect, become close again. And the exact opposite happened. I lost him forever."

She takes a deep breath then continues, her voice lower, more serious.

"One year ago he quit everything. At the height of his fame, just like that, overnight. He's not on any social networks anymore, he deleted all his accounts. Only the Happy Recess videos are still online because my mother was still in control of them. Sammy moved house, changed his phone number, I don't know where he is. No one knows. I don't see my parents anymore either. I write to my father from time to time, a short email to tell him how I'm doing. He replies within the half hour, he worries about how I'm doing, he asks me when I'll be coming to visit. Sometimes, after all these years, I get the impression that my father has begun to have his doubts. It might be just a word, or a memory, something between the lines that I can read, his regrets or his sorrow. I haven't been back in the south for a long time."

Kimmy breaks off and looks around, as if she's surprised she's still there. Then, her voice suddenly fainter, she adds, "You know, deep down, my mother got what she wanted. Now and forever, for an entire generation, she became, and will always be, *Mélanie Dream*, the mother of Kim and Sam. But Sammy . . . I don't know if he's happy."

The silence that follows has the same intensity as her story.

Sadness has taken possession of her face. Emotion is circulating just beneath her skin, little electric charges, hard to contain.

Clara looks at her watch. Right now, she is supposed to be at the mortuary for the autopsy of a boy they found last night: it had been made, unconvincingly, to look like a suicide. This time she really has to end their conversation.

"I'm really sorry, Kimmy, I have to get going . . . I'll see what I can do. I can't promise anything, but I'll be in touch."

The young woman's face clouds over.

She stares at the pen and paper Clara is holding out to her

as if they'd been dug up from an archaeological site, then she realizes she has to write down her contact information.

When the elevator doors close behind Kimmy Diore's tall figure, Clara murmurs to herself, words as clear as the ones that sometimes still wake her at night:

"She came to look for her brother."

Upon leaving the Bastion, Kimmy heads toward the metro. With a bit of luck, she'll find an e-bike at the bike station. She might have managed to see Clara Roussel, but she's not sure she was able to convince her. She didn't have time. She would have liked to tell her everything, from the day Élise Favart first brought her to that glass building with its labyrinthine corridors, up to her eighteenth birthday, when she decided to go back there. She has often wondered why she remembered that woman, when her memory had erased the other faces, all those adults with their gentle voices, full of care, who examined her body and asked her questions. Seeing her again this morning, such a little woman, and at the same time so magnetic, Kimmy thought that maybe it was because Clara was no taller than a child.

She would have liked to stay all day in that office. She would have liked to release her anger, her guilt, her sorrow. Leave behind, in those walls, the years of fake joy and unspeakable malaise.

She hadn't been able to find the right words.

When she looks for the sweet moments of her childhood, it's always Sammy she thinks about. She goes back to him. Her big brother.

When he would sneak into her room, once they'd turned in for the night, to tell her a "real" good night.

When he told her stories about Scotch, the invisible little boy he'd made up.

When he stuck up for her, because she'd forgotten her lines or refused to dress up in a pink tutu. There were days when only Sammy could coax her into wearing a costume she'd refused to put on.

When he would leave the biggest slice of pie or cake for her.

And those games that belonged to them alone: don't step on the cracks in the sidewalk, count the electric cars, hide Dirty Camel somewhere he couldn't be found, so he wouldn't have to go in the washing machine.

One day, during the time she had the tics, Sammy got into a fight because a boy at school had made fun of her in front of other pupils.

For a long time they'd managed to keep their world to themselves, off-camera. They even had their own language. That little world of brother and sister, a coded version, and their parents knew nothing about it. But bit by bit Happy Recess had eaten into their games, their vital space, imposing its style, its words, its stock phrases repeated a hundred times over. Happy Recess had won.

Sammy had always pandered to their mother's every whim without ever standing up to her. He was the perfect son, his mama's little boy. He always said yes, she could count him in. He worked hard and didn't complain. The more Kimmy shied away, the more docile he became; the more she'd sought to rebel, the more he proved his willingness to go along with his mother. Because Kimmy said no, he said yes. And because he said yes, she could say no.

All through those years he had put up with insults, mockery, and nicknames. Waves of hatred and sarcasm. He had never answered back. As if nothing could make him doubt. He explained to anyone who was prepared to listen that he was constructing his future. That he would become famous and make a lot of money.

She had been angry with her brother for wanting to be the

perfect child. She'd despised him for his obedience. She hadn't realized how much he was taking on. How much he was making up for.

But now she understands.

By leaving her the room to rebel, he made it possible for her to escape.

S antiago Valdo has recently acquired some voice recognition software, and its technical performance, he has to admit, is rather amazing. The microphone is so powerful that he can dictate his presentation while walking around his office. With a single word he can open his archives or other documents during dictation; he can hunt down quotations or illustrations. The software points out repetitions and any mistakes you might make in syntax or grammar, and even suggests solutions.

Over recent days Santiago has been writing an article about the development of *homing*, a key trend conceptualized by an American sociologist.

As he dictates his sentences, he sees them appear on the white page as if by magic, with no errors or spelling mistakes.

If he wants to correct something, all he has to do is say "go back," and indicate the number of letters or words in question.

Pacing around the room, he is trying to formulate his conclusion.

"People can now, from their sofa, live lives other than their own. All they have to do is subscribe to a paying platform, choose their formula—immersive, to varying degrees, depending on the material they have at their disposal—and allow themselves to be guided. The market is expanding fast. When it comes to the commercial availability of proxy lives, virtual reality has been meeting with undeniable success (for only a few euros, you can spend twenty-four hours in a villa on stilts in the Maldives, with excellent color reproduction), and the *real story* (also known as 'home reality TV') is occupying an increasingly important share of the market.

"Over two thousand real lives, anonymous or famous, are currently available in the Share the Best catalogue: men and women, single or in a relationship, of all genders and sexual orientations, families of every size, pensioners. Package deals with preferential rates make it possible to experience two or three lives at once.

"Many people—"

He breaks off to correct himself.

"Go back: two words."

He thinks for a moment then continues his dictation.

"Increasing numbers of young adults no longer leave the house. They work from home, or no longer work at all; they do not go to the theater, the cinema, or even the supermarket anymore. Everything they buy and use (food, cosmetics, electrical appliances, cultural items, etc.) is delivered to their door, and they communicate through various increasingly sophisticated interfaces or video games. At that price, they feel safe."

He stops. Figures he'll finish later. He has to take a bit of distance, come up with a more incisive conclusion.

The pathologies that Santiago studies, all related to an early overexposure to social media, appear during adolescence or, more frequently, at the onset of adulthood. Addiction is one of the main symptoms. Essentially behavioral (gaming, the Internet), this addiction can also spread to psychoactive substances such as alcohol or drugs. Addictive disorders can arise when the subject has the feeling that their audience or media coverage is dwindling (at which point everything unfolds as if the subject, deprived of their dose of gratification—number of views, comments, and various signs of subscription—is compensating for that lack by means of another substance that is now more accessible), but these disorders also arise at the height of their celebrity, in order to appease the anxiety brought on by fame along with the isolation it can cause in certain cases.

Moreover, other psychiatric disorders which have been, until now, observed on the American continent, have been identified in Europe and are leading to new forms of research: Santiago, along with twenty or so hospital practitioners and colleagues from the university, has established himself as one of the leaders in the field.

Now that he has had two phone conversations with Sammy Diore, he is almost certain that the young man is showing the most characteristic signs of what is known as the Truman Show delusion, first observed in Los Angeles in the early 00s. A few cases have been described in Europe, concurrently, although they have not led to any university publications. This syndrome, which used to be viewed as an undiagnosed psychiatric disorder (paranoid delirium, schizophrenia, bipolarity), is now held to be a fully-fledged pathology. Its name comes from Peter Weir's 1998 film, which Jacques the Shirker has summed up as follows:

"*The Truman Show* tells the story of a young man who, as he is about to turn thirty, discovers that he has been filmed from the day he was born, and that he lives surrounded by actors. His wife and his best friends wear earphones and are paid to play opposite him, and his entire existence has been orchestrated by the crazy demiurge who is running the show. Unbeknownst to him, Truman Burbank is the internationally renowned and adored hero of a major reality TV show. When he falls in love with a minor player, he decides to run away, to make it to the real world."

Santiago has been working on this subject for a long time. Patients suffering from Truman Show delusion are convinced they are constantly being filmed and that every minute of their life is being rebroadcast somewhere: on a virtual reality TV show, on a sharing platform, in the depths of the Darknet . . . Everyone around them is part of the conspiracy: friends, colleagues, family members are all playing the roles assigned to them in advance, and making their victims suffer, or helping to hide the truth from them.

The extreme anxiety—most often occurring prior to the delusion—these patients experience finds a rational explanation in the idea of a generalized conspiracy. Convinced that everyone's attention is focused on them, that they are being watched by an invisible audience, they actually help, in this way, to legitimize their anxiety.

In the case of Sammy Diore, his disorder is not merely a representation: he feeds off precise childhood memories that are, in all likelihood, traumatic.

In the most serious forms of the pathology, the subject thinks that their mind and body are being controlled by advanced or experimental technologies. Surrounded by connected devices, the subject lives as if they too are an object, controlled remotely by an invisible, evil authority. The patient may go as far as to hear voices, which they believe are directly produced in their brain by various systems of transmission, while their memories appear to them like images that have been implanted without their knowledge. They then become convinced that not a single organ in their body can escape from this stranglehold.

Over the last five years, twenty or more diagnoses of Truman Show delusion have been made in France, affecting patients born after 2005 and who have been on display on sharing platforms or social media since their infancy. At this stage, the incidence of this early exposure remains nevertheless a working hypothesis.

Clara is heading home, on foot. She is walking at a steady pace; she knows no better method to work off her stress. Gradually her solar plexus opens up, and the feeling of oppression disappears. She notices the silence. An unreal silence, something this city is not used to. After a long battle in parliament, the law forbidding gasoline-powered vehicles in the twenty arrondissements of Paris has just come into force. Walking gives you another perception of space, she thinks, one that reminds her of winter days when she was a little girl, back in a time when it still snowed.

Her thoughts follow one another, to the regular movement of her body: they are circulating. When they move around like this, they seem easier to approach, to circumvent, or even to avoid. They obey the same momentum as the one propelling her forward, and in that very cadence, they disappear or become clearer.

She thinks about Kimmy Diore and her strange request.

She thinks about the body of the young man, the false suicide.

She thinks about the vermilion dress she could wear tonight, and the lipstick that would go with it.

She thinks about the offer Cédric made, the last time they had lunch together at the cafeteria. He would like for her to transfer to the Child Protection Squad. A leadership position will soon be available on his team. She came up with a series of objections (she hasn't worked in the field for a long time, she doesn't have children), but he quickly cut her off: he needs her.

As Clara is walking past the park, a man overtakes her.

He turns around to look at her, unabashedly, then continues on his way, visibly disappointed. She knows that from behind she still has a very youthful adolescent figure, which attracts gazes. From face on, she's a woman with no makeup and a tired face. She smiles.

As she gets nearer her building, she starts to walk faster. She likes this slight exhilaration caused by the change of pace, when she manages to keep it up over the final kilometer.

When she reaches the entrance to her building, the door opens automatically. After seven in the evening the night watchman is in his lodge. She greets him with a wave and a smile, via the camera. They have their little secret. One evening when Clara came home the worse for drink after a dinner party, she stopped to chat with him. She didn't feel like sleeping. They talked about this and that, about an incident that had happened a few days earlier, about the sudden tiredness that sets in at four in the morning when you work at night, about the winter that is no longer winter. And then, through some obscure association of ideas, he'd asked her if she knew how to play poker. His face suddenly lit up, and he ushered her into his lodge as if he were inviting her into a château. He reached into a drawer for a deck of cards and a bottle of whiskey. The game had lasted all night long. By early morning he had won, and he accompanied her back to her apartment, all above board, a proper gentleman.

Since that day they have met at least once a month. He excels at bluffing, she beats him with strategy. They put on their best clothes for the occasion: a dress and high heels for her, a light-colored shirt and black shoes for him. They're not just playing poker, she knows that. They are also playing the seduction card. He's much younger than she is and he's very attractive. Things could go off the deep end. But every time, they manage to stay on the verge, each of them camped on a ledge.

They are sure-footed. They've already seen it all. Maybe because they know what they have to lose. And that nothing is more delightful than the present moment prolonged, like no other, this moment of promise and desire, and this unique, singular connection being woven by the game, and by danger.

Tonight she'll wear her red dress, and at about midnight she'll head down the stairs.

On the twentieth floor of the Khéops tower, at the edge of the Chinese quarter, Santiago Valdo rings at door number 2022. After trying one last time—in vain—to persuade the young man to come to his office, he has agreed to make a house call.

The peephole briefly goes dark, and then Sammy Diore opens the door. For a few seconds he stands motionless facing the psychiatrist, as if hesitating to let him enter. He is wearing worn tracksuit pants and a white T-shirt that is not very clean either, but his immaculate sneakers look as if they have never been beyond the threshold of his apartment. After a moment of mutual observation, he eventually invites the psychiatrist to come in. Before closing the door he stretches his neck in either direction of the corridor, and Santiago is instantly reminded of a spoof of a spy movie, aware at the same time that the young man is not displaying any self-derision in his exaggerated gesture.

The furniture has been reduced to the bare minimum—armchair, table, and two chairs—and the walls are bare. "A little phobia of clutter," thinks Santiago in silence. One glance in the bedroom is enough to conclude that this room obeys the same constraints of bare austerity. Anyone would wager that the place is uninhabited.

Sammy Diore invites him to take a seat, and he sits down across from him, his elbows on his thighs, his hands joined, his back forming a long curve that looks as if it could bend even further. "He's become spineless," thinks the psychiatrist.

The young man stares at him with suspicious attentiveness, and Santiago realizes why: he's making sure his visitor isn't fitted with any equipment capable of recording or filming him.

His features are drawn, there are shadows under his eyes, and his face is wearing the frozen mask of someone who has difficulty sleeping. In spite of his rather loose clothing, or maybe because of it, his thinness becomes obvious.

The psychiatrist leans back against the chair, prepared to listen and let the young man do the talking.

The silence lasts a few more seconds until Sammy eventually begins to speak.

"I don't know how to get out, Doctor."

Santiago nods his head, aware that he is on the verge of caricature, but he has found no better way to encourage a patient to continue, without directing their thoughts.

"I can't to go on like this. I'm constantly hounded. Wherever I go. I can't . . . Do you know they've been filming me since I was six years old?"

Santiago takes this as a real question, one he cannot avoid answering.

"Yes, that is, I know you made a good number of videos with your family for various platforms, YouTube and Instagram in particular."

Sammy seems relieved not to have to tell his story from the beginning.

"The problem is that she lost control."

He pauses. His gaze is looking for somewhere to rest. The young man seems to be wondering how to go on, visibly in the grip of great confusion.

"My mother . . ."

Santiago notices his hands are trembling slightly, and he wonders yet again whether Sammy might be undergoing treatment. Then with a smile he encourages him to go on.

"She ran everything. For a long time. Nowadays she's not in control of anything anymore. Nowadays my entire life is re-broadcast, live, I don't know where or who by. There's a good possibility it's a paying platform. I don't know which one, or how those people communicate with their subscribers. No matter what I do or where I go, I'm being filmed. I've taken refuge here, at home, because it's the only place they haven't managed to bug. I've checked everything: the furniture, the walls, and a few items I've had to keep. But I can't be sure we're not being filmed right this minute while I'm speaking to you. Maybe you're one of them . . . All the people I've seen recently were equipped with retinal cameras. All of them. I can't be sure how honest you are but, in any case, given how things stand with me, I have no choice."

Santiago decides it's time to break his silence.

"You may place all your trust in me, Sammy. I don't belong to any organization, I have not been fitted with any equipment and, what's more, I am bound by medical confidentiality. Is that clear to you?"

Sammy, in turn, merely nods.

"On the telephone you mentioned a young intern at Sainte-Anne hospital who you'd been in touch with . . . Did you see her at the hospital?"

"It's because of the bakery."

"Go on?"

"They have cameras, too. It's supposed to be just CCTV for security, but nowadays there aren't any systems that can't be hacked. The same thing with public transport and local administration. People think the National Commission on Informatics and Liberty can protect them, but it can't do a thing. They've been overwhelmed for a long time. Every company gets its images stolen, when they're not selling them . . . A few months ago I went down to buy some croissants. I had just entered the store when I saw the camera pivot toward me with its lens that opened all of a sudden. Ready to swallow me. I don't know what happened. I broke down. I just remember shouting. I was thinking, 'Who's shouting like that?' It was unbearable. I found out later that it was me. The fire department came and they took me to the hospital. I explained everything to the intern. She told me I had to stay there for a little while, long enough to get some rest. She said that I needed sleep. She was right. But I refused. They might drug me and sell the images."

"You thought she was in on a plot?"

"No, she wasn't, I don't think. She was just one of those people who don't want to see the truth. Who don't want to know what it's all about. Because anyone on the hospital staff could be an accomplice. So I came home. And I haven't been out since."

"Did she prescribe any medication?"

"Tranquilizers, but I didn't take them. I'm afraid they'll sedate me and make me less vigilant—isn't that what would happen?"

"You can show me the prescription, and we'll discuss it."

Santiago knows that the ball is in his court now. It's up to him to show he can listen to what his patient says—without, however, encouraging his raving thoughts.

"Sammy, I'd like to go back over one or two things, if you don't mind, to get to the bottom of your current situation. During your childhood you were filmed for the YouTube channel your mother had created. And then you had your own channel, which was doing really well. I think you were testing video games and that you gave advice on how to become an influencer, am I right?"

"Yes, yes. Among other things."

"And you left it all a few years ago, from one day to the next."

"Yes."

"Do you want to tell me why?"

"The whole time I was at school, everyone wanted to be a YouTuber. Most of the pupils dreamed of having my life. They wanted to take selfies with me, to be invited to my house . . . Of course there were always a few who didn't give a shit about me. Little jibes, as if they were nothing. 'Tell us then, Sammy, do you have any toilet paper left?' or, 'Who's in charge of your life, Sammy, Instagram or your mom?' or else, 'Let Sammy pay, he's rolling in it..' It didn't take me long to figure out that I'd never be like them. That's the price you have to pay. But on the networks it was hatred. I even got death threats. I stood my ground, you know. That's not why I quit. That's what people like to say. They want to believe that I'm suffering from depression because of the haters, or because the videographer Michou always had more followers than me. That's not true."

"So what happened?"

"Last year I met a girl who went for her coffee in the morning at the same café as me. She was really pretty and I could sense her looking at me. We started talking, first at the counter, and then we arranged to meet. That was the first time I ever felt I could trust someone. She knew who I was but it didn't seem to matter much to her. I got a lot of private messages from fans on Instagram: photographs, love letters, propositions. I never did anything with any of them. I wanted to have a real-life encounter. One evening after a few beers, she invited me over to her place."

His voice has changed, and he clears his throat before going on.

"She lived in a big studio. When I went in, the first thing I saw were the mugs, because she had the entire collection on display on a shelf. The Happy Recess mugs. With my photo and Kimmy's, at every age, more or less. And the photograph of my mother. She had the diaries, the posters, the pens, the makeup bags, an entire collection of objects all arranged, like in a museum."

He pauses, overcome by emotion. Santiago waits for a moment then encourages him.

"How did you react?"

"I started crying. I couldn't say a word. She probably thought it would be a nice surprise, that I'd be glad to see all that stuff. But I'm telling you: it finished me. I left her house, I never went back to that café, I never saw her again."

He sat up straighter in his chair.

"For a week or two I was so out of it that I stayed in bed. No posts on Instagram, no videos on YouTube or TikTok. That's when it started, I'm sure. They thought I was going to pack it in. I just needed to take a break, but they freaked out. They contacted people and they began following me. After a while I understood that my neighbors, my concierge, and even some of my friends had been recruited."

Santiago observes the young man: his anxiety is more and more palpable.

"Is that when you deleted all your accounts?"

"Yes. But you can't stop just like that. When people need to see you, to know where you are and what you're doing, when they need your advice and your jokes, when thousands of people depend on you and on your life and the mood you're in, and they're willing to pay for it, you don't have the right to vanish."

Sammy stops for the time it takes to adjust his breathing in an exercise that is apparently meant to calm him down. He closes his eyes. He fills his lungs several times, then empties them, very slowly. Santiago remains silent. After four inhalations, the young man continues as if nothing had happened.

"There's still way too much money to be made. And if I don't take advantage of it for myself, others will do it for me."

"Who?"

"I told you, I don't know. What I do know is that they're very well organized and they're everywhere. It's impossible to hide. That's what I realized the other day at the bakery. They've activated all their networks, they've got optical and tactile sensors, and infrared cameras, and drones, and all the listening artillery."

"What about your sister, where is she now?"

"The last I heard, she's in Paris, but I don't see her anymore."

"Do you think she's also part of this . . . this organization?"

"No. I'm sure she's not."

"How would you explain your estrangement?"

"She doesn't love me."

"And you, do you love her?"

Sammy is caught unawares. All of a sudden, his eyes fill with tears. So, with a child-like gesture, he hides his face behind his hands.

C lara has spent a good part of her day searching for information about the aftermath of the Diore case and its various protagonists. Within the space of a few hours, thanks to helpful colleagues, she's found out a fair amount. She's been on the phone, made photocopies, compiled documents. Enough to make up a little file which will almost certainly be of interest to Kimmy.

Every evening, as soon as she gets home, she starts by taking off her clothes, as if she's shedding a dead skin. Whether she has spent the day in her office or outdoors, she tosses them into the laundry basket.

Sometimes she wonders how many people change their clothes when they get home, the way she does. How many put on boxers, old tracksuit pants, and slippers, or throw on a big loose pullover or a shapeless sweatshirt. How many of them, instead, choose a robe, a lacy nightgown or a silk négligé. How many take off their contact lenses and put on their glasses. How many, by doing this, dissociate their outdoor self from their indoor self.

Her indoor outfit depends on her mood. She likes long dresses and cotton trousers.

Cédric called her this morning to follow up on his job offer. He's been increasing his angles of attack. He says things like, "You have to change gears," "I have some cases you'll find thrilling," or "Think about the evolution of your career."

He also says, "This position was made for you."

Or more direct: "It's time to get out of your office."

He alone, perhaps, can gauge all her doubts. It's not just a question of the department, or the posting. The decision is far more significant than that.

He alone, perhaps, knows that she's stopped growing.

For some time now, she's felt as if she were living on the wrong side of the world, in an impossibly deep recess, at the edge of those supposedly "social" networks saturated with fake love and authentic hatred; at the edge of the World Wide Web of illusions, stuffed with selfies and glib phrases; at the sidelines of everything that moves at the speed of sound.

She's the woman who cannot keep up with the city she no longer loves, where everyone is in a hurry to get home to order something and shop online, or to obey the imperious itinerary of algorithms. She is the feverish woman whose excessive vigilance prohibits sleep, the woman with her unavowed melancholy who can no longer follow the crowd.

Is it because she never saw her parents grow old that she feels so distant now—an anachronism, even though she's only forty-five years old?

On reflection, she doesn't really value this life of staring at a screen, talking with some artificial intelligence that only ever asks her to look up to obey the requirements of facial recognition. She doesn't want to sit, the way others do, deep in her sofa with her smart phone grafted onto her finger, her wrist, her palm, in search of ever greater thrills, waiting and watching for tragedy to appear on her screen, the attack and the hero *du jour*, who'll already be forgotten by the following morning.

The world is beyond her comprehension, and she has no purchase on it. The world is insane, but there is nothing she can do about it.

Maybe it's this feeling of helplessness that has become

unbearable. This feeling that she has never tested her muscles, her courage, her resistance, that she it's too late to go to the front. This feeling that she's let herself slip down a slope, and now she feels too tired to climb back up.

Maybe Cédric is right. It's time to move. To find another way to do her bit.

A few days ago the company doctor asked Clara, during her annual check up, "Do you ever have suicidal thoughts?"

"No, not explicitly," she replied.

"And indistinctly?"

Indistinctly . . . she avoids going near open windows.

But she didn't tell him that.

Every evening when she gets home, she feels she has reached a safe place. And she knows this is not a good thing.

She knows that indoors (the sofa, the closed curtains, the gentle warmth of her apartment) is a privilege and a trap.

This evening, as soon as she gets home, she taps Kimmy Diore's number on her watch.

The young woman takes the call on the first ring.

By the time she picks up, there is no longer any hesitation.

The next day, Clara walks across the Seine. The light is strangely bright for the end of the afternoon, white, dazzling, as if projectors had been set up to illuminate the river, she thinks, gazing at the sky.

Walking quickly, her hand shielding her eyes, for no apparent reason she thinks about her uncle Dédé. According to family legend, which never leaves out any of the quainter episodes, he died the day the leftist singer Renaud kissed a cop. She thinks about her cousin Elvira, who went to live somewhere in the Caribbean, and her cousin Mario, who became an economist. She thinks about the friends she's lost touch with, because she hasn't had the time to devote to them.

She has an appointment with Kimmy Diore.

In a café on the Boulevard Raspail, which Clara chose because it has a dark room at the back and few customers, they sit facing each other.

Clara, for the second time, has to figure out how to deal with the young woman's gloomy gravity, her fluctuating gaze, her anger simmering just below the surface.

She begins by explaining that she doesn't have the right to pass these documents on to her, because Kimmy was a minor at the time of the events. Normally, Kimmy would have to submit a request to the Commission for Access to Administrative Appeal, a rather fastidious process which could take some time. Nor does she, to be honest, have the right to use the instruments of the Criminal Investigation Department to find someone's contact information for her personal use.

Kimmy's face immediately clouds over, her lips purse, her breath is halting, her legs start jiggling under the table.

She doesn't know how to hide her emotions, thinks Clara, immediately putting an end to her introduction.

"But anyway . . . in certain cases, we can find a way around it."

Kimmy is hanging on her every word.

"I found the transcripts of your two interviews conducted by the Child Protection Squad. And Élise Favart's, as well. There are several of them, you'll see. I also found out what happened to her. When she got out of prison, she regained custody of her son, who had been entrusted to her mother while she was in custody awaiting trial. She went to live in the Morvan region, where she met her future husband, who is a special-needs teacher. He worked, and still works, at the institution for disabled children where Ilian went. They got married and she took his name. They have a little girl, who's five years old now. Élise found a part-time job at a doctors' office."

A fleeting smile passes over Kimmy's face: she is visibly relieved to hear the news.

"I've also included a few summaries that I had written up at the time, which give a broad overview of the investigation. And I have something else for you."

Kimmy leans closer to Clara, even more attentive. Clara pauses for a moment before continuing.

"I found out where Sammy has got to. It wasn't easy, because he's trying very hard to disappear. He hasn't seen anyone for months except for a psychiatrist who has been to his house twice. I'm not sure he's doing all that well. I would even venture to say he needs help."

Kimmy grabs the documents and stuffs them into her bag.

For a few seconds her gaze drifts around the room, as if lost, before landing again on Clara.

Scarcely audibly, she murmurs her thanks.

Then she stands up and leaves the room.

The anger hasn't always been there. It came to Kimmy the day she wanted to know. When she began digging. The day she found the articles in the major papers of the time, about Élise Favart's trial. The day when, in the summaries of the hearings as described by a renowned legal columnist, she read that all through the trial, her mother had not once looked at Élise. All through those days, according to several witnesses, Élise had tried to catch her former friend's gaze, to no avail. Even when, with a catch in her throat, she begged Mélanie for forgiveness.

It was reading that detail a few months earlier that roused her anger. Prior to that, it was silent. Or else it had been taking another form, secret, below the surface.

That evening Kimmy finishes going through the file Clara Roussel has entrusted to her.

She reads the words she had spoken as a little girl. The way she described, on two occasions, the eight days she'd spent with Élise. She is relieved. Everything has been recorded in the transcripts. Her hesitancy, her silence. Her clear attachment to the young woman. She tells of an interlude with no conflict, no fear. Then she describes the last evening, which Élise had evoked during her first hearing, that evening when she understood there was something not right.

The photograph she finds, inside a folder, of the wall painting she'd made with Ilian, overwhelms her. The anger recedes for a moment.

*

In Clara's summary, it is noted that the morning after Kimmy's return, her parents asked the president of Children at Risk to immediately refund the €500,000 deposited to the association's account. They had not posted the video as requested, therefore they were under no obligation to honor the donation.

Kimmy has closed the file.
The anger is there again, and it has won.

Every morning the alarm clock rings and Mélanie hurries into the bathroom to freshen up. She wipes a cotton swab soaked in flower water over her face, does her hair, puts concealer over the shadows under her eyes and a trace of blush on her cheeks, then she goes back to bed. From her bed she launches the live broadcast of her everyday life.

On Share the Best, the day has begun. The alarm clock rings again, she stretches in a beam of light. She sits up in bed and says good morning to her subscribers.

Using a single tiny box, which she can hold in one hand, she directs every aspect of the production: she activates, or de-activates the microphones remotely, and can alter connections herself from one axis to the other. Between the house and outdoors, twenty or more cameras have been installed, each one capable of detecting and following movement in a perimeter of four or five meters. It's incredible, the technical progress they've made. The box is the equivalent of the "mixer" once used by TV directors to make their programs. She no longer even needs to have a microphone on her person. The sound equipment has been installed more or less everywhere in the house and is powerful enough to capture and transmit whispering voices several meters apart. And in *Vlog* mode, a more recent development, she can address her audience whenever she wants: all she has to do is look at a camera face on for that image to be broadcast in priority. Her words can be read from a banner on the screen, transcribed live by voice dictation software, so that subscribers can enjoy them wherever they might be, even when they cannot activate the sound.

She thinks it's wonderful.

Mélanie now lives in a sort of *Loft* reserved for her alone, where all other competitors have been eliminated. That was what she was thinking the other night as she got ready for bed. A *Loft* that she runs with a master's hand, where she is producer, director, and lead actress all at the same time. Her editorial policy, for the most part, is focused on practical and domestic life, but she also tackles psychological issues. Her subscribers love to hear about her moods, and listen to her thoughts and her aphorisms; she has gathered a lot of material to enrich her remarks.

Once a month, on a Thursday evening at eight forty-five, she streams *Live Dreams*. Among hundreds of contestants, she chooses a few subscribers from Mel Inside to take part in a live exchange with her. She listens attentively, answers compassionately, and is generous with her advice and confessions. Bruno sometimes joins in. He intervenes on the more masculine issues (choice of domestic robots, household safety and protection, swimming pool maintenance, and so on), generally at the request of other husbands. Lately Bruno has had to be cajoled into taking part, but Mélanie insists on it. Her community adores him and her viewing figures go up when he is there. People need to dream. To see a fine couple like Mélanie and Bruno—stable, so close-knit. It reassures them. It does them good. She does people good. That's all there is to it. She has become a fairy, yes, a modern fairy. She doesn't need a magic wand, just a few cameras and a lot of love to give.

Over the last two years, over the holiday season, Mélanie has broadcast a "Best of" her life. A veritable fireworks display: it has beaten all the viewing records.

After enjoying her breakfast (a ritual sponsored by a brand of low-cal jams: she must be sure to place their label prominently on display), Mélanie has her shower. During this time the program is interrupted and a *Memory Album* replaces the live feed. Her first assistant is responsible for doing the montages, made up of images filmed when Kimmy and Sammy were little. On top of nostalgic, copyright-free background music, Wilfrid mixes archival material, with a great deal of sensitivity: picnics, excursions to amusement parks, vacations, meetings with fans. Most of the Mel Inside subscribers used to follow Happy Recess, and love seeing those moments again. They are deeply moved.

As soon as she's dressed she returns to the live broadcast: in a confidential tone, she reveals the name of the fashion brands she is wearing (she changes her outfit every day and never wears the same clothes twice), then acts as if she is putting her makeup on for the first time that day, sharing the names of the products she uses with her community and extolling their virtues. Then she has to have her first espresso of the day, courtesy of the Friendly brand. Her contract stipulates two cups a day; after twenty years of upscale positioning, with capsules presented as if they were precious jewels in their cases, the brand has returned to a more family-friendly position, more respectful of nature, and now it is counting on Mélanie to reach a target audience that is more *down-home*, as they call it, in English. The problem is that her doctor has advised her not to drink coffee. Because of her nerves. And so, when she can, very discreetly she avoids finishing her cup, or furtively pours it down the drain.

This morning, as Mélanie finishes getting dressed, she can't seem to find her usual energy. A faint fatigue, "a drop in my blood pressure," she muses, delaying the moment when she must pick up the live feed again. Lately she's been feeling as if she were on a roller coaster. Sometimes she's full of energy, as excited as a Mexican jumping bean; other times she's exhausted, abnormally feeble. The last time she had a video call with Dr. Roques, he found she was tired, but the data recorded on her watch were normal. He suggested it might be psychological fatigue.

Fortunately, Wilfrid always factors in a safety margin in his archival montages, so she has at least twenty minutes to spare.

She relaxes, staring a little into space, then she decides to switch on the radio; she might hear some news that she can comment on during the day. The *happy few*, as she calls them now, like to have her opinion about the major issues impacting the planet.

The nine o'clock news has just started. She listens to the headlines, then her mind drifts and wanders. She thinks about how to plan her day, the variations she might find to her morning *routine*, the contract she is about to sign with a major cosmetics firm, the angle of camera number eight, far more flattering to her profile than camera number nine . . . until the news anchor's voice ruthlessly bursts the bubble where she'd found refuge.

"This news just in: Kimmy Diore, the former YouTube star, has voiced her intention to take legal action against her parents for unlawful use of her personal image, breach of privacy and poor choices with regard to her upbringing. This makes Kimmy Diore the fifth child influencer to file a complaint against her parents on coming of age. We will return with more details regarding this breaking news in our one o'clock edition, but we have already been able to obtain an explanation from Maître Buisson, a practicing attorney in Paris who has assisted several former child influencers and YouTubers, in particular Little Dorothy, who is now twenty-two years old with a fortune estimated at €4 million, and who is now accusing her father of failing to respect the law."

Without thinking, Mélanie switches off the radio.

For a few seconds, in this silence, she struggles to catch her breath.

She's not sure she heard right. She must have misunderstood. She types a few key words on her telephone, and sees to her horror that the press release has already been republished dozens of times.

Kimmy? It can't be.

She can't go back on live. No way.

She's already been through a media frenzy. She knows what's coming.

Wilfrid's montage is still playing. She'll have to let him know, so that he can take over the broadcast and follow up with more archival material.

But right now she doesn't have the strength.

She has to calm down.

Her daughter . . . her little girl . . . her little Kimmy is suing them . . .

She feels horribly alone.

Bruno left at dawn to visit a Jacuzzi showroom in order to choose a model for their garden from the range the maker was offering them. Could he have heard the news and kept it from her?

Or maybe it's that registered letter she hasn't picked up yet at the post office?

No, it can't be. She can't believe it.

Her little Kimmy is suing them . . .

An SMS from Wilfrid rouses her from her torpor: he'll take over.

She'll just go on sitting there and wait for her husband. In silence.

Her *sweeties* will be worried.

She'll be getting tons of messages, because they panic over the slightest thing.

That's just too bad for her *sweeties*. For once they'll just have to be patient, Goddamn it. They go too far sometimes. She already gives so much. Sometimes her *sweeties* are a real pain in the ass.

She's going to drink some coffee. Screw it. She doesn't care. She feels so tired.

Hey, yes, there's a thought: she'll test all the capsules—yellow, green, pink and, best of all gold. Lots of gold.

She's a fairy, after all, she's not afraid. Fairies cannot be touched. Fairies aren't afraid of anything. Fairies know the difference between good and evil. Fairies are above the contingencies of the world and the vile attacks it can spawn.

The old-timers in the Criminal Investigation Department call her "the Professor," to keep the tradition alive. But ever since the stunning, spectacular, return of a grammarian presenter from the 70s and 80s on the Vintage platform (although this presenter actually died long ago), the younger police officers now call Clara "Master Capello." In the Crime Squad and elsewhere, challenges are set and bets are made. Most of the time this means slipping an incongruous word or improbable expression—generally chosen at random—into a report. Her new team is very fond of this sort of game. You have to have something to keep yourself entertained. The other day Clara had to insert the word "pulverulent" (relatively easy) into a summary to be sent to the prosecutor's office. The previous time she landed the word "gadzooks" (more treacherous). This time, she had to place the word "fulminate" somewhere in a summary, a rather old-fashioned but efficient word. She wins every time.

She has spent the entire day in an online training session on nonverbal behavior prior to aggression.

Back at home, Clara turns on the radio. She never made the switch to any of the continuous news channels, and with the exception of the TV news and a few daily shows, programs from over-the-air channels or TNT have almost all completely disappeared.

While she's opening her fridge to see what there is to eat, the name Kimmy Diore suddenly catches her attention.

She goes over to the speakers to listen.

A woman's voice, confident, expert, seems to be providing a detailed explanation.

"These lawsuits brought by children against their parents do not only concern former child stars. The movement to disconnect, and to reduce one's digital footprint has been gaining traction among young people. As they reach adulthood, a certain number of them are becoming aware that they are already burdened with a heavy digital liability that precludes any hope of anonymity. Citing their right to safeguard their personal image and to have a digital clean slate, they generally decide, therefore, to turn to the justice system to demand that their parents remove their photographs or videos, which have been published and tagged on social media throughout their entire childhood. Some of them even go so far as to seek compensation."

The journalist, whose voice is familiar, takes over again.

"Let's return to the story that concerns us today, that of Kimmy Diore. She is suing her parents for unlawful use of her personal image and poor choices. Let me ask you, Corinne Buisson, what does this mean exactly?"

"Legally, until a child turns eighteen, the use of their personal image is the responsibility of their legal representative. They are there to protect the image, but do not own it. As a rule, parental rights must be exercised in the interest of the child. Some parents are not aware of the fact that their child was born with rights to their image. They behave as if they were the owners of that right. Parents are finding themselves in court now for not only failing to protect the child's right, but also, as some argue, actually abusing it."

"I'd like to remind our listeners that a law aiming to control the commercial exploitation of child influencer's image on online platforms was passed in 2020. Does this mean the law has served no purpose?"

"No, I wouldn't say that. France was the first country to legislate on the matter, which was symbolically important. It has made it possible to say to parents: Watch out, you can't just do whatever you want. Some of them have subsequently back-pedalled. But as often happens, we haven't given ourselves adequate means to enforce the law."

"Do you mean that there hasn't been enough control?"

The lawyer takes her time before answering.

"For a start, the law limits the number of hours in a day children can be on set, depending on their age. In this regard the law was based on the regime governing children who work in the entertainment industry. For example, it authorizes a six-year-old child to film three hours a day, and a twelve-year-old, four hours. When this applies to time spent at a photo session or on a film set, both of which, by definition, can be limited in time, it makes sense. But on the scale of an entire childhood, when the children are filmed by their parents every day, that's another matter altogether. You also mentioned the issue of control . . . How many families have seen a work inspector show up at any time over recent years?"

"But with regard to the financial aspects, some real progress has been made, wouldn't you say?"

"I won't go into details on the air about the ways parents have found to circumvent the law. There are many, and most of the families concerned found them sooner rather than later. I'll just give you one example. One of the leading channels in this domain featured two little twin boys, and over several years it had generated millions of views and a few million euros. A news site unveiled the financial arrangement: the boys' legal representative—their father—went through a modeling agency in order to pay his sons, and he then declared and paid for a certain number of hours every week, within the regulatory limits. This money was deposited in an account with the Deposits and Consignments Fund, as required by law. But this father, who also saw himself as the author, director, and producer of the videos—which, in fact, he was—and had invested in the equipment necessary for the videos' production, went on collecting most of the money disbursed by the brands, not to mention the income generated by YouTube. Who can claim to control this distribution of funds? That's just one example . . . and I haven't even mentioned the issue of family *vlogging*, which is developing rapidly, where the entire family performs and the children are no longer even considered to be actors but simply extras . . . thus totally evading any legislative framework."

"I'd like to turn to you now, Santiago Valdo. You are a psychiatrist and psychoanalyst, and you raised the alarm long ago about the psychological damage caused by this premature exposure. Can you tell us something about it?"

"The children's desire is shaped very early on, and they themselves often end up believing that it came from their own volition. In reality, they have no choice. They are prisoners in terms of the emotional stakes—their connection with their parents—and the financial stakes, since most of the families in question are living off this income. Moreover, the young people who are filing lawsuits at present have been confronted, from their earliest childhood, with demands no children should ever be subjected to: they are expected to be charming, promote products, respond to fans, manage their image, and so on. Today many of them are paying the bitter price for it all."

"Why is this harmful to children?"

"We have noticed that they place a limited amount of trust in their own parents, and that they have difficulty establishing healthy relationships with their peers. We have also observed that as adults they lead lives of great solitude, are very fragile when it comes to addiction, and they often have other symptoms that are far more severe.'

'Allow me to play the devil's advocate for a moment: haven't there always been child stars? It's not exactly a recent phenomenon. Britney Spears, Macauley Culkin, Daniel Radcliffe, Jordy here in France: every generation has its icons.'

'Among the names you've cited there have been a few prominent psychological breakdowns. The difference—because there is a difference—is that the children we're discussing today, and who are now adult, have been made to perform from early childhood on YouTube or Instagram; they weren't being used to make just one film or one series, promote it, then go home. These children are being made to play their own role, every day, at home. In their own bedroom, in the living room, in the kitchen, with their own real parents. And 'role' is the operative word here, because in reality no one is ever their real self in front of the camera. It's very tiring to play a role, you know.'

'I would nevertheless like to point out that some of these children have been spectacularly successful. The younger son in the Cuddly Toy Gang has gone on to become a renowned actor, and the eldest daughter from Minibus Team has had an exceptional career.'

'I don't deny it. Fortunately, some children, even the ones most at risk, do make a life for themselves.'

A musical interlude follows the conversation. Clara hurriedly sits down.

When the music ends, the journalist picks up the thread.

'A few months ago Pablo the Boss received compensation from his mother for a significant amount, and he also obtained the destruction and confiscation of any images that featured him. His mother had filmed and published every stage of his childhood, and the most notorious video remains the one where she pretends to be a special correspondence on the scene of the event and declares to her subscribers that her son has just done his, quote-unquote, 'first poop on the potty' (the video had several million views). Similarly, we anticipate that quite a few of the babies filmed by their parents for the famous Cheese Challenge will one day demand the deletion of these videos. I would like to remind our listeners that this challenge, which enjoyed success worldwide, consisted in the parents throwing a slice of cheese at their baby's face and filming their reaction. Santiago Valdo, can we conclude that these recent court decisions in favor of children are a positive sign?"

"Yes, of course. But the right to be forgotten was already incorporated in the law passed in 2020. The truth is that it is impossible to enforce. Images of these children have been reproduced and commented on ad infinitum. They can never be erased. On the Internet, as you know, nothing is erased. Consequently, the law remains powerless."

"Thank you, Santiago Valdo, for your perspective. I'd like to remind our listeners that our guest is a psychiatrist and psycho-analyst, and the author of the book *In the Event of Prolonged Exposure*, published by—"

Clara switches off the radio. She is lost in thought.

Move when something comes up. When the wind changes direction. When it's the right moment.

She dials Cédric Berger's number and without even saying hello, she announces, "I'm in."

On the other end of the line, she hears a whoop of joy. Then he adds, "I promise you that never again will I use 'between you and I' in the place of 'between you and me.'"

Kimmy is getting dressed to go and see her brother. Like every day, she puts on a neutral outfit, for all occasions, a camouflage that has become instinctive, the shapes and color carefully thought through so that she will blend into the crowd. She will never be free, she will never be invisible, she knows that. In spite of the hood, the cap, the drab gray colors, there will always be someone who'll stare insistently or burst out laughing there in the street. She will never be cleansed of all those gazes that have tarnished her, worn her down, spoiled her, with the help of the screen.

In the street she keeps her gaze down, and slouches to make herself appear shorter. She has tucked her blonde hair into a black beanie.

Sammy lives in one of those tall towers in the thirteenth arrondissement that are visible from the beltway, on the twentieth floor, he specified. He didn't want to go out and she had a lot of trouble persuading him to let her come to him. On the telephone she could sense that he was anxious and feverish; in spite of time and distance she can decrypt the tiniest inflections in his voice. He didn't seem to trust her, she could tell that much. She managed to talk him round by telling him that she needed him.

She promised to come without a bag, empty-handed.

Until today, recent events had seemed like nothing more than a blurry, unstable sequence, dictated by anger. First there was her visit to Clara Roussel (she got up one morning, drank a coffee, and set off for the Bastion, though she'd never thought about doing it before), then the decision to take her parents to court: all on impulse.

She doesn't care about the money. She already has plenty. She wants the damage to be acknowledged. Her stolen childhood.

Now she knows that all of this is converging toward one single purpose. She wants to see Sammy, to join forces with him. Because she's understood one thing: she can live without her parents, but she cannot stand the thought of losing her brother.

As she is leaving the overground metro, a lovely butterfly flutters around her. She just has time to see the blend of colors, ochre and orange, and to think how rare they have become, particularly during this season. There in the middle of the city's gray buildings she sees it as a sign of beauty, the poetry of nature.

The sun has not yet broken through the shapeless milky veil that seems to have been placed on the buildings like a lid, diffusing its light as if through a lampshade. The rue Dunois is just next to the metro. She punches in the code and enters the tower.

In the elevator mirror, her pallor betrays her apprehension.

As soon as she rings the bell Sammy opens the door. He looks behind her as if to make sure she hasn't been followed, then ushers her into the living room.

They sit on the chairs at the little round table.

She is suddenly overwhelmed by the flagrant kinship of their posture, their crossed legs, the way they seem to be trying to make themselves smaller, and their hands flat on the table, to keep from swaying.

She begins to speak and tells him about all the years gone by. The ones they spent together, the ones that drove them apart.

It's a flow of words too long restrained, the chronology soon gets lost, she wants to share her memories, she wants to remind him of the sweeter moments, she wants to tell him how much he matters to her, everything she has been able to do thanks to him, she wants to tell him she understands that he, too, has suffered.

Sammy listens in silence.

They look at each other, and stop speaking.

And then Sammy takes her hands.

A butterfly comes in through the open window, the same one as before. Kimmy thinks for a second that maybe it has followed her, then she tells herself, that's impossible.

In a beam of light the insect flutters above them.

And then she hears a faint, barely perceptible whirring. In fact she's not even completely sure. The insect goes up toward the ceiling. She raises her eyes and for a split second, it's strange; she thinks she can see a tiny camera planted between its wings.

Once night has fallen, she likes to look at her own reflection in the black pane of the picture window. As a rule, this is the time when she settles into her sofa, facing camera number three, to share her mood and her impressions with her subscribers, and to comment on the news. It's also an opportunity for her to offer some tips of a practical nature, or for personal development, because lately Mélanie has been dipping into the three Ws, a new method of positive psychology based on three fundamental principles: *watch, want, win*. Then she heads to the kitchen and starts preparing dinner, thus honoring a few ongoing obligations she has with regard to product placement.

But today, she's silent.

Today, she hasn't done anything.

She hasn't been back on her live feed since yesterday, causing a veritable panic among her fans. In the space of a few hours the comments, questions, and pleas began pouring in, in ever greater numbers, on all her networks, everyone contributing a theory or an explanation.

She cannot reply. She doesn't have the strength.

She needs this silence. What it might be made of, she does not know, she's been living for so long in the noise that she herself has to make to satisfy all the people who love her.

What she does know, is that she can't stand hearing those words anymore—*trial, law, summons, justice*—because they make her want to vomit.

Everything is so unfair. Why won't people understand that she's always done her best? She sacrificed her private life, her youth, so that her children could be happy and famous? It's not as if she's killed anyone.

This evening, all she does is post one written message to apologize for the temporary interruption in her broadcast. She could entitle the message *Bye-bye sweeties*, or better still, *Fuck you sweeties*, ha ha, that would be so funny, she could tell them, "Go fly a kite," or "Get off my case," or "Mind your own business," like her mother used to say—her mother, well, well, what's she doing here, it would be so funny, yes, "Fuck the *sweeties*," oh my goodness, so funny, well maybe not, they wouldn't take it very well.

Bruno hasn't come home.

Yesterday afternoon she tried to reach him several times, to no avail, and he eventually called to tell her he'd be staying the night in a hotel.

Initially she thought he'd been held up or got stuck in traffic. But after an endless silence, where she could hear his breathing, amplified, halting, he confessed that he didn't want to come back to the house, to their home, anymore.

He said, "It's over, Mélanie, I can't go on living like this."

Initially she thought she'd misheard, then he said the same thing again, in that dull, muffled voice. It's over.

Bruno, her buoy, her rock, her most loyal supporter . . .

She can't help but think about the video she'll film, maybe tomorrow, if she feels better. It could be a real hit. *When you're a woman in your 40s and your husband flies the coop . . .* Or what about, *Women always end up struggling on their own.*

But no, it's absurd, she mustn't panic.

Bruno just needs some space.

It's not for good. He'll be back tomorrow. To talk about it.

He wants to breathe.

He's right, actually, it's important to breathe. In fact, she's going to switch on the new essential oil diffuser the Biolife brand provided, a perfume of flowers, with earthy, woodsy undertones, a real balm. Delightful.

Actually, she doesn't feel too good. For the first time she can't get her priorities straight, it's all muddled.

She has a slight headache. Feels queasy.

Maybe she drank too much coffee.

Kimmy is suing them and it's almost worse than when she went missing.

Bruno is hurt, that's all. Mortally wounded, in fact . . . He's cracking up. It's no surprise. But he'll get his act together, she knows he will.

She's a fairy and Bruno is a big teddy bear. Oh yes, that's it. *The fairy and the teddy bear*, it's so funny. So funny you could die of laughter.

She has to survive. Survive for both of them. The title of her next video mustn't give way to sorrow. On the contrary, it has to be upbeat. More than ever.

Join forces in the storm, that would be a magnificent title. Or something like, *One gust of wind can't bring down a tree*.

She'll talk it over with him.

This time they'll decide together.

And life will go on, like before. Everything will go back to normal, she mustn't worry.

Everything is fine.

Everything is fine.

Everything is fine.

Delphine de Vigan has published several novels, a number of which were nominated and won major literary prizes in France, including the Prix Goncourt, Prix Goncourt des lycéens, Prix Renaudot, Prix de Libraires, Prix du roman Fnac and Gran prix de lectrices de Elle. She lives in Paris.